A DEFEATED MAN'S DESTINY

Casey James

ISBN: 1536876615
ISBN 13: 9781536876611

PART ONE

CHAPTER ONE

David Lewis's life, to put things lightly, had not turned out like he'd hoped it would. And now, after the night he'd just experienced, he was more than ready to end his journey. He had the gun and the pills to accomplish this task, but he wouldn't use them. No—David wasn't one to make things easier on himself. He would trudge forward through the mud like he always had, never being permitted to travel on the paved roads of life.

He collapsed onto his bed face first as he slammed the door behind him. It was dangerous for him to lay like this. Soon he would be asleep, and he had things that he needed to do in order to heal properly. As he lay there, each heartbeat made his beaten face ache and his brain throb with a dull pain. Eventually, before sleep claimed him, he staggered back to his feet.

The steam built in the shower while he slowly and painfully removed his clothes. Once naked, he looked at the mess in the mirror. He had a large mouse living below his right eye and five stitches squeezing together a mound of flesh above his left. His upper lip looked like it belonged to a bimbo porn star. Finally, he looked at his throbbing right hand with contempt for failing him once again. He leaned onto his sink, peering into blue eyes tucked behind swollen cheeks, trying to see past them into his soul, marveling at his broken down meat vessel. Somewhere behind those eyes resided his true self.

As he gingerly stepped into the shower there was one question on his mind: *Why am I doing this?* The pool around his feet turned dark red as the dried blood washed off of him. After twenty minutes of letting the water strike the back of his neck, he washed up and got out.

He limped outside to his balcony with a cigarette readied in his mouth. Leaning against the railing, he ignited it and took a deep inhale of his first smoke in two weeks. He was proud of his break from the cancer sticks, but this relapse was well deserved, and quite amazing, he thought. Below him, Larry, the owner of the liquor store located below his apartment, locked up shop by sliding a metal gate across the front entrance. He looked up at David and gave a subtle wave before walking around the back of the building to wherever he laid his head at night. The I-5 freeway hummed above David; the yells of the homeless fighting off all sorts of demons rang out below. He took another incredible and lengthy drag from his cigarette and looked up at the stars. Unlike in Los Angeles, a couple hundred miles south in San Diego one could still see the stars on a clear night like this one. Orion's Belt took the center of the sky, an infinite ocean of neighboring stars packed around it. He didn't know what other constellations were out there or which star was actually Venus; he just knew that the grand mystery of what was happening out there was the only thing that gave him peace. The only thing that kept him sane.

That night, David slept a dreamless sleep. He liked when this happened because his dreams were usually nightmares.

⋇⊹⊱

The morning light crept up David's body until it reached his eyes, causing them to open slowly. He rolled onto his side in order to escape the annoying sunlight. The resulting pain was excruciating. He let out a scream that echoed off the walls of his small apartment and returned to his back with a sigh. He felt like he had been by a truck, when in actuality he had been struck my another man's hands, knees, shins, and elbows a great number of times. Back in his original position, he felt around for his phone that was lost amongst his blanket. When he found it, he discovered the time—12:30 pm—and a text message.

The text was from Mike Thompson, his coach. "I know it's a tuff pill to swallow. But we'll learn from this loss. Can't just be a banger anymore. Get some rest and recover. We'll get you another fight ASAP."

A look of disgust flashed across David's face as he read the message. He set the phone aside, reached his hands into the sky and contorted his body in a stretch until a loud pop in his back shocked him into a very brief state of ecstasy. He let out a yawn, threw his covers to the side, and slowly got to his feet in the fashion of a ninety-five year old man. Sitting atop the fridge in his kitchen was a container of strong pain killers. He took three in his hand and washed them down with some milk.

Eggs quickly sizzled from clear to white in the pan as David cracked them in with his good left hand. As he flipped the eggs, he thought about the fight—things he should have done differently, things he did well, and how on earth his rugged opponent didn't go to sleep after receiving a right hand bomb on the chin. *Some people just can't be knocked out,* he thought, shaking his head.

After breakfast, his belly was full and his face was itchy. The pills were doing their job. He had enough strength to go get his check, and he intended to do so. *That's why I do this shit,* he remembered.

With only his left hand on the handlebars, David rode down Sports Arena Boulevard sporting a hoodie and large glasses to mask his swollen face. He stopped at the Rosecrans intersection, taking deep breaths and soaking in his surroundings. The Saturday morning traffic was light. The sky was rendered grey from the morning fog sweeping in from the harbor. There was a time when David would feel a high after his fights, win or lose. But those days were gone. The novelty of being a cage fighter had worn off. All he felt now was pain and frustration.

A mile further up Sports Arena, he pulled a right into a small mini-mall parking lot and rode up to the left side of the building where he locked his bike up to a sign's pole. The actual sports arena—the one the street was named after—towered a couple hundred yards behind the small lot. All of the spaces in the complex were vacant and boarded up except for one, the one he had come to. He walked past some windows that were foggy from inside perspiration and entered through a door that read "The Bear's Den".

Inside the gym, twelve men were going to battle on a mat behind a cage wall. In pairs of two, they took turns shooting their bodies in on their partners' legs, wrapping them up with their arms, and taking them to the ground. Walking amongst them and watching intently was a thick man with grey hair. He had sharp features, protruding cheekbones, and a look on his face that would make babies cry instantly.

"Good Ray . . . thirty seconds!" the grey-haired man bellowed with ferocity. His pupils grunted and groaned as they struggled to get up after each takedown. "Finish the drill!" the man shouted. There was more battle for the longest ten seconds of the students' lives until their coach shouted "TIME!" Several of the men collapsed to the ground after hearing the call. The grey-haired man finally noticed David, who was sitting in a chair and watching the action with his arms crossed. "Okay boys, circle up," he called to the group of young fighters. The men who were lying down picked themselves up from their pools of sweat and joined the circle. The scary man, known as Coach Mike, raised his hand in the center of the human ring. The others did the same with much more difficulty. "Good practice boys. I'm seeing a lot of improvement in your wrestling. This shit is important. If you need proof, ask the guy sitting over there." He pointed at David, who was sitting emotionless behind his large glasses. "That motherfucker he fought last night couldn't dream of standing with David. But you don't see David in these practices very often, do you?" No one dared say anything; they were in hearing distance from the man being discussed. "This is MMA, not boxing or kickboxing or muay thai. You gotta be a well-rounded fighter to survive in this game, alright? Go get some rest. We got team practice at five and Jiu Jitsu at six tonight if you can make it. If you wanna be a champion, you'll make it. Alright fellas, team on three. One, two, three—"

"TEAM!" the crew shouted in unison.

The sweaty men began filing out into the entry area where David was sitting, some giving David props for his performance as they passed. To David's right was a long bench that ran the length of the gym. Underneath the bench, the fighters' smelly bags were piled on top of each other. This was the closest thing the Bear's Den had to a locker room. The men congregated here as they caught their breath and changed clothes.

Mike came out off the mats last and looked down on David. "The only time I can get you to wrestling practice is when you got a check waiting for you, huh?" Mike usually wore a face that looked angry even when he wasn't. He was wearing that face now.

David nodded. "That's about right."

"Come on." The coach turned for a small door that led to his office. David got up and followed him in. The office was bare save for two pictures on the wall of a younger Mike Thompson stomping on men's faces in an old-style boxing ring and a desk in

7

the middle of the room stacked high with papers and an ancient Macintosh. The two men took seats on opposite sides of the desk. They engaged in a long, dense silence.

"I'm proud of you, David," Mike said, breaking the stillness. "You fought well."

"You got the check?" David replied calmly.

Mike shook his head slowly as he grabbed an envelope off the top of a stack of papers. "There was a time when it wasn't about the check," he said, sliding the envelope across the desk. David grabbed it and ripped it open with his teeth and left hand. He examined the check for two hundred and fifty bones.

"Woulda been more with the win, obviously," Mike said, seeing David's displeasure.

David just nodded while looking at the check, hoping to change the numbers with his mind.

"There's good news from this. Brian Holliday loved the fight. He says you're gonna get more fights on TV despite the loss. Shit the fight mighta been better for you than him. You're gonna get some good fights from this."

"No I'm not," David replied, folding the check and putting it in his pocket gingerly.

"What do you mean?"

David began to massage his swollen right hand. The pills were wearing off. "I'm done," he said eventually.

Mike dropped his head a few inches, surprised by what he was hearing. But he wasn't too surprised. Something had changed in David, starting before his most recent fight. He was growing more distant and uninterested in the career he had chosen. "David, it's the day after the fight. You shouldn't even be here right now. Sleep on it."

"I don't need to sleep on it. There's no future in this sport for me. We gave it a good run Mike, but I think now it's time for me to find something else."

"What are you gonna do? Go back to robbing people? You gonna go work at Kinkos?"

David shrugged.

"David, you're a born fighter. Most those guys out there, they're just athletes that try to outpoint people like it's a fucking karate class. You go out there to *kill*! There's a fire in you that you're either born with or you're not. All you have to do is dedicate yourself just a little to this thing. Just a fucking little!" He held his thumb and pointer close to show just how little.

David took his glasses off. "Look at me Mike." He leaned forward and pointed at his disfigured face. "I can't live like this anymore. Not for two hundred dollars. That's not even enough to pay for the x-ray to tell me the hand that I already know is broken is broken." David leaned back in his chair. There was another brief silence.

"This is the life we chose kid," Mike said, restraining himself from pointing out the many scars on his own face. "It's your decision. And I know the one you'll eventually make, because I know *you*. We're cut from the same cloth. And I know why you're acting this way right now. I get it man. What I want you to do is go to the hospital and get that hand taken care of, on me. Take a week off, then see where your head is at."

"I'm not going to the hospital," David said, rising from his seat. "And my mind is made up. I'm done mopping the mats, I'm done teaching kids how to box, and I'm definitely done getting in that cage." David left.

"See ya next Monday!" Mike called loudly. David slammed the door, making him jump slightly. "Door works," he mumbled to himself.

CHAPTER TWO

When David got back to his house, he had a bottle of Jim Beam in his back pocket and went straight for his pain killers. He took a pill in his hand, re-considered, then grabbed an extra and washed them down with the bourbon. He reclined on his couch and turned on his small TV that sat atop a stack of books. An ESPN program was breaking down the top ten plays of the day. David dozed off before they made it to number five.

A pounding at the front door woke him several hours later. As he slowly got up, he struggled to register what planet he was on. Louder knocks came as he stood, and the world steadied around him. The clock on the wall read 8:13 p.m. David walked over to the door, looked through the peephole, and turned on the porch light. He saw only the top of a short man's head, but he would recognize the shiny, grease-job hairdo anywhere.

He went through his series of four locks, twisting and sliding them to their unlocked positions. He opened the door to a short man with brown skin wearing a blue suit neatly tailored to his slim frame. The man was adorned in gold jewelry at just about every location he could place it. In his right hand was a manila envelope that was bulging from what it contained. His name was Jorge Lombard.

"Got something for you," Jorge said, extending the envelope. When David reached for it, Jorge pulled it just out of reach, like a bully teasing one of his victims. "The boss is real mad."

David angrily snatched the envelope with a second swipe. "He can be mad all he wants as long as he pays me." David looked inside the envelope. A large stack of cash rested on the bottom.

"He knows you didn't try to lose that fight. I know it too. Anyone who watched that fight knows it."

"Bullshit," David said, lobbing the envelope onto his couch.

"No you're the one telling bullshit." Jorge had a thick Cuban accent and didn't quite have the American lingo down.

"Listen numbnuts. What we're doing is illegal. I would be in deep shit if I didn't make that fight look real, so that's what I did."

"You can explain that to Terry when you meet with him tomorrow."

"I'm not explaining shit. You can tell him I said that. He can be happy with the money he made and leave me the fuck alone. I'm done with you guys. You can tell him that too."

Dense silence pierced the air. Slowly, Jorge's white teeth emerged in a condescending sneer. "What were you gonna do if you won?" he asked. "I was watching that fight and thinking 'man this guy wants to die or something.' So tell me, what would you have done?"

David stared intensely at the man with the sinister smile. Thoughts of escorting Jorge over the railing behind him bounced around in his head. He let that thought bubble fill and ultimately burst. "Run along now Jorge. Have a nice life."

Before the Cuban could speak again, David slammed the door shut. He locked his series of locks then limped the short distance back to his couch, where he dumped the contents of the envelope onto the table before him. Not only did a large stack of bills fall out, but also a small bag of white powder. At first, David stared at the objects like they were tainted by some evil hex. He rubbed his hand through his hair and let out a long sigh. After his moment of reflection, he grabbed the stack of cash. The bundle contained fifties and hundreds. He removed the rubber band that held the bills together and began to count. It was all there, all ten thousand dollars.

David turned his attention to the bag of coke. This gift wasn't part of the deal he agreed to, just a little bonus from Terry.

"Fuck," David muttered to himself. He took another swig from his Jim Beam and emptied the coke onto the table. It had been a month since he touched the booger sugar. He vowed to be done, but he'd told himself that lie once or twice before. He rolled up one of his crisp new bills and snorted a line with it. Within minutes, he wasn't concerned with the pain in his body. In fact, he felt no pain at all.

David walked the streets afterward, clenching his jaw and inhaling deeply, high as a kite. His cigarette flashed like a broken stoplight with each drag as he trudged down the sidewalk. It was a cool night, and premature signs of the holidays were popping up in the neighborhood: some early Christmas lights, plastic snowmen, and wicker reindeer. He made his way off the residential block to the more happening Garnet Street. It was a Saturday night, which meant the streets were flooded with drunken people having a good time. David looked around and saw happy couples walking hand in hand down the street, kissing and laughing as they came and went from the bars. Ahead of him, as he made his walk to nowhere in particular, a group of women, made up and looking good, walked in his direction. He made eye contact with the one on the far right, the woman who would have to pass closest to him. After meeting David's eyes, she quickly looked away, and her smile slipped from her face.

David didn't look like he had been to prison. He didn't have any tattoos, his head wasn't shaven, and he didn't dress in clothes that were three sizes too big for him. He looked like your average guy, maybe even a little better than that. But they *knew* he had been to prison. He was sure of it. Somehow people could smell his dark past like a dog smells fear. The distance that was given by this group of women proved this fact. He paid them no mind, just walked, smoked, and thought.

Jorge was right about his accusations earlier that night. David wanted to win his fight and forgo his payday he had just collected. But he was unsuccessful. To David, this revealed two dire truths. One, he was a spineless bum for even agreeing to the deal. And two, he wasn't even good enough to right his wrongs when he decided to. He wasn't just a bum; he was an untalented bum.

Rock bottom—he didn't hit it in prison, for there was still hope that he could turn his fortunes around when he got out. But now, with opportunities to be a better person recognized and audaciously turned down, he was there, laying flat at the dirty bottom with flies swarming around his head.

⇥⊹⇤

The Silver Fox was a bar in Chula Vista owned by Terry Watkins, the leader of one of San Diego's fastest growing gangs—The *Perros Locos,* The Crazy Dogs. The exterior of the joint did little to draw customers in. In fact, new clientele was the last thing Terry wanted. The bar was a front, a place to clean his dirty money, and a headquarters for his crew of thugs and coke-heads. The bar sat on the corner of Madison Street and Racine Avenue. An untrained eye would swear they were in Mexico, and there weren't many differences. Shanties that appeared to be barely standing lined the street. The few properties that had yards were long dead and uncut. Prowling those yards were dogs with murderous intent, pacing and barking at anything that moved. Tonight, the bar was full with the clientele Terry did want: the low-lifes, the gunslingers, the hookers, the wise-guys, the dopers, and the con-artists, all the people who could help Terry make a buck.

Terry had a strong partnership with one of the main exporters of cocaine across his secret tunnels into California. Their partnership gave Terry a strong hold on the cocaine trade in San Diego County. The gang was a mixture of several ethnicities, a rare thing in the crime world, and this was evident in the bar. White men who looked like they could be stockbrokers were mingling with Mexicans who looked like they had just crossed over. Many had. Tonight they joined under this roof with the same objective in mind: getting loaded. Women were dancing on the bar, wearing clothing that left little to the imagination. Cocaine was being snorted at every table. The dance floor (really just a space between tables) was filled with mediocre performers. People were stumbling, dancing, laughing, and having a grand ol' time.

Jorge Lombard stepped through the front door into the chaos. Some people called his name as he began walking through the bar. He waved or nodded back to them but didn't change his course, which was toward a hallway in the back of the bar. He squeezed through bodies until he made it to his destination. He came to two doors; on the right was the filthy restroom, and on the left was a door that read "Employees Only". Jorge knocked on this door lightly a couple of times. A moment later, a round-faced man with hair greasier than his own opened the door for him.

Inside the office was a more subdued environment than the bar. The entry area was the office, but twenty feet away the room turned into a warehouse. This area housed supplies for the bar, but in certain locations—inside barrels, behind walls, above the ceiling plasterboards—kilos of cocaine and an armory or weapons were hidden.

A group of seven men in suits sat on leather couches in the office area. A tripod with a map propped on it was in the center of the circle. Standing next to the map was a man in the nicest suit of all, Terry Watkins, a man who looked like he could be president of the United States. He was around forty and had a neat, tight haircut. His face was always cleanly shaven every morning. His teeth buffed an impossible white.

Jorge's entrance paused the meeting that was taking place. All eyes turned to him. "Having a meeting without me?" Jorge asked rhetorically.

"What did he say?" Terry asked.

"Says he's not coming," Jorge said with a smile. "Says that you can be pissed off all you want, but he ain't coming."

The men broke out in scoffs and whistles. Terry was the only one in the room without a smile. "He's an ungrateful guy, isn't he?"

Jorge nodded slowly.

"Is he saying he wasn't trying to win?"

"Yes."

More laughs followed. Even Terry couldn't stop himself from laughing. "We'll figure out what to do with the kid. Right now we got some other shit to deal with." Terry turned his attention back to the map in the center of the group of men. Jorge took a seat and lit up a cigarette. The map was of a city block in an east-downtown area called Lincoln Park, home of the LPB, The Lincoln Park Bloods, one of the *Perros Locos's* largest and most ferocious rivals.

"Sunday it goes down," Terry said, pointing at the board. "Those fucking niggers will be all over the place, doing whatever the fuck they do with their worthless lives. We're gonna pull up on Washington Street. Make sure we're not on opposite sides of the park or we'll take friendly fire. The mission is to take out as many bloods as possible. Simple as that. Maybe they'll learn to not step on our toes anymore."

The men in the room nodded in agreement. Jorge's crazed smile made another appearance.

CHAPTER THREE

La Jolla elementary was a factory of excellence—at least that's what the sign in the lobby said. Millionaires of all varieties sent their kids here for their formative years. This morning, Jamie Hurley found herself in the principal's office. Her son, Ryan Hurley, was on her left. Across the mahogany desk in front of them was the principal of the school, Mrs. Linder. The old war-horse had dyed blonde hair that was meticulously curled for hours that morning. She wore a purple dress suit and had pale skin that was excessively contrasted by her pink cheek makeup and maroon lipstick. She stared at the mother and son with eyes that sat at the bottom of wrinkled sockets.

"Mrs. Hurley, I'm going to have the same conversation with you and Ryan as I did with the other boy and his parents. Violence will not be tolerated at this school. I have a very tough decision to make here."

Ryan sat broodingly in his chair, looking at the floor in front of him. His brown hair was ruffled, a bruise was forming quickly on his left cheek, and his eyes were red, indicating he had been crying. Suddenly he burst out "He started it! I was just defending myself!"

"I don't care who started it," the principal replied calmly.

Jamie told her son to be quiet and rubbed his shoulder. Then she looked to the principal and tried to reason with her. "Mrs. Linder, Ryan is really sorry. Isn't that right?"

Ryan didn't look up from the ground as he said "no".

Jamie shook her head at her son's lack of gamesmanship. She would have to handle this on her own. "What is it that you want him to do when a kid starts hitting him?"

"Tell a teacher, or come to me. Let us handle it. There are many options, but fighting is not one of them. Wouldn't you agree?"

Jamie was a young mom, and she wasn't appreciative of Mrs. Linder—or anyone for that matter—taking on a motherly tone with her. "Not at school when he can get in trouble. Do I believe in defending yourself? Absolutely."

Mrs. Linder tilted her head. Her eyes narrowed. "Well I see where some of the problem is coming from then."

Jamie saw red. She didn't leave the restaurant where she worked during the breakfast rush—forgoing good tips—to be lectured on how she should raise her son. Before blowing a gasket, she decided cut to the chase. "Is he expelled or not?"

The two women stared at each other for a moment. Jamie began to think that Mrs. Linder's hearing aid had gone out. Finally, she spoke. "No. We will give him a one week suspension. But if it happens again, he's gone."

"And what about the other boy?"

"That boy was beaten bloody, Mrs. Hurley. He's suffered enough."

With that, a small hint of a smile touched the corners of Ryan's mouth.

⤜⊹⊹⤛

Jamie drove her black Mercedes through the palm tree lined streets of La Jolla on her way home with Ryan sitting shotgun beside her. She kept taking glances at her son. Every time she looked towards him, she saw the large bruise on his cheek, making her blood simmer inside. She decided she had to keep her cool so that she could be a good example for her hot-headed son. "You have to control yourself, Ryan," she said after a glance.

The boy didn't respond; he just watched the world go by through his window.

Jamie carried on, seemingly accustomed to one-sided conversations. "Stay away from that boy. Another fight and you're going to be expelled."

There was still no response. Jamie's knuckles turned white as she gripped the steering wheel tight.

"Look at me!" she shouted. This time the boy obeyed. When she spoke again, her voice was lower and calmer, but the anger was still detectable. "I just got called out of work for this. That's a big deal. And you just got suspended for a week. You're lucky I'm not making you walk home."

Walking in the seventy-five degree weather would hardly have been torturous, but Ryan refrained from stating this. "Mom I'm sorry," he said, sounding genuine. "I was defending myself. I scored a touchdown and next thing I know I'm being pushed from behind. I almost fell down he pushed me so hard. And when I turned around, he was coming at me swinging."

"And then what happened?"

"And then he got beat up."

Jamie stifled a laugh. Ryan was known to throw in an unusually grown-up response from time to time, but it never stopped being hilarious. Now Jamie was the one not responding.

"What do you think Dad's gonna say?" Ryan asked.

Jamie let out a sigh. "You let me handle that."

❂

The Hurley residence sat among the mansions and swank restaurants of the La Jolla village. Theirs wasn't the biggest house, but it

19

certainly didn't stick out as if it didn't belong. It was only one level, but the hand carved angel fountain, the white pillars, the double door entrance, and the perfectly kept grass lined by beautiful flowers and gnomes were indicators of the residents' wealth.

The sun was fading over the Pacific in the view their backyard provided, burning the sky a beautiful red while Jamie was in the kitchen making dinner. She wasn't the best cook; that honor fell to their house keeper, Lupe. But tonight's meal was spaghetti. Even Jamie's novice skills couldn't mess that up.

As she drained the noodles of the boiling water they rested in she called for her son to come to the table. Ryan came into the room with wet, spiky hair and without a shirt. The bruise had turned to a full blown black-eye. He quietly took his seat while watching the television. The evening news was on, talking about a nasty car accident on the freeway and the resulting traffic. Jamie made a plate for her son and poured her secret sauce on top of the steaming noodles. She placed the plate in front of Ryan and told him to dig in.

Ryan did just that, twirling a saucy bundle of noodles together with his fork and shoveling the bite into his mouth. With his mouth full, he asked "Where's Dad?".

"He's working late," Jamie said from behind her son with a hint of anger. She made a plate for herself and grabbed her glass of wine as she went to the table to eat with her son. "How is it?" she asked as she took her seat across from him.

Silenced by his mouthful, Ryan looked at his mother and nodded his head up and down in approval. Jamie smiled at him. *He might be an elementary school rebel, but I raised a good boy,* Jamie thought as she smiled. She began eating her food in a much more delicate way than Ryan did, but still quickly. On the television, the news story changed from local tragedies to sports. The sports anchor, George McGuire, was reporting about some local MMA fights that had taken place over the weekend. After introducing the story, footage of the fights was shown. Ryan watched with keen interest as fists and shins collided with faces and abdomens. Once Jamie caught a glimpse of the hand-to-hand violence and the look on Ryan's face, she scrambled for the remote.

"Let me see this!" Ryan pleaded.

Jamie gave her son a death stare, but the returning look from her son showed that he really wanted to watch. *Why does he like this shit so much?* she wondered. *He certainly didn't get it from his dad.* Finally, she released her grip of the remote and let Ryan watch.

Among the series of quick highlights were some shots from a fight that featured a man with short, messy, dark brown hair and a set of eyes that looked like burning blue coals. The short clips showed the blue-eyed fighter throwing haymakers while biting down hard on his mouthpiece. Other clips showed the blue-eyed man's opponent taking him to the ground and beating on him. The final shot of the highlight featured the latter getting his hand raised in victory.

Then George McGuire was on the screen again, this time on location. He had a mic in his hand with a shot of the small but packed arena behind him. In the frame with McGuire was a big, grey haired man.

"Mike, that was a tough loss for your top prospect David Lewis there. Tell us how you saw it." McGuire poked his mic into the coach's grill.

Mike stood with his hands on his hips, not looking his interviewer in the eyes but off in the distance. "Yeah like you said, it was close. Could have gone either way, but he didn't do enough."

"You had several other fighters on the card tonight. Seems like you've got a good thing going at that gym of yours."

This snapped Mike out of his daze and brought his attention to the reason he agreed to do this interview in the first place. "Yeah I appreciate that. We got a lot of good up and coming guys, but we also offer classes for all levels. We have plenty of women who train with us, and we also offer kids' classes, which are taught by David himself. He's an excellent coach."

The interview ended with Mike telling viewers how they could find the gym. "It's called The Bear's Den, and it's located at the corner of Rosecrans and Sports Arena Boulevard," Mike concluded. Ryan would not forget this.

Then McGuire was back in studio with his white teeth shining. He discussed the Chargers' upcoming game against the Seahawks before tossing it over to the weatherman. Ryan had stopped eating. All he could think about was the grey-haired man saying "Kids classes . . . taught by David himself".

"I wanna do that," Ryan said, turning to his mother.

"Do what?" Jamie asked as she took a bite of noodles.

"I wanna go to that gym."

"No way in hell," Jamie said quickly, dismissing the idea.

"Why?"

"Ryan, you just got suspended for fighting. Why would I send you to a gym that teaches you to fight?"

"Because I would get all my frustration out there!" Ryan pleaded, "I wanna learn something that I love. I wanna be a real life ninja."

Jamie again had to stifle her laughter. Picking at her spaghetti helped her achieve this task. "Absolutely not."

"I promise I would never fight at school again if you let me go."

Jamie didn't respond.

"I'll run away like a little girl, I promise!"

"No," Jamie said, but the look on her face showed a small opening. Ryan saw it. He was an expert at reading his mom's expressions just as she was of his. "Let's talk about your punishment instead of things that you want after just getting suspended. How do you plan on filling your time with the week off?"

"I don't know."

"I have an idea. Every morning, you are going to start your day writing 'my butt should be in school' one hundred times."

"You're kidding!"

"I'm dead serious. There's two T's in the butt I'm referring to. And after that, you will be Lupe's slave. She will be delighted to have some help around the house."

Ryan lowered his head. His vacation from school wasn't going to be as fun as he thought.

"If you're good, maybe I'll consider taking you to that gym."

Ryan's head sprang up like a dog hearing the sound of its leash jangle. "Will you *really*?"

"You have to be a saint this week. If you are, I will consider it like I said."

Ryan got up and walked around the table to hug his mom. It was a cheap tactic, but an effective one. "Alright, alright, that's enough. Are you finished with your food?"

"Yes."

"Go rinse your plate and hit the sheets then."

Ryan did so, leaving Jamie alone in the kitchen. She looked at the clock. It was closing in on nine. She shook her head in aggravation. There was no word from her husband. Nights like this had become the norm in the Hurley residence.

CHAPTER FOUR

For the next couple of days, David was free to do a whole lot of nothing. Mike had given him the week off from his obligation of teaching the kids' boxing class. David planned on extending that week forever. With each day, his body felt better. His lip went back to its normal size, the bruise under his eye went from a dark blue to a light pink, his ribs didn't feel like broken glass, and his right hand was looking less and less like a blown up latex glove. He could even ball it into a fist again.

Monday came and went without much action. He left the house only once to pay the much overdue rent and to buy a bottle of whiskey on his way back. Tuesday was about the same. The pizza boxes were stacking, clothes were piling throughout his studio, and flies were beginning to swarm in the kitchen. Wednesday arrived with high levels of health and boredom, so David decided to take a walk down to the bar. Not only to catch a breakfast-buzz, but also to look for new employment.

The Lodge was a bar owned by an Italian man named Sal. Although the place had a kitchen, it was ill-advised to eat the food that it produced. David came here occasionally when he wanted to watch a football game that wasn't being aired on his modest cable plan. The reason he liked this place was that unlike many other bars in the area, nobody ever came to The Lodge. He usually had the place to himself and a handful of other drunks.

David strolled into the dark restaurant and removed his glasses. The place was decorated in a tacky, laser-tag theme with neon lights running up and down its S-shaped bar. Surrounding the bar were around twenty unattended, circular tables.

Sal, a short, bald fellow, was behind the bar talking to a customer when he saw David strolling up. "Aye!" he yelled. "Just the man I was hoping to see."

"Who me?" David replied with a smile as he placed his wallet on the counter and got comfortable.

"Yeah you." Sal walked over to the line of tap beers and neatly poured a glass of Modelo, then walked over and set it routinely in front of David.

"Thanks, Sal. What's been goin on?" David asked as he took a sip of his beer.

"Same shit, just tryna keep the doors open, you know?"

"I hear ya. What did you want to see me for?" David asked, although he was pretty sure he knew the answer.

"Well," Sal began, folding his arms, "after all the time you been comin here, you didn't tell me you was a fighter, man."

David smiled and shook his head. "The black eyes never gave you a clue?"

"I just figured you were gettin in scraps on the street. None of my business. But I didn't know you was a *cage* fighter, and a damn good one at that."

"I lost that fight, Sal."

"Yeah but you looked good doin it! Sometimes that's all that counts. It's an entertainment business, and brother, that fight was entertaining!"

This praise was like salt in an open wound. David hid his anguish with a forced smile. "Well, I'm glad you enjoyed it."

"Shit yeah! They're gonna replay the whole card on Friday if you wanna come down and watch it."

"The Warriors game will be on, Sal. Don't do that to these people."

"Nonsense. Our boy put on a scrap and we're gonna watch it. Fuck that baseball crap."

"It's basketball Sal, but do what you want. I won't be able to make it. I got some stuff going on." David sipped his beer some more and looked around. He planned to ask for work, but after seeing just how far downhill the place had gone, he wasn't so sure he still wanted to. But after some thought, he realized he was in no position to discriminate. "Hey Sal, you got any work you need help with around here?"

"Are you kidding? Look at this place."

David smirked and nodded. "Just thought I'd ask."

"Fighting not paying the bills?"

"No. I'm actually done fighting." David downed the last of his beer and twirled his finger in the air, signaling for another.

"What? Why?" Sal asked as he turned, poured another beer, and replaced the empty glass.

"A lot of reasons really. You know of any bars that are hiring?"

"Shit, all the ones with business. Turnover in those places is ridiculous. Unlike here." Sal looked over to the bar-back who was cleaning glasses. "Julio's been here ten years man."

"I know. That's why I came here first. I don't know if I can handle working for some of these other places. A little too much commotion for me, you know?"

Sal looked at David and drummed his fingers on the counter. After a moment of deliberation, he finally spoke. "Alright, tell you what. I can give you a job. You'll do a little bit of everything, work the door, bar-back, mop the floors. I could use a versatile fella like

26

yourself. Makes it so I don't have to hire multiple people. We're co-min into the holidays, so things should pick up a bit. But it's gonna have to be for minimum wage."

David considered for a moment and came to the same realization he had before. "That works," he said. "When do you want me to start?"

"Let's do Monday. You look a little banged up still."

David gulped down his second beer and set it down along with a twenty dollar bill. "You're the man, Sal. I won't let you down."

"I know. Good to have ya."

David came home with a slight buzz and went to the fridge to add to it. He sat down on his couch, twisted the cap off of his Jim Beam bottle, and took a long chug. The length of his drink and the lack of a grimace when he finished showed just how far along the road of alcoholism David found himself. A bar whipping-boy was the job he had just obtained. Thinking about this, David laughed as he took another sip. When he was in prison, he developed a master plan for his life when he got out. He was going to clean up, leave the *Perros* and do what he knew best: fight. He woke up every day before breakfast and busted out a hundred pushups, squats, and crunches. He shadowboxed in the yard while everyone stared at him like he was a crazy man. He *was* crazy—crazy for success. Now David realized he was also crazy in another sickening way; he was crazy for thinking he could ever be something more than mediocre.

David drank until these hurtful truths faded from his mind. Eventually he drifted away to the land of sleep. As he slept, he had the dream he feared would come every time he shut his eyes.

On a rainy summer night between David's junior and senior year of high school, David is strumming his guitar aimlessly under the watch of his

Michael Jordan posters when he hears his father come home. He's drunk as usual. David knows he's drunk because he's singing an ACDC song badly. David stops strumming for a moment to listen to the imminent argument between his parents.

His mother is downstairs washing the dishes. She darts a look at her intoxicated husband. "Where have you been?" she asks sternly. David's father opens the fridge and peers inside.

"No beer?"

"Maybe if you didn't kill a twelve-pack every night you'd have some left."

"Don't give me that shit," says Walter, slamming the fridge door shut.

"Where the hell were you?" Sarah demands an answer once more.

"I don't have to answer to you, woman. I put food on this table. If I wanna let loose with my friends after a hard day's work, something you know nothing about, then I will. Okay?"

David's mother stares at her husband with big, enraged eyes, but there is nothing she can do. Not without getting the shit beat out of her, and she doesn't feel like getting the shit beat out of her this night. So she turns back to her sink of soapy dishes and returns to scrubbing. But she feels something— her husband's eyes on her. Her mean, drunk husband's eyes. He was in the mood for something that seldom took place in the Lewis household. He came up behind her slowly and put his hands on her waist, resting his head on her left shoulder. "You look good in that blouse," he says.

"Don't, Walter." She moves her head away from his rank breath. His hands drift down to her crotch. She swipes them away and turns around quickly. "Don't! You're drunk! Go watch TV or lay down and beat off! Because that's not happeni—"

WHACK! The back of Walter's right hand stops David's mother in her tracks. David's father grabs her by the arms and begins to kiss her neck. "NO WALTER! YOUR SON IS HOME, WALTER!" He throws her to the ground like a rag doll. She begins to scoot away on her butt towards the wall with a terrified look in her eyes. But Walter grabs her feet and pulls her back to him. He unfastens his belt with his left hand and pulls his pants down while holding her ankle with his right. "Walter, please," she says quietly with tears streaming down her cheeks. But her horny husband doesn't listen. He climbs atop his wife and begins to have his way. He is too drunk—both with alcohol and deranged lust—to notice his son emerge in the doorway.

Walter is a few unwanted, torturous strokes into the raping of his wife when a baseball bat shatters his head, causing him to collapse onto his wife's chest instantly. The loud CRACK of his father's skull was something David would not soon forget. He stands above his parents on the kitchen floor with his Louisville Slugger in his hand.

"She said stop!" David screams like a child. He thinks—and somewhere deep down hopes—that his father is still alive. But he isn't. David's mother pushes the limp body off of her and stands up next to her son. She is creepily stoic. Her blouse Walter had fancied is now coated with blood. They both look down at Walter as the puddle of blood begins to spread rapidly across the tile floor. There's a sense of horror, but also a sense of relief between them. They both feel it.

"What do we do?" David asks, his voice having returned to normal.

"I think we gotta call an ambulance."

"I think he's dead, mom."

"We'll call anyway."

"What are we gonna say?"

"The truth—all of it. You did nothing wrong, son. Whatever happens with this, don't forget that." She takes her son, who was now becoming a muscled man, into her arms.

David sprang upright on his couch, his heart beating violently in his chest. That fucking dream. He was a prisoner to it. Since that night, it had come to him in many forms. But this one was as real as the night it occurred. It was two in the morning. The moon was casting long shadows from his kitchen window. He grabbed a cigarette and sparked it. As he smoked and reflected on his quickly evaporating dream, he realized he had done what his mother told him not to do that night: he had forgotten that he did nothing wrong. In fact, he didn't believe that. The courts did, his peers did, but *he* never did. Ever since that horrible night he'd been haunted by his father's ghost and condemned to a life of misery.

CHAPTER FIVE

In the midst of his one week suspension, Ryan's hand was cramping as he finished writing his ninetieth line of "My butt should be in school". He fought through his fatigue for ten more lines while propping his right wrist up with his left hand, finishing his first daily task. He spent the rest of his day folding clothes, washing dishes, vacuuming—doing whatever his long time nanny asked. Lupe Hernandez had seen a lot of Ryan, even bathed him when he was younger, but she had never seen him work so hard before. To Ryan, every bit of work he did that week was worth it because there was a light at the end of the tunnel.

⟨⊹⊹⟩

On Thursday, the sun rose over the eastern hills of Julian and set against the Pacific Ocean with very little happening in David's life. His stubble was growing into a mini-beard, and his belly had lost all definition and was now covered with a nice layer of fat, like that of a polar bear getting ready for a long, foodless winter. His eyes normally had a piercing, enchanting affect, but now they were dull and empty.

When Friday night came, David was on the couch flipping through the channels when he stumbled upon the rerun of his fight that Sal has spoken of. He was struck by a wave of shame and embarrassment that caused him to change the channel immediately. But something brought him back.

His last fight was his first ever to be aired on television. When he got the news that he would be fighting on TV, he was over the moon. The bout was only broadcasted on a local channel, KFMB. The network had shoddy production, but they still pulled significant San Diego viewers. He wanted to watch it, and no matter how painful it may be, he was going to. This fight was supposed to be his prison aspirations taking form in reality. Leading up to the fight, David could see his master plan starting to unfold. Then Terry gave him the call that changed the dynamics of the fight completely.

This deal was in place until the cage door was closed behind him and David met eyes with his opponent, bringing him back to the streets of his youth. After that, all bets were off—literally.

The close up of David's face was so intense that it even gave him the willies. The bell rang, and David walked into the center of the ring. His opponent was on his bicycle from the start, staying on his toes and trying to keep his distance. David did his best to cut off the ring; he ate a few jabs for his troubles. Around a minute into the first round, he got his opponent backed against the cage and unleashed a vicious right-hook left-hook combo to the body, then finished with a right-hook upstairs—*WHAP!-WHAP!-WHAP!* The shots thundered off of his opponent's flesh. The crowd and the announcers applauded the effort. David's opponent circled to his right, away from David's right hand. He couldn't eat many more of those shots. David could smell blood in the water and plodded forward quickly. But his opponent shot in for a double-leg takedown and completed it successfully. He was able to ride David, and David was unable to get up. David never cared for grappling; he preferred seeing who could knock the other man out, a weakness of his that Coach Mike repeatedly lamented. The rest of the fight played out in a similar fashion—David throwing terrifying shots at his opponent's head for the first half of the round then getting taken down and pounded on for the second half. David squirmed in his chair throughout the viewing, as if doing so would change the outcome. It was a close fight, but his opponent got the nod. David lost the fight, but in doing so probably saved his life.

David turned off the TV and set the remote down, surprised by what he saw. He thought of a saying that Mike had told him: "Things are never as bad or as good as they seem". He agreed with his coach in this instance. He was furious with his performance before watching his fight. Furious and ashamed. But after watching the rerun and hearing the praise from the commentators, he felt some pride resurfacing. He also began to feel something else: the urge to fight again.

David went out onto his balcony with a cigarette in his mouth and gave it life with a match. The stars were out again, and David was powerless not to marvel at them. *Is this my destiny?* he thought. *Am I really destined to live out my life in mediocrity? Am I really just a bundle of cells that randomly came to be on this flying rock through space?* . . .David shook himself free of this line of reasoning. *No way. That can't be the case. I'm here for a reason. I can feel it. I have this thirst for greatness for a reason—it's there because one day I'll achieve it."* As he made this realization, a shooting star darted across the sky. His bright smile emerged through his dark beard. He looked at his cigarette with some distain, and then he snuffed it out.

David thought he was ready to give fighting another shot. It would be his last chance for glory and his last chance to become a person he could be proud of. He would have to put down the bottle, and the coke. He would also have to revert to a former mindset, the mindset that once helped him earn five knockout victories in a row. Before he started his journey up the steep mountain again, he had another neglected errand he needed to see to. The following Sunday, he did just that.

He spent the majority of the morning taking several busses out to the border so he could pay a visit to an old friend and mentor at Donavan Penitentiary. David had been back to his former home only once since his release nearly five years prior. A spooky familiarity pervaded the air as he walked through the doors. The smell of plastic and cold metal brought back many bad memories. Even though he didn't see any guards whom he recognized and he was wearing street clothes, he still felt the eyeballs of every officer in the building. Just like the women of David's interest, cops could sense his criminal past.

David checked in at the front desk and was sent to a waiting area where a handful of people were seated. After about twenty minutes of flipping through various magazines, David was allowed into the visitors' room. The room was a row of cubicles facing a long wall of glass. David sat in the third cubicle and waited for his inmate to arrive. He was nervous. He wished that he had more good news to bring to his old friend. He didn't have much to show from his years of freedom, and that was a shame.

After several minutes, Mark Summers waddled his chained legs into the booth across from him. The past five years had not been good to Mark. He was almost twenty years older than David, but that number looked closer to forty now. He was down thirty pounds, and his pale face was gaunt. David tried his best to hide his concern upon seeing his old cellmate. Mark smiled big as he took a seat across from David on the other side of their barrier. The smile made him look younger and in better condition. He reached out with his bony hand and removed a black phone from its holster on the wall.

"Well isn't this a pleasant surprise," Mark said into the phone.

David smiled back. "How you doing, Mark?"

Mark looked around mockingly. "Just living the dream."

David chuckled briefly. "You've lost some weight."

"You noticed, huh?"

David nodded slowly.

Mark turned his palms up and sighed. "Just not as hungry as I used to be. I'm getting old, my man. What brings you all the way out here to this shit-hole?"

David adjusted his ass in the uncomfortable plastic chair as he thought about his answer. "I don't know. I guess I've just been thinking about you lately."

"What would you do that for?" he asked. "You know what's going on with me. Same shit, nothing's changed, except I got my own cell now. Fifteen years in this place finally earned me some seniority. But I gotta say, I'm glad you came. I haven't had a visitor in a long time. The only person who comes is my crazy nephew and his crazier wife."

"I'm sorry I haven't been out to see you."

Mark waved a dismissing hand. "Don't worry about it. Everything going good on the outside?"

David cleared his throat. There was an excess of phlegm from his return to cigarettes. "It's not all roses. But it's better than being in here."

Mark nodded. His smile carried David past his initial concern. "How's the fighting? You haven't sent me a letter in a while."

"I've won seven and lost seven now . . . My most recent L came about a week ago in my first televised fight. So I'm not really setting the world on fire like I had hoped."

"Just gotta keep with it. You're establishing yourself; you got a career going. You're on television for Christ's sake. Have some resolve, kid."

David nodded. He was happy to hear this from Mark. Mark changed David's life when the cell door was slammed behind him at the age of nineteen. The tall man the inmates called The Doctor—he was the only guy in the joint with a PhD—hopped down from his bunk and immediately made David feel welcome in an extremely ominous place. Mark put a book in David's hands and taught him about life, especially about the forces. It was only through Mark's encouragement that David embarked on his journey as a fighter, the reason David felt so much shame for his lack of success and his relapse into his old ways. "I plan on it. But . . . "

"But what?"

"You know how you always talked about forces taking you off your path?"

Mark smiled. "Oh yeah."

"Well, they're strong, real strong in my life. You remember that guy I used to work for?"

"Terry something right? I hear he's big time now. Got some young punks in here that are in his gang."

David nodded his head. "He is. I've kept my nose relatively clean, but he asked me to throw my last fight."

"And?"

"Well . . . I accepted . . . but I tried to win the fight. I just lost."

"You got a death wish or something? What did you do that for?"

David shook his head, still hurting from the decision he had made. "I don't know. I thought things would be different when I got out. I thought I'd never go back to my old ways . . . It's hard man."

"Fuck yeah it's hard," Mark said, his voice raising several octaves. "Being in here is fucking easy man. Easiest shit in the world. It's fucking adult day care for Christ's sake. Being out there is way harder than the monotony of this place. But you can do it. And it's gonna be glorious when you overcome those obstacles. It's one day at a time. Remember that—". Before he could finish his thought, Mark burst into a storm of vicious coughs.

"You sure you're doing ok?" David asked.

"I'm fine; I'm fine," Mark said, waving that dismissive hand again.

David thought Mark looked far from fine. But he remembered that Mark was getting old in prison, not Club Med. "You should be getting out in a few years, right?"

Mark looked up at David and for a while said nothing. David became more and more suspicious that Mark was keeping something from him. "Yeah, I got a shot in sixteen months," Mark said unenthusiastically. "We'll see what the parole board has to say."

"They'll let you out. Everyone loves you in here, even the guards. We'll have a big party for you when you get out." David paused and smiled. "Even if it's just you and me at a bar, it'll be a party."

A ghost of a smile emerged on Mark's face. Then it disappeared. For a moment, a look of frustration replaced it. Then that disappeared. He looked David squarely in the eyes and spoke softly. "I want you to do something."

"What?"

"You know where Telcolote Canyon is, right?"

"Yeah."

"There's a willow tree in there. I don't see many willow trees in San Diego. There was lots of em in Montana when I was growing up. Anyway, this one's got big ol' roots that jump in and out of the dirt. The biggest root points down at the ninth green of Telcolote Golf Course. That might be a good way to get there, through the course. Buried five feet away from that root is my life's savings— among other things. I want you to have it."

David's eyebrows jumped up, wrinkling his forehead. "No way. Get it when you get out."

"I want you to have it. You seem like you could use some money."

"Who couldn't? But I'm not gonna do that."

"Why the fuck not?"

David leaned forward with a perplexed expression on his face. "Because it's yours. You've been here fifteen years."

"You could hang on to it for me then. Make sure it's there."

"If it's there now, it'll be when you get out. They can't do any construction in that valley. It's a protected area. Did you wrap it good?"

"Of course I did."

"Well you're good to go, then." David paused and looked around.

Mark sighed. They sat in silence.

"I'm gonna get out of here Mark. It's really good to see you."

Mark's comforting smile made him look well again. "Thanks a lot for coming in."

"I'm gonna overcome the forces. I'll do it for you. Keep an eye out for me in the papers."

"Don't do it for me, kid. Do it for yourself."

Mark put a fist on the glass, and David met it with his own. They both hung up their phones. David watched as Mark rose and waddled away into the depths of the prison.

CHAPTER SIX

Lincoln park resided just east of downtown over several small foothills. The area held San Diego's highest African-American population. The local gang, the Lincoln Park Bloods, had a strong hold on the gambling, prostitution, and drug trade in the area. If you were a young man in Lincoln Park, you had ties with the LPB. When the *Perros Locos* tried taking their action downtown, the result was always bloodshed. The latest disagreement left three of *The Perros's* best men dead in the street. They were found by police missing their shoes and wallets.

That Sunday morning, revenge was on the way.

The LPB's headquarters was the Granite Oaks projects building, fifteen floors of decaying red bricks and barred windows. Outside of the projects was a park scattered with splotches of dead grass, a basketball court with terrible rims and backboards, and homeless drug fiends throughout. Despite these poor qualities, the park was the favorite hangout of the community. It was their home. Accordingly, that Sunday, like every Sunday, Lincoln Park was busy with activities. Men in red clothing stood in small clusters everywhere, smoking blunts and drinking beer. The sounds of basketball dribbles could be heard as a five-on-five game raged on. Kids were using the park to run around and play hopscotch. Despite their poor neighborhood, bright smiles shined from their dark faces as they sang songs while skipping rope. The clusters of boozing Bloods were also enjoying themselves in their alternative ways.

At least their last moments on earth were joyful.

"Pass that shit motha fucka," a shirtless man said to a hefty fellow who was holding the blunt a little too long for the shirtless man's liking. He sipped his beer then glanced to his right and noticed two black cars at the edge of the park. People—outsiders—were stepping out of the cars quickly. The shirtless man had time to yell "AYE—" before ear-shattering sounds of machine-gun fire pierced the air. Bullets ripped across the park. Bodies dropped everywhere. Many ran for cover. Those who pulled their guns and fired back were quickly shot down. The children collapsed into piles as their jump rope flew through the sky.

The Perros stood in a line of eight. Every man had a machine gun exploding in their hands. Jorge was among them. His mouth clenched shut; his eyebrows furrowed as he panned back and forth with his weapon. When he was empty, he reloaded and unleashed one more clip. Eventually the fire came to a stop. All that could be heard was the screams of witnesses coming from the surrounding buildings and the screams of agony coming from those who were only wounded instead of dead. The Perros moved quickly towards their cars. All of them except for Jorge. He lingered as he lit a cigarette. After briefly surveying his handiwork, he joined the others. The duo of cars pulled away.

The war had begun.

CHAPTER SEVEN

O n Monday morning, Coach Mike entered The Bear's Den at 7:00 a.m. with a coffee in hand. He flipped on the lights of the empty gym and went into his office. Moments later, rap music blared from speakers located throughout the gym. Mike emerged without his coffee and made a B-line for the treadmill. Every day for the past eighteen years, he had run three miles to begin his day. "If I don't do it, I'll kill someone," was his famous saying. This notion may have been true. His students never doubted it. As he ran, his face never grimaced. Each breath methodically went in through his nose and out through his mouth. After finishing his run, he showered up before people started filing in for his 8:00 a.m. Jiu Jitsu class. When he emerged from the shower, he was surprised by what he saw. David was sitting on the bench by the front door. Mike walked over while drying his hair.

"I expected you back," Mike said. "But not this early in the morning."

David stared at him for a moment before speaking. "I watched the fight."

"And?"

"And it wasn't as bad as I thought it was."

"It never is." Mike sat down next to David. He looked at him like the father he had become to him. David had never told Mike exactly how his father died. He told him that the old man died in a work accident. But Mike never bought that. He figured it was something big by the way David avoided the subject. The lack of a male influence in David's life was evident by the way he interacted with others. David cared very little about a firm handshake or maintaining solid eye contact.

"I want another fight," David said, turning to Mike. "And I want to do it right this time." He had reverted to the man Mike had grown to love. The man who walked into his gym fresh out of prison looking to take on the world.

"Ok," Mike said. "I can do that for you. But I'm gonna hold you to your word. We're gonna do this thing right. You were right last week when you said it's not worth getting beat up for two hundred dollars. That's why you have to rise to your full potential and stop getting beat up." Mike looked at David, who was staring through the cage wall at the mats that would soon be filled with people grappling. "How's your hand?"

David looked at it then showed its progress to Mike. It was still puffy and red but not nearly as bad as it was when he'd last seen him .

"You're a stubborn fucker, you know that? Why didn't you go to the doctor? That thing should be in a cast."

"It's good. Just a hairline fracture. Another week and I'll be good to go. I'll still teach the kids and get my cardio right on the treadmill. Does that work for you, Coach?" David looked at Mike and gave him a coy smile.

Mike smiled back. It was strange seeing their two stone faces bare their pearl-white teeth. He patted David on the head and said "That works, kid."

That week, David began his transformation. He called Sal and thanked him for the opportunity to work at The Lodge but told him he had decided to continue fighting. Sal was happier about the decision than David was.

David showed up every morning at seven to run three miles with Mike. Then he would return home and eat breakfast. The morning cardio helped him drop weight quickly. The fat he had gained from eating nothing but pizza the week before quickly disappeared, revealing a slab of hard muscle. At four in the afternoon, he would come back to the gym and do a strength workout that didn't involve using his right hand, which was rapidly getting better—a strength workout of a core or a leg variety. At five, a group of young kids would file into the gym, and David would do what he was paid most for. The kids were glad to see their coach back after his week long absence, and he was happy to see them. Even though he had no prior experience with formal boxing before joining the gym, David was able to take the basics that Mike had taught him over to the kids' classes. And after five years of teaching (and learning), he had become a damn good coach.

David gave high-fives to every kid as they came in, leaving no one out. He had been the one who was left out often in life and knew how much it could affect a child. If parents came in, he was sure to shake their hands as well. This week, he did so with his left mitt. "Alright guys, you know the drill. Grab your ropes and get to ropin." The kids—ranging from the ages of eight to fifteen—jumped rope sloppily for ten minutes to begin each practice.

"Tiiiime!" David shouted to the now glossy skinned children after ten minutes had expired. "Alright, wrap up and glove up. Let's box!" After the warm-up, David usually taught a technique or combination to the class. Practicing a particular technique consumed the majority of his hour-long class. He taught all the rules of boxing: keeping your hands high and elbows tucked, throwing strait punches, rotating your knuckles—all of the things he himself didn't do. But he taught these golden rules to these young assassins because he knew it would benefit them. Eventually they would develop their own style of utilizing these techniques, as some of his advanced students already had. This day's lesson was how to land a left hook to the body by first setting it up with a straight right hand to the head, a simple but effective technique.

While David taught the class, Mike sat at the front desk reading through emails, winding down after teaching killing techniques for the majority of his day. The front door chimed as a blonde woman entered. A small boy with brown hair trailed closely behind her. Mike looked up from his computer and stood to greet them.

"How's it going?" Mike asked, smiling bigger than he would for a guest without breasts.

"Good," Jamie said, smiling back. "I've come here interested in signing up for some classes for my boy here."

Mike looked over his desk at the boy she was referring to. The kid's face appeared to only consist of two giant blue eyes.

"Well you picked a good time to come," Mike said. "The kids' boxing class is going on right now. Do you want to check it out?"

"That would be great," Jamie said.

Mike walked around the small counter that separated them and reached out his big hand towards Ryan. "What's your name, young man?"

Ryan shook Mike's hand, amazed at the roughness of it. "My name's Ryan."

"Nice to meet you, Ryan. I'm coach Mike. You want to learn how to box, huh?"

"Let's just say he's got some energy he needs to expend," Jamie answered for her son.

Mike laughed. "You've come to the right place." He motioned toward the side of the room where David was teaching class. "Follow me."

Jamie and Ryan followed Mike along the front window on their way to another section of the gym. As they walked, Mike played tour guide, pointing out the Jiu-Jitsu and wrestling area. As they rounded a wall that cut the gym in half, they encountered a large, empty cage. Beyond that was an open area where a conglomeration of kids with boxing gloves was punching each other slowly. Walking amongst them was the man they had seen fighting on television.

David walked through the rows of students, examining their technique. He watched closely as they punched straight with their right hands, got their heads off center (leaning to the left), and whipped their left hands into their partner's livers. For the most part, the group of kids looked damn good. This was no accident. David taught them well. He encountered a pair of his younger students who were struggling to get bend with their left hook. He pulled them aside and began giving them a more in-depth tutorial on the technique that he loved so much.

Jamie and Ryan watched intently but with their focus on different things. Ryan was looking at a black boy named Xavier, one of David's oldest and best students. He marveled at how he moved like a professional at his young age and wanted to be like Xavier. Jamie's attention was focused on David. She noticed his diligence when working with the boys who appeared to be Ryan's age. His care for them was evident. His eyes, voice, and body language were all she needed to see to confirm this.

After twenty minutes, a timer on the far wall sounded its alarm. The kids ceased practicing. David stopped teaching his younger students and stood up to address the class. From his new angle above the group of five-footers, he saw Mike standing in the corner with what appeared to be a mother with a new student. "Alright boys, get some water, get some oxygen, and get ready to spar!" he yelled. Then he walked over to the newcomers standing with Mike.

As he approached, he smiled without teeth and said nothing. He noticed Jamie's beauty right away. When he got close enough, he could smell her perfume. *They always smell as good as they look* he thought. He waited for Mike to do the introducing. Mike was better at that kind of thing.

"David, this is Ryan and his mother Jamie. Ryan wants to learn how to box."

David looked down at Ryan and folded his arms. A bigger, more genuine smile emerged on his face. "Is that right?"

Ryan nodded his head. Jamie watched the interaction between them with a smile on her face, a smile that came from nervousness rather than genuine amusement. "I watched you fighting on TV," Ryan said.

Everyone's seen me lose he thought to himself. "Right on, you saw me get my butt kicked?"

Ryan shrugged. "It looked like you were winning."

David chuckled. "Thanks, bud. But the judges saw it differently." He turned his attention to the nice smelling woman. "I think we're going to get along."

"Is it safe?" Jamie asked.

"Absolutely," David replied. Jamie's question reminded him that the class he was teaching was not over yet. He turned his head and yelled at Xavier to run the sparring portion of the class that day. Then he turned back to Jamie, taking a moment to get back on his train of thought. "I've been teaching for three years now and haven't had any serious injuries. Not in class anyway. Maybe a few black eyes here and there. But it looks like Ryan's already got one of those going. So he should be fine."

Ryan smiled, the first one he'd cracked since he walked in the door. He looked up at his mother. With that eye contact, he knew he had her. Jamie turned and looked at David. "Ok, we'll try a month. He'll probably only be able to come one day, maybe two a week."

"Sounds good," David said. He was ready to return to his class of students when Jamie did something he didn't expect: she willingly continued the conversation with him. And, call him crazy, he thought it could have been a flirt.

"Are you here every day?" she asked.

"Monday through Friday. This is my office," David said with his sheepish smirk.

"Good," Jamie said. "I like how you teach the kids. And by the way, I thought you won too."

David didn't know how to respond. This woman clearly lacked the ex-con-detection system that all of the other woman he encountered seemed to possess. There was a gleam in her grey eyes. She wore a polo with the name of a restaurant on it, a name he couldn't read. The black shirt wasn't very flattering, but she managed to make even it look good. Her snug khaki pants *were* flattering, showing the legs of a very fit woman. He admired her for bringing her young son son to an intimidating gym to learn how to box. Suddenly, painful thoughts surfaced of his mother coming home from work to an empty apartment while he was out committing crimes. *How beautiful she was, and what an asshole I was*, he reflected in anguish. Eventually, he realized he had been staring into Jamie's eyes for an inappropriate amount of time and looked away.

Mike, noticing, uncomfortably brought the meeting to a close. "Ok well, we're really looking forward to having you guys."

"Thank you for the tour," Jamie replied and then looked to David once more. "Nice to meet you, David." She put her hand on her son's head. "Come on Ryan."

Ryan fought off his mother's grasp and looked up at David. "Will you teach me to punch like you tomorrow? I wanna punch as hard as you do."

A smirk rose at the corners of David's mouth. "You got it bud."

The boy turned around and joined his mother as they left. He watched them go for a moment then turned to his class.

"Alright punks, let's spar!"

⫷╌╌⫸

At five o' clock the following day, David was fresh out of the shower after an exhausting workout. Across the gym, David's students were filing in for his class. The attendance of his class varied each day. Some kids came frequently; others stopped in once a week. The only kid who came every day, rain or shine, was Xavier. Knowing this, David didn't pay much attention to who was present at his class unless there was an extended absence. But today was different. He was eager and hopeful to see his new pupil, Ryan, and Ryan's mom. Adding a new student was nice; David liked seeing his class grow. And Jamie—there was something about her. Something about her presence. When he recalled her image, she was surrounded by a soft light. Whether it was by his making or not, it was there. He was excited to see her again (and had finally shaved for the occasion). But she and Ryan never came that day. They didn't come the next day either, nor for the rest of the week.

Jamie didn't plan the absence. She thought she'd be able to get off work with enough time to get Ryan from school to the gym, but she couldn't. With the holiday season entering its prime, The Capital Cafe—the popular restaurant where she worked—was busier than usual. She was upset, but no one was more upset that Ryan, who felt like he was being lied to by his mother. He had learned that lying was all his father was capable of, but his mother had always been truthful with him—sometimes brutally.

While Jamie was being swamped by rude tourists and hoards of wealthy La Jolla foodies, Ryan was on the bus towards the after school program he attended: After School Matters. It was regarded as one of the best after school programs in the area. It had great counselors, a big screen TV with a Playstation hooked up, every board game under the sun, and even a small indoor court for soccer and other activities. Despite all of these amenities, Ryan hated After School Matters. He cried the first time he attended. Everyone saw, and everyone laughed. He spent most of his time drawing and the rest of his time staring out the window, waiting for his mother to arrive. The worst part about the place came from a new development. It was not far from the gym he had recently signed up for and was now being denied access to. Ryan could see the large Bear sign towering high in the sky several blocks away. He begged his mom to let him walk. She considered but ultimately declined. The area was seedy, not the neighborhood any reasonable mother would want her nine-year-old kid walking through alone, no matter how short the distance was.

This day, Ryan rode the bus with his head rested on the window, sulking throughout the entire ride. At After School Matters, he sketched. Normally he drew animals, eagles being his favorite subject. But today and throughout the entire week, he drew fighters.

CHAPTER EIGHT

The following Tuesday, David was out for a run, punching the air as his feet pounded the pavement. He didn't like to run with music in his ears like most people. With his ears free from blasting tunes, he could feel his breath plunging deep into his lungs and exiting rhythmically. He liked to hear the noises of the cars passing, people yelling, and dogs barking. He could feel his body becoming ready for battle again. He was once again back on the right path, which alleviated him of the demons that constantly resided in his subconscious. He came full circle back to his apartment after a good five miles. He was high. Not the high he got from the coke. To David, it was much, *much* better.

When David got inside his apartment, he saw that he had missed several calls from Mike and had a text from him as well. The message read "Give me a call."

David picked up his phone and dialed, pacing around the living room that was also his bedroom.

"We got a fight," was how Mike answered.

David's eyes widened as he felt a surge of nervous energy. A strange, anxious feeling always came over him when he heard he was scheduled to fight another man. "When?"

"Seven weeks. December twenty-third. Holliday and his promoters are calling it a Christmas card special. Get it? Anyway, this is a big deal."

"Seven weeks? Shit, that's the longest notice I've gotten for a fight."

"Yeah, well, we're gonna need that much time. This is a big one. The dude you're gonna be fighting is a beast. His name is Arnold Loder, a badass Muay Thai guy."

The name was familiar to David. The guys in the gym talked about him frequently. "I've heard of him."

"I'm not surprised. Dude's tough. You guys will be the co-main event. Holliday is really stoked about this fight."

"What's the money situation looking like?"

"Four hundred to show, four hundred to win. And a lot of recognition for knocking this guy off."

David pinched his lips together and shrugged. "Alright."

"It's about the opportunity, David. This is big."

"I know, Mike. I'm excited."

"How's the hand?"

David looked at his hand and balled it into a fist. "Good to go. Tomorrow, let's have at it."

"Ten-four."

When Mike pulled up in his truck to the gym the next morning, David was standing by the front door waiting for him. David pretended to look at a watch he wasn't wearing as Mike parked. Mike smiled as he exited the truck, excited at David's eagerness to train. He gave his pupil a fist bump as he walked up with his bag hanging from his shoulder and a coffee in his free hand.

"You ready to go?" Mike asked while he fumbled around for his keys.

"More than ever," David replied, taking notice of his coach's struggle. "Let me help you out." He took the keys from Mike and opened the door himself.

"Thanks," Mike replied. They entered the gym.

The two men ran side by side on neighboring treadmills with their sweaty shirts plastered to their chests.

"You got any film on this guy?" David asked between breaths.

"There's tons. I'll show you some on Youtube later. The guy's got a hell of a highlight reel. He's solid everywhere but definitely prefers standing up and trading, which is good for us. But we're gonna be ready for anything, even taking him down if we have to."

The look David gave Mike said what he was thinking: *that's never gonna happen.*

Mike sensed the disbelief in David's look. "I'm telling you man, it may come to that if you want to get this W."

Instead of going home to eat after the run like he had done the previous week, David stuck around for something that he hated: the 8:00 a.m. jiu-jitsu class. The class's attendance was a mix of amateur and pro fighters. After a warm up jog, the class broke into forty-five minutes of training in a certain technique. The last fifteen minutes were dedicated to live sparring (it wasn't a coincidence that David ran his boxing classes in the same fashion).

David practiced with his partner, another pro fighter named Dillon Embry. Dillon was a brute heavyweight but a nice guy. The two fighters practiced a move called an arm drag, which is used to take the back of the opponent. David hated the monotony—and the intensity—of grappling practice, which is why he so often avoided it. But drilling these techniques over and over again is what makes great grapplers. Eventually, the body learns to do certain things in certain situations without the mind being present at all. David knew this, so he drilled, and drilled, and drilled. Back and forth, David yanked Dillon's massive arm, taking him off balance, and wrapped his legs around his back quickly, sinking in a choke. Then Dillon would do the same.

After class, David and Mike sat in the office watching tapes of David's upcoming opponent. Arnold Loder was the hottest up-and-coming fighter out of San Diego. He had a record of eight wins and one loss. His lone loss was his first fight, where he was tapped out by a rear naked choke. This was a possible weakness for David to expose, but he had to remember that it was also Loder's first fight. Loder's grappling had improved greatly since then. His last eight fights had all been knockouts, seven of them in the first round. He was widely considered to be on the fast track to a big league organization like the UFC or Bellator MMA.

Loder's highlight tape showed exactly why he was so highly touted. He looked the part of an elite MMA fighter. His body was tattooed from head to toe in colorful ink, he had a closely shaved head, and his physique looked like it was chiseled out of granite. But his scariest feature was the way that he *moved*. He was trained by the Muay-Thai legend Krak Yen, and his style of striking was a mirror image of his master. He plodded forward like a coiled snake with his hands high to protect his head. He was light on his front leg, which he used to block incoming strikes. Every punch and kick he launched was technically perfect—straight down the pipe and vicious. He was the antithesis of David—a wild man who threw looping punches—but they were similar in their supreme aggressiveness and effectiveness at putting their opponents unconscious. David and Mike shouted "*ooohhhh!*" progressively louder while holding their fists over their mouths as they witnessed Loder ruthlessly destroy each opponent on film.

After the display of carnage was finished, David leaned back in his chair and looked at Mike, who was hovering above him. "He's as good as advertised."

"Yup, sure is," Mike said. "But he's a man. He breathes the same air as you and puts his pants on one leg at a time just like you do. And he'll go to sleep if your fist meets his chin."

David spun around in his chair and nodded. He was envisioning the fight already. This was an opponent who was finally going to trade punches with him. He liked that idea, and the smile on his face showed it. "I'm gonna finish him."

Mike smiled. "I like the confidence. Be ready for anything, but I like it. And I can very well see it happening. Anyone who bangs with you is in danger."

David sat in silence. Mike noticed his pupil's fists clench and his weight shift slightly in his seat. He was going through the fight in his head. Eventually, he snapped out of his daydream. "I should head home for a bit," he said. "Just to get some food in me, maybe watch some TV. I'll be back later to teach class."

"Good call. Nice work today." Mike patted David on the shoulder and headed for the door. His wrestling class was starting soon.

"Hey," David said, stopping Mike from his exit. "What ever happened with that new kid that signed up?"

Mike smiled. "Are you wondering where *he* is, or are you wondering where *mom* is?"

A returned smile was David's answer.

"You like her, don't you?"

"How could you not?"

"Fair question...I don't know. I need to give her a call," Mike said. "They paid for the month already, so they're wasting cash not being here."

"I can call if you'd like," David said, still brandishing a stupid, boyish smile.

"You, make a business phone call? Jesus you must be in love. Didn't you see the rock on that finger, Romeo?"

He hadn't noticed. He was too fixated on those unusual grey eyes. A small bubble of fantasized hope burst inside of David's chest. "It's not about that," David lied. "The kid was so excited. I just want to make sure everything is alright."

"Hey, be my guest. His name is Ryan Hurley. Mom was Jamie, in case you forgot. His info is in the computer."

David twirled around to the computer again and pulled up Ryan's info. He punched the listed number into his cell phone and looked at Mike as he heard the ring. "Do you mind?"

Mike smiled and shook his head as left the room.

The phone rang for a long time. David was beginning to think it was one of those phones that didn't have an answering machine and would just ring forever if you let it. He went to hang up when he heard that angelic voice. "Hello?"

"Hi, can I speak to Jamie?" David said, feeling and sounding like a telemarketer.

"This is her," Jamie replied, ready to hang up on the solicitation.

"Hi Jamie, this is David. I teach boxing at The Bear's Den. We met last week."

"Oh yes, the fighter."

"Yeah . . . I was just calling to see if everything's alright. I was excited to work with Ryan and haven't seen him since that day."

"That's nice of you to check in. Trust me, I'm in the doghouse with my boy for not bringing him. I'm just having some difficulty arranging a way for him to get there from his after school program. My work schedule has been hectic lately, and Ryan's father works very late."

"Well is there any way we can make it work? I'd hate to see you waste your money, and he seems like a good kid. I was excited to work with him."

"Well his after school program is just down the street from your gym. I can see that big ass bear sign you guys have from the parking lot."

David chuckled. "Hideous, isn't it?"

"A little bit. It worked though; it got me in the door. Anyway, like I said, it's just down the street, but you know that's not the nicest area. I think he's too young to walk there by himself."

"Yeah, I'd agree with that." David hesitated before making his next offer. "I could walk him over . . . I mean, I know you don't know me very well."

"I don't know you at all. All I know is that you're a fighter. So that's starts you at negative one."

David shrugged and tilted his head. "Fair enough."

"I'm kidding, David. You seem like a nice guy. I could see it in the way you talked to my son. You weren't faking that. I know faking when I see it. His father is great at it."

David didn't know how to respond to that, so he didn't.

"You know where the burrito shop is across the street?" Jamie began again.

"I eat there every day," David replied, almost laughing.

"His after school program is three blocks behind it. It's called After School Matters."

"Ok—I think I know the place you're talking about."

"Should I call them and let them know you'll be checking him out today?"

David was in shock over the situation he found himself in. No one had ever trusted him like this. "Sounds like a plan to me."

"Ok I'll do that then if you promise me he's in good hands."

You mean the hands that gripped the bat that shattered my dad's skull? David thought. "He is. I promise."

"Ok I will give them a call and let them know that a strapping young man named David Lewis will be coming to pick him up today. There shouldn't be a problem; just bring some ID."

David's smile turned gigantic. His cheeks were turning a tint of red. "Awesome Jamie. Will you be able to pick him up at six when class is over?"

"Yes, that should be fine. In fact, you're really helping me out here. It's busy season at my restaurant. That's why I haven't been able to bring him. I just can't make it there by five, but six should be perfect. So thank you. I appreciate it, and I know Ryan will too."

"My pleasure Jamie. I'll see you later."

David hung up the phone and leaned back in his chair. She was coming back, and he was petrified.

CHAPTER NINE

At 4:45, David jaywalked his way across Sports Arena Boulevard towards Jose's Taco Shop. Usually he made this short trek to obtain a greasy California Burrito. Today, his journey was for a new student.

Inside After School Matters, chaos was surging as was typical. Music was playing loudly. Kids were running around, laughing, crying, and screaming. The big-screen TV was surrounded with children eager to play the winner of the Madden game that was taking place. A game of monopoly was turning heated, as it always seemed to. Ryan Hurley, however, wasn't participating in any of these activities. He was sitting on a little plastic picnic table and staring out the window. When it came to the last hour of his stay, Ryan started to long for his mother. Time ticked by slowly in that hour, but with Zen like patience he waited, unaware of the surprise he was in for.

From around a corner to his left, Ryan saw David emerge on the sidewalk outside. He was looking around, momentarily lost, but then he spotted Ryan's location and started to head his way.

A bell chimed as David entered kid heaven. An older lady at the front desk greeted him warily, having never seen him before. "Hi there."

"Hi, I'm here to pick up Ryan Hurley. His mother said she would call to let you guys know that I would be picking him up."

"She did." The woman looked David up and down. "I'm just going to need a picture ID from you, David."

Just as the woman spoke these words, Ryan came running around the corner with his eyes wide. "What are you doing here?"

"I'm here to pick you up, big guy. You ready to have some fun?" David pulled out his wallet and removed the ID, placing it on the counter. The woman looked at it, smiled a big fake smile, and handed it back.

"What are you guys going to do, Ryan?" the woman asked to Ryan's head as it was just poking over the barrier from the front area they occupied.

"David's gonna teach me how to punch really hard," Ryan said plainly.

The woman raised her eyebrows and looked over to David. He lifted his shoulders and smiled back at her.

"Alright champ, let's roll."

Instead of jaywalking, David took the long walk down to the crosswalk with Ryan. As they walked, they talked and got to know a little bit about each other. David found that he liked this kid. He was very subdued, his voice never reaching over a set, calm level.

"How do you like that place?" David asked. "Seems like they got a lot of really cool stuff in there."

"Yeah they do. They have the new Playstation."

"That's pretty cool. Do you have one at home?"

"Duh."

David laughed. "Well excuse me. I never had one."

"Really?"

"Really. My favorite thing to do as a kid was play basketball. That was like my video game."

"I like basketball too. Kids at school don't pick me though because I'm not very good."

"I'm sure you're plenty good."

"No I really suck at it."

"Don't say that man. All it takes is practice. Just like we're about to do with boxing. Today you might not be very good, and that's ok. But in time, you can be the best. The only person that can stop you is *you*. Maybe one day we can practice basketball together, too. But let's go one sport at a time, alright?"

Ryan pondered David's words for a moment as they began to cross the sidewalk. "You really think I can be the best?"

"Absolutely. To me, the 'best' is just the person who works harder than anyone else and has an undying belief in their heart. But you can't lie to yourself; you have to outwork everyone. And we're going to start today."

Some of David's students had already arrived when he and Ryan strolled through the door. Three boys of varying ages were sitting on the long bench in the front of the gym talking about whatever young kids talk about. Xavier was also early, but he wasn't sitting around gossiping—he was shadow-boxing in front of the mirror. Ryan watched with fascination as the lean black boy punched the air in fluid combinations.

"Hey Xavier, come over here real quick," David called.

Xavier walked over, his skin shimmering with sweat. "Ryan, this is Xavier, one of my best students." They exchanged a little kid handshake. "You can learn a lot from him. See how he's boxing in front of the mirror before class has even started? That's what champions are all about." Xavier smiled, pleased by his coach's praise.

David knew everything he was saying was true. He had the keys to every door he needed in life. That's what made him a great coach for the kids. He could only hope that these kids were better at taking his advice than he was. What he didn't tell Ryan, Xavier, or any of his students is that life is a cold, obtrusive motherfucker, and its forces against your will for greatness get stronger as you age.

That day David had the class go through their routine, letting Xavier take the lead while he taught Ryan the basics off to the side of the group. Equipped with mitts on his hands, David went down on two knees in front of Ryan, making him the same height as his student. Ryan looked at the gloves on his hands with wonder, like they were equipped with magical capabilities. David clapped his pads together. "Alright big dog, we'll start with the most important punch: the jab." David slowly demonstrated the punch, extending his left arm straight and rotating his fist, bringing his right hand up to protect his face at the same time. "The power comes all the way from your legs. You can even pivot your front left foot a little to generate some torque."

David had Ryan try the punch on his mitt. When he did, David was impressed. When David usually taught punches to students as young as Ryan, they ignored everything he had instructed them to do. They just attempted to punch as hard as they could, throwing technique out the window. Ryan, however, executed a slow, thoughtful, perfect jab into the pad. David raised his eyebrows and smirked. "That's perfect, Ryan. Now let's learn a right straight, the knockout punch."

As class was ending, students began heading out the door, but David and Ryan were still working. Jamie slipped into the gym to pick up her son. She slid her glasses atop her head and looked around. As she rounded the corner to the area where she first met David, she discovered he and her son were on the mats, still practicing.

David was now having Ryan throw combinations instead of single punches. "One, two, three, two!" David shouted, then—*WHAP-WHAP-WHAP-WHAP*—Ryan would blast off the four-punch combo.

Ryan was tired, but David kept pushing him. "One, two, three, two!"—*WHAP-WHAP-WHAP-WHAP*. Ryan struggled as he got this final combo off. They were done, and Ryan was left with wet noodles for arms. "Good job my man," David said. The sound of Jamie's clapping made them turn to the bench area where she was standing. Ryan ran over and gave his mom a sweaty hug while David rose to his feet.

"Oh my god son, you're drenched!" Jamie said, pushing her son to an arm's length and examining him. Ryan smiled and nodded.

"He got a good workout. Learned lots," David said, walking over.

Jamie smiled at David, then looked down on her son again. "You have a good time?"

"Yeah."

"What do you say to him?"

"Thanks David," Ryan said, his big eyes bulging through strands of wet hair.

"You're welcome. You did really well bud. I'm impressed. Just remember what we talked about, alright?"

"I will."

Jamie smiled at the exchange between student and coach. She was very happy to see her son treated so well and that he was discovering new interests. "Ok Ryan, take your gloves off and go wait in the car. I'm going to talk to David for a bit, ok?"

David waved his hand, dismissing Jamie's request of returning the gloves. "Keep em. We got tons."

"Are you sure?" Jamie asked.

"Absolutely. Just throw em in the washer. They're pretty ripe."

"Yes!" Ryan yelled as he ran off to the car.

Jamie turned to David, noticing that he had broken out in a slight sweat as well. David saw the ring on Jamie's finger this time. It was quite a rock. *How could I have missed that?* he wondered temporarily. But when his attention shifted to Jamie's eyes, he realized how he had overlooked the ring. There was something about her, something hard to put his finger on. It was more than her beauty. It was the way she behaved. She felt more open to him than any woman he had met before. He somehow felt comfortable around her despite her beauty. Maybe she gave off this vibe to everyone. David thought this was probably the case, but he hoped otherwise. He wanted this feeling to be reserved for him, and him alone.

"I just want to thank you, David," she said. "You're really good with these kids."

"I appreciate that. I like teaching them. It makes me better at what I do. Keeps me sharp."

"That's what they say, huh? Teaching makes you better at the skill you teach."

"That is what they say. Whoever they are."

Awkward laughter followed from both parties. "So, is this going to work for you, bringing him over here every day?"

"It's a piece of cake for me. Seriously it's no trouble at all. As long as you're okay with it."

"Is there any reason I shouldn't be okay with it?

David took a moment to respond. "Nope."

"Ok." She smiled, and David smiled back. "Well, it's time to get home. I'm sure my boy is hungry."

"I have a feeling you'll see him eat like you've never seen before tonight, so make double."

"That's a scary thought, but I'll do that. It's taco night, so that should be easy," she said with a laugh. "Thanks again David."

"See you tomorrow," David said. Jamie walked away. When she was out of hearing distance, he said it once more.

David's right hand was as close to one hundred percent as it was going to get, so that night he began hitting pads with Mike again. Unlike grappling, this aspect of training is where David shined. The pads seemed to explode when David connected with his punches. The gym was empty now except for the two of them, and the blows sounded like gunshots bouncing off the walls.

Mike shuffled around after each combo. David stalked him, then let loose a series of punches, grunting and yelling with each strike. After five rounds of intense work, they called it a night.

Afterwards, David sat on the bench breathing deeply, trying to slow his heart rate, just like he would between rounds on fight night. Mike was haphazardly cleaning the gym, throwing some pads in a corner nearby. "You're looking good man. Real good."

David only nodded, breathing close to normal now.

"You just gotta keep with the wrestling. It'll come," Mike said as he finished his organizing of the gym for the next day. He walked over and took a seat next to David. "You realize what's gonna come after you win this fight, don't you?

"Eight-hundred dollars," David replied, playing dumb to the real rewards.

"A hell of a lot more will come if you beat this guy . . . *when* you beat this guy, you'll be on the map. And you know it."

David looked down at the ground and nodded again. He was exhausted, and he had four more weeks of this training to go. In spite of the difficulty, David knew the opportunity he had. A win in this fight would make him a big name on the San Diego MMA circuit. Most of the world except Mike was picking against him. Not even the other fighters in the gym thought he stood a chance against Loder. This doubt made the prospect of winning even sweeter for David. Finally, with his breathing slowed and heart rate down, he looked at Mike. "I want it bad, man. Real bad. I'm ready to start making real money, and I'm ready for people to know my name."

"They will." Mike put his hand on the back of David's neck and leaned his head in close. "Five weeks, and they will know who David Lewis is."

CHAPTER TEN

A prison hospital is a sad place. The room is constantly packed with patients faking their ailments, like they faked their way through their failed trials. Mark Summers, however, was here for a legitimate reason. He had throat cancer, with the bloody coughs and the unbearable pains to prove it. He had the strange sensation of feeling and witnessing himself die, but somehow, he didn't seem upset about it. He lay with a newspaper in hand while his doctor examined his test results on the opposite side of a curtain.

On the front page of the paper that day was a story with a headline reading: "Massacre In Lincoln Park Leaves Thirteen Dead, Nineteen Wounded." Mark glanced over this story without much heartache or interest. *More San Diego gang violence*, he thought dismissively as he turned to something that interested him more, the sports section. The lead story was about how terrible the Chargers were—another tired story for Mark. He glanced at the Padres' stats from their last game against the Giants. Then, just as he was about to set the paper aside, something caught his eye:

Rage Cage Promotions presents: A Christmas Card Special

On December 23rd, Pechunga Casino andResort will host Rage Cage Promotions for a night of exciting hand-to-hand combat. The main event features a heavyweight bout be-tween Jamal "Tank" Johnson and Khabib Nabokov for the Rage Cage Belt. The co-main event features a welterweight bout between San Diego natives Arnold Loder and David Lewis. Just two days before you open your presents, Rage Cage is delivering a present of its own. Tune in to your local stations or buy your tickets on ticketfinder.com to experi-ence the excitement live…

Mark's eyes darted across the page as he read the short adver-tisement. His heart rate began to speed up. *I know that man*, he thought. *That's my old cellmate. That's my friend.* Mark and David had a deep history. Mark essentially raised David and gave him the education he never received—and wouldn't have received even had he paid attention in school. When David stepped into his cell many years ago, he was fresh off a failed bank robbery and was hav-ing devastating withdrawals from the many drugs he consumed daily. He entered prison having no idea there was more to the world than the disturbed bubble in which he had grown up. Mark gave David a crash course on philosophy with Socrates, Plato, and all the world's greatest thinkers as his aides. Soon, David came to the realization that he was hurling around a star in the infinite cosmos on a giant rock, and somehow, some way he came to be on that flying rock. When this realization is made, it becomes hard to stress about bills, reality TV, congressional debates, even being in prison for a few years. He made it to the race. It's a difficult race, but at least he had the opportunity to participate, and that was beautiful in itself. David couldn't believe a man in prison could be so upbeat. But that was Mark; that was the Doctor. After some time, the acceptance of this strange journey rubbed off on David.

The curtain next to Mark was pulled open. The doctor (the medical doctor) was back with some paperwork in his hand. "This isn't good, Mark."

Mark folded the newspaper and put it down on his lap. "You're telling me," he said with a smirk. "I can't even take a shit without pain. Used to be my favorite part of the day."

The doctor smiled and shook his head. Everyone liked Mark. "The cancer has spread from your esophagus into your lungs. We need to get you on treatment right away if you're going to have a shot at beating this thing."

"I don't care if I live," Mark said bluntly. "I just want the pain to stop. Give me some painkillers or something. The good stuff."

"It's required by law that we get you treatment, and we can't give it to you here. You'll need to be transferred to a hospital with the necessary equipment and staff. Look on the bright side if you can; you'll be allowed to get outside these walls."

Outside these walls.

An idea struck Mark. He didn't have much longer to live, and he knew it. He didn't want to spend his final days filled with tubes pushing lethal toxins into his blood stream. He wanted to spend those days breathing fresh air, eating good food, seeing the few loved ones he had left, and most importantly, watching a particular fight. He didn't have a chance of escaping prison—he'd seen the failed attempts of many in his time. But escaping a hospital? That was something he was willing to attempt.

CHAPTER ELEVEN

David wasted quite a bit of water in the shower that evening (his water utility was free, so fuck em). As the hot water struck the back of his neck, David thought about many things. He thought about Arnold Loder, who was out there somewhere preparing to go to war with him in five weeks. He thought about the young boy he trained earlier that day and how much he reminded him of himself. He thought of Terry and if he would make an appearance in his life once again. And inevitably, the greatly unwanted thoughts of killing his father crept through his defenses, as they so frequently did. But mostly he thought about Jamie, her golden hair that sat just below her shoulders; her freckled, full cheeks; her soft, grey, eyes; and that confident, playful attitude she carried. She was the one that could make him whole, and he knew it. But she was a married woman, he also knew that. Even if she wasn't married to the wealthy man that bought her the bolder she wore on her ring-finger, she could never love David. He was an ex-convict who had killed his father. He wasn't meant to be whole. That was reserved for everyone else.

Everywhere he went, he saw happy families with kids living in large homes. They had built-in networks of people who loved them unconditionally. David only had two. One was behind bars. The other, his late mother, was buried in the dirt. These people David saw were living the life he never had. He longed for that life, but it had always been beyond his grasp.

After showering, David sat on his couch wrapped in a towel and feeling melancholy. The muted television flashed across his face and the wall behind him, making those surfaces change colors. He was most susceptible to his addictions during times like these. One line of coke, one drag of a joint, or one pull from a flask would take all his problems away. He looked to his nightstand where one of those relievers was calling to him.

David opened the drawer and fumbled around until he found what he was looking for. He pulled out the bag of coke Terry had given him after his last fight. He hadn't touched it since, but he hadn't trashed it, either. It was waiting for him, whispering to him as he slept. Terry knew David was a slave to this shit, that he couldn't help himself. That's why he gave David this freebie; to keep him coming back.

David was once one of Terry's best soldiers, with a specialty in robbing rival drug dealers. Terry plucked David off the streets at the ripe age of seventeen, just a couple months after the death of Walter Lewis. David became addicted to the drugs Terry provided in a time when they were greatly needed, but eventually he became even more addicted to the high he got from robbing people. For two years, The Kid—as he came to be known—was on the rise in the crime world. But like all drugs, the effect gets weaker as tolerance builds. That's what happened for David and his new favorite drug. He became bored with robbing pimps and crackheads. He needed a bigger dose of this opiate—like a bank. David came up with the plan and scouted the place for weeks. Terry sanctioned it, providing guns and a driver. David didn't mess with the safe, just the drawers. A gun to the unsmiling manager's head gained him access to the bullet-proof, glass encased room. David was already counting Benjamins in the get-away car when he saw the blue lights flashing in his rear view mirror. After a short chase, and a deadly one for the driver, David was arrested and sentenced to five years in Donavan Penitentiary.

Terry thought he would get his old gun back easily when he was released from prison. The contrary was the case. Instead of becoming a more hardened criminal in prison—the effect being locked away had on most people—David appeared to be a new man. A man who didn't want to rob; he wanted to fight. But Terry didn't get to his position by easily taking no for an answer. He eventually got in contact with his old soldier. And although David would no longer rob for him, Terry found other ways for David to be of use.

No more, David thought, *no more*. He carried his bag of coke through his small apartment—all fifteen feet of it—to the toilet where he dumped the remains into the water, then flushed it with satisfaction.

That same night, under the same crescent moon, Ryan was in his living room punching the air like a wild man while Jamie took plates from the table to the sink. They were alone again. After rinsing her plates, Jamie grabbed a hefty glass of wine she had readied and walked into the living room where her son, she thought, was quickly losing his mind.

"Will you take it easy Muhammad Ali?" Jamie requested of her newly crazed son.

"Can't," Ryan replied between a combo. "Gotta work harder than everyone else if I want to be the best."

Jamie smiled, but she was exhausted from a long day. "Ryan, *stop*, seriously. You can practice more tomorrow."

"Fine." Ryan let his hands fall down to his hips. Breathing heavily, he walked over to the couch and sat next to his mother, laying his head on her crossed legs. She lifted her glass of wine to avoid spillage and planted a kiss on the top of his head. "Where's dad?" Ryan asked, even though he knew the answer.

Jamie's face had an expression of sadness and disappointment at this question. "Working late again, it would seem."

"I wanted to show him what I learned today," Ryan said from the comfort of his mother's lap.

"Tomorrow you can. It's time for bed."

"Okaaaay," Ryan said with great disappointment. He got up and headed down a hallway for his room.

"Make sure you brush those teeth!" There was no response from her son, but she knew he would do as told. Despite what Mrs. Linder thought, Ryan was a good kid. Jamie turned on the television and watched the evening news while she sipped her merlot. Sitting above the television on a shelf was a picture of her with her husband (flanked tastefully by candles and other ornaments). The man in the picture was the kind of man you would imagine Jamie being with—broad shouldered, tan, perfect teeth. And in the picture, taken during the seventh inning stretch at a Padre game, they both looked very happy.

However, that picture was very old.

An hour later, as Jamie went to pour her third glass, lights flashed though the kitchen as a car pulled into the driveway. She looked towards the lights with disdain as she walked back to her perch on the couch. Minutes later, a man in a suit entered the door. Max Hurley was a tall, handsome man. He was thirty-eight, making him ten years older than Jamie. "Hello," he said in a distant, tired tone as he headed for the fridge. From that fridge he pulled out a plate of tacos wrapped in plastic. "These for me?"

"Yup," Jamie replied without looking his way.

"Thanks," Max said, heading for the microwave while unwrapping the plate. The room was silent save for the television and the hum of tacos being radiated. Once done heating, Max took the plate and began eating at the table. After one taco down, he spoke again.

"You giving me the silent treatment again?"

Jamie sipped her wine, looked at him blankly, then turned back to the television that was now playing a *Friends* rerun.

"Why don't you just speak your mind? It's been a long day."

"What am I supposed to say?"

"I don't know, maybe 'how was your day?'"

"How was your day sweetie?" she responded dryly.

"It was long, as you can see." Max took another bite from his taco. His chiseled jaw tore the chicken to shreds.

"I sure can."

Max polished off the taco then got up and walked into the living room, rubbing his hands together. He took a seat in a recliner adjacent to the couch where Jamie was sitting.

"Look, I just have to get through the holidays. Then things will be better."

"Things are always going to get better according to you. When here, in reality, they steadily get worse."

Max gave an exasperated look and rose to his feet again. "I guess I'll have to let my actions speak for me." He went to the kitchen to finish his meal.

"This isn't working, Max."

Max stopped and turned around. "It's not? Looks like it's working pretty well to me. You got your comfy clothes on and your glass of wine watching a forty-two inch plasma television. That not working for you? Is that Benz not working for you?"

"You really think I give a shit about all that?" Jamie barked. "Do you think that's why I married you?"

"More and more, yes," Max said tiredly. That calm, nothing-is-wrong-here tone was enough to make Jamie want to rip her hair out.

"Why do you think that? Because I won't fuck you? Why would I let a man who I never see, who never sees his son, share a bed with me?"

"I don't know, maybe because you had the brain to realize that the reason I'm away so much is because I'm trying to provide for you and Ryan and doing a pretty bang-up job at it."

"I want a husband who loves me, and Ryan wants a father who loves him. That's all. We don't need any of this shit."

"I do love you guys. And you know it."

"I *don't* know that. I know you love your job. I know you love people bowing to you. I know you love having a young hot wife to show off at your holiday parties."

"Don't be so full of yourself. You've had one too many glasses of that shit."

"Oh I've built up quite the tolerance over the past couple months."

"Good for you." Max grabbed his plate and dumped his remaining taco in the trash. "I'm going to bed." He grabbed his coat and headed for their bedroom. At the entry way, he turned back to Jamie. "Are you coming to bed?"

"This is my bed, Max. You know that."

Max shook his head and walked down the hall.

In his room, Ryan lay in bed with his eyes open, listening to his parents engage in their nightly fight. He heard a door slam, then turned over and hoped to finally sleep.

CHAPTER TWELVE

The next day was Sunday—David's lone day off from his training. He slept in to 9:00 a.m. It was the longest he could go these days; his body was conditioned to the early mornings. He rolled to the side of his bed and brought his feet to the ground. Outside, the sun was shining and birds were singing their morning songs. Another beautiful day in San Diego, the kind of day that would be wasted staying inside reading a book or watching *Sportscenter* over and over. He would go stir-crazy if he did that on this glorious day. So he decided he would eat some eggs and then go for a walk.

David went through life as a loner. Even as a child, he never made much of an effort to make friends. His mother always told him he had to "get out there," if he was going to meet people. "Things will happen. People will come to me," he would always tell her. He often turned out to be right, and on this day he was again.

He strolled slowly through the neighborhood with a cup of Starbucks coffee. Eventually, he left the collapsing brick buildings of Point Loma and found himself in the sleepy town of Ocean

Beach. He made an effort to observe everything—a practice he read about in a book on meditation that Mark made him read. He noticed squirrels agilely playing and fighting over an acorn, lizards scrambling across the sidewalk below him, the grooves in the trees, and figs falling from those trees. He took it all in, and he felt wonderful. When he was constantly drunk, he was incapable of appreciating nature's divine beauty. At that moment, her grace was crystal clear. Noticing his surroundings was supposed to free him from the prison of unwanted thoughts that he so often found himself in. The technique worked. There were no thoughts of prison or the horrifying atrocities he witnessed there. No thoughts of the night he killed his rapist father or the *crack* of his skull. There were no thoughts at all, just the joy of being alive in that place and time.

Eventually David found himself walking alongside a park barricaded by a tall chain-link fence. The park had a large field that only stopped when it reached the vast and blue Mission Bay. There was a jungle gym with children climbing it and a basketball court where six black men were playing a game of three-on-three. David stopped once he got close to the game. He grasped the fence and began to watch the game intently.

What he saw on the court somewhat surprised him: these guys could play. The ball was moving around well from teammate to teammate. There was good jump shooting, better defense, and of course a lot of shit talking. While all six of the men seemed adequate, one was clearly the bull-hen. He stood around six-two. He had a long, slender build and a distinct swagger about him. David watched him call for the ball at the top of the key. Once he had it, he started to back down his opponent, the way Michael Jordan did so prolifically in his later years after he had lost some spring. David thought he would give a shoulder-shake then spin for a fade-away jump shot like Michael. But instead, after the shoulder shake, he spun for the basket, leaving his defender behind. As another opponent came to support, the slender man took flight. He cocked the ball far behind his head in one hand while he shoved his opponent's face down with the other. Then he violently slammed the ball through the hoop.

"Oh my god," David said to himself, a big smile on his face.

The metal chain combined with the force of the score caused the ball to go flying to the right of the court in David's direction. It rolled to a stop in front of him, rattling the fence.

The man who did the slamming jogged over for the ball. When he saw David, something happened in his eyes. A brief flicker of curiosity. David noticed but didn't understand what the look was for. He didn't recognize the slender man. As the man grabbed the ball, he smiled and said "You like that?"

"Impressive," David replied. He looked around the man to see the court better. "I think your boy busted his ankle."

A scream of pain on the court verified David's suspicion. The man who had attempted to block the shot had come down on another player's foot and rolled his ankle.

"Man get the fuck up," the slender man said as he turned around and walked towards the court where the injured player was writhing in pain with both hands wrapped around his ankle. The rest of the players crowded around him.

"Fuck you Nigga!" the injured man screamed. "My shit's broken!" The rest of the men broke out in laughter.

"Your shit ain't broken nigga," one of the other men said. "You just sprained that shit for the millionth time. Roll your ass off the court, you good."

The injured man got up slowly with aid from the others and hopped off the court on his good foot. He collapsed onto the first row of a set of bleachers positioned at the side of the court.

"I guess that's game then," one of the men said.

"Nah fuck that," the slender man replied. He looked in David's direction. But he was no longer there; he was walking away down the sidewalk.

"Aye!" the slender man called, stopping David's easy stroll. David looked back. "Aye man," the slender man said. "You wanna fill in for this punk?" The slender man's accessories looked at him skeptically as he made this request.

"Fuck you nigga," the injured man called in his defense once more.

David looked around and considered the offer. He hadn't picked up a basketball in close to a year, but he greatly missed the game he grew up obsessed with. He looked down at his clothing. He was wearing a t-shirt and jean shorts, but on his feet were Nike running shoes, the kind of low cut shoes that could easily leave his ankles looking as large and red as those of the man in the bleachers. He didn't think that would happen, however, nor did he think these guys knew what they were in for. "Yeah I'll play," David said. But when he looked for an entrance to the fenced off court, he didn't see one. "How do I get in?"

"It's all the way on the other side," the slender man said. "I'd just hop that shit if I was you."

David did. As he climbed the fence and hopped over the top swiftly he was reminded of the many times he he had done so when evading the police as a youth. He walked over to the group of men. The slender man had the ball in his large hands. He looked around at the others. "New game?" They nodded in agreement. He looked at David. "Playing to eleven. Ones and twos." David nodded. "We'll shoot for teams."

The slender man dribbled over to the top of the key and launched a shot. Swish, nothing but metal net. He passed the ball to the next player. His shot spun around the rim a couple times before it left the hoop. The next man's shot hit the back iron and spat the ball back out towards the shooter. The next man missed the rim completely and hit the injured player on the bleachers directly in his injured ankle. He screamed once more before throwing the ball onto the court in disgust. The ball rolled over to David's green

Nikes. As he picked up the rock, the players looked on silently. David looked back at them. A smirk tilted his lips. He dribbled over to the top of the key, pounding the ball hard into the pavement, getting his feel for the orange ball back. He looked at the basket, gave the ball a spin in his hand, then let go a pretty jump shot and sank it.

The players looked at David, a bit shocked. The final member of the group sunk his attempt, and the teams were established. The first three shot makers formed one team, the ones who missed forming the other. One of those strange, slightly unfair agreements of street basketball.

"Shoot for take," the slender man said, then shot once more and drained the attempt. "Our ball."

During the game, David took his time finding his offensive groove. He looked to pass the ball when he got it rather than shoot. This seemed to be a good strategy because the slender man was scoring at will. The defense was testy. The man he was guarding, the shortest of the men, called for the ball often, thinking he could take advantage of the white boy. But he couldn't get past David, who was crouched down low with his arms extended, a technique his old coaches would have been proud of. Besides his first shot of the game—which banked in—the short man could do nothing against David. The one time he broke free to the basket after receiving a screen from his teammate, he had his easy layup attempt swatted into the grass by David, who had recovered with blinding speed to catch him. The blocked shot received shouts of joy and mockery for the blockee.

The score was ten to seven, game point for David's team, when the slender baller went cold. He couldn't buy a bucket. David took the opportunity to take the winning shot. The slender man brought the ball up the court, sweat dripping off of his bare chest. David called for the rock. The slender man gave it to him and accompanied the pass with a look that David perceived as confidence.

David motioned for his two teammates to clear out of the way. It was his opponent and him alone, *mono y mono*. The scrappy defender bent down low, pulled his shorts up, and extended his arms. "What you got, boy?"

David drove hard to the right on his way to the basket, but his defender stayed in front of him well. But David was close enough to the basket. He jumped in the air and spun clockwise. The motion allowed him to break free from his defender. As he finished his rotation, he switched the ball to his left hand and laid it home. Game over.

Shouts and laughter followed as David's teammates walked over to him and gave him high fives. "Fuck yeah boy!" one man said.

"Good shit," the slender man said.

David gave high-fives all around. Then he headed to the bleachers, where the injured player was smiling and shaking his head in disbelief at what he had just witnessed. David took a seat next to him and tried to catch his breath. The injured man introduced himself as Jabari and proceeded to jabber into his ear as David sucked wind.

After a minute of rest, he heard someone say "You don't recognize me, do you?" When he looked up, he saw the slender man.

"No," David replied. "Can't say I do." But that wasn't completely true. There was something familiar about this man. David was now certain that he had seen him before. He looked around at the men as they were putting their shirts on. Every one of them had *red* shirts. These men were bloods. And David was once a member of their biggest rival gang. His heart instantly picked up its pace to the rate it had just dropped from.

"I was locked up in Donavan," the slender man said without malice.

David breathed a sigh of relief. For a moment, he thought it was a man he had robbed when he was younger. He didn't remember robbing any bloods, but there were many things he didn't remember from those days. "Really? Now that you mention it, you do look familiar."

"It's all good. There wasn't a whole lotta white and black minglin goin on in there," said the slender man, taking a seat next to David.

David laughed. "No, definitely not."

"I remember you were one of the good ones though. Stuck to yourself. You were cellys with the Doctor, weren't you?"

"I was," David said, feeling some nostalgia. Other than Mark, it had been a long time since he had interacted with anyone from prison. Donavan was a large part of his life, an unfortunate but large part. It shaped who he was, whether he liked it or not.

"He was a good dude. Helped me write my way outta that place with the appeals process."

"When did you get out?"

"Shit I'm fresh out. Just got out a week ago. Just after he escaped."

David's head snapped back. "He escaped?"

"Yeah man. You don't keep in contact with no one inside? Can't say I'm surprised. You was always readin or shadow boxin in the yard. I gotta admit, I thought you was crazy. You damn sho could ball though. That's why I asked you to play."

David was still dumbfounded. "Hold up a second. How did he escape?"

"He got cancer, bro. He was being transported to a hospital in Hillcrest and escaped from there. It's all over the news."

"Jesus," David said quietly to himself. *Mark's out there...on the run. Best case scenario, he's drinking Margaritas in Mexico. Worst case... he's dying of cancer in the streets without treatment. He's got connections though. Seems like everyone who came to the prison knew him...maybe he's taking advantage of those connections.* David's mental straining continued. *But why not just take the treatment? A hospital room beats a prison cell. There's gotta be a reason . . .*

"How's the free life been to you?" the slender man asked, snapping David out of his daze.

David was almost too distracted to carry on the conversation. But he liked this guy, so he engaged with him despite his state of shock. "It has its ups and downs, but anything's better than rotting inside Donavan."

"I hear that," the man said. He looked around, enjoying the fresh air, the sunlight, the smell of the freshly cut grass. After surveying these pleasures, he repeated himself. "I hear that."

David smiled, recognizing what had just occurred. "What's your name?"

"Darnell. Darnell Williams."

"I'm David." Darnell looked at David's extended hand for a moment, considering, then shook it. This act was something that would have, at the very least, gotten them a stern talk from their respective race brothers when they were locked up. Darnell was still operating on this level.

"We plan on playin here every Wednesday. Our spot keeps gettin shot up." Darnell paused and sighed. "Prison is hell, but at least you ain't gotta dodge bullets."

"You from Lincoln Park?" David asked.

"Born there, bred there, and I'll most likely die there."

David nodded his head, expecting this answer.

"Anyway man, feel free to come out and ball if you want."

"I might just do that."

"Aight then. Take down my number."

David took down Darnell's number then said goodbye to the group. He watched the ensemble head out. They had to walk the long trek around the fence thanks to Jabari's busted ankle. Once they were gone, David found that his previous practice of taming his thoughts was impossible. All he could think about was Mark. "*What's he doing? Is he alright? Why hasn't he tried to contact me?* his thoughts raced. He got up and started home with the intentions of grabbing a newspaper on his way back.

David hopped the fence again, a feat considerably harder to accomplish after an intense game of hoops. When he landed safely on the other side and began to walk homeward, something caught his eye. Across the street, a car was parked. A car he recognized—a black Lexus, the vehicle favored by a band of thugs he was familiar with. The windows were heavily tinted, but the driver's window was slightly open due to the heat of the day. Through the open slit, David could see sunlight glistening off of something inside. The reflective surface was greasy, black hair. He was certain that that hair belonged to a certain Cuban he knew. He started towards the car with the intention of dragging Jorge from his vehicle. When he made it halfway across the street, the car sped of, confirming his suspicion.

David stopped at the liquor store below his apartment, not for booze, but a gatorade and a *UT San Diego* newspaper. Once inside his apartment, he sat down on his couch and began to search. He was about to turn to another section when he found what he was looking for on the lower half of the front page.

DONAVAN ESCAPEE STILL AT LARGE

The search for convicted felon Mark Summers continues, officials say. Summers was able to escape detainment Thursday after being transported to USCD medical center in Hillcrest to receive treatment for throat cancer. The officer in charge of surveying the prisoner said that he turned his back for a moment and summers was gone. Summers, a former Junior college philosophy teacher, had accumulated several drug possession charges before he was imprisoned in 1999 after a field of marijuana plants was discovered on his acre of land in Julian. An ensuing raid found an arsenal of weapons in his home . . .

The short article went on to describe Mark's crimes that landed him in prison and also his ghastly, eroding features to aid in his capture. A flurry of emotions rushed through David: worry, excitement, despair, hopefulness. But the strongest emotion was guilt. How could he have ignored the clear fact that Mark was dying before his eyes? The truth was that he knew Mark was dying; he just refused to believe it. That's why he declined to dig up the money Mark buried. Doing so would have confirmed what he was trying so hard to deny.

What brought David out of his spiraling decent towards a full blown nervous breakdown was the pleasing image of Mark outwitting the cops in a hospital gown. Then another thought put him at ease. Mark would contact him. This was a certainty. He was waiting for the right time, but he would come forward when the time was right. What David needed to—what mark would want him to do— is focus on his upcoming fight. That's what David did.

CHAPTER THIRTEEN

While David was making new friends in Ocean Beach, a black Lexus—having different plates than the ones he encountered in Ocean Beach—arrived outside of The Silver Fox. The rabid four-legged neighbors were barking and leaping in the nearby shanties. The dogs leaped so high that it was a mystery how the poorly installed fences contained these savage animals.

Muffled screams could be heard coming from the parked Lexus. As the driver's door opened, the screams became audible then diminished again as the door was closed. The driver was a giant man—six-five and over three hundred pounds. The behemoth opened the rear door and once again the screams were clear. "PLEASE BILLY, DON'T DO THIS! . . . PLEASE! SOMEBODY HELP!" Billy dragged the screaming man out of the back seat, dumping him onto the pavement. The man's hands were tied behind his back. His glasses, which had managed to stay on through the ride, crashed onto the ground. Billy picked up the man by his belt and carried him like a briefcase into the bar.

The closed Silver Fox was empty save for a small group of rugged men playing cards and drinking away their hangovers. These men noticed Billy carrying the screaming man through the otherwise quiet bar. But not one of them looked up or acknowledged what was happening.

Terry was drawing a picture at his desk in his smoke filled office while he waited for Billy to make his delivery. The well done drawing was of a samurai holding a bleeding, decapitated head. The cigarette responsible for the smoke in the room was dangling from Terry's lip. On a record player, the upbeat sounds of a Neil Young's Greatest Hits album were playing. The tunes were drowned out when suddenly the door was pushed open with the screaming man's head.

Billy tossed the small man onto the ground. He rolled over and saw Terry staring down on him. He stopped screaming, petrified by Terry's presence. Terry could tell the depth of the man's fear by the fragrance of fresh piss he now found himself basking it.

"Put him in the chair, Bill," Terry said calmly. He took one final drag from his cigarette before crushing it on the samurai's face.

Billy picked the smaller man up once more and slammed him into the chair across from Terry. The man was quiet now, his bottom lip quivering. Terry could see the wheels turning in his head as he frantically tried to come up with any type of alibi that could save his escaping life.

Terry leaned back in his chair and reached behind for the record player. He switched it off, cutting the cheery music. The room was now silent. Above that silence was the heavy exasperated breathing of the terrified man in the chair. Terry turned and looked at the man named Zach Marshal. He bounced the pads of his fingers together, not saying a word, just staring, letting Zach drown in the quicksand of his thoughts until he could no longer stand it.

"Terry, let me explain myself," Zach said desperately.

"What is there to explain?" Terry asked calmly. "You killed one of my girls—One of my best girls."

"I didn't mean to! And she fucking tried to rob—"

WHACK! Billy's fist clobbering the back of his head silenced the prisoner.

"No more talking," Terry said with his hand up. "First, you don't have my money for three months now. I let that slide. I still provide your shitty brothel with my girls, and clients, and protection. All of this while you slander my name every time you open your stupid, drunk trap."

"Terry I nev—"

"SHUT THE FUCK UP!" Even Billy, standing with his arms crossed behind Zach, winced at this shout. "Then you fuck and kill one of them? These girls aren't yours—they're mine. Of course she was going to rob you, you stupid fuck! That's why she let you between her legs in the first place!"

Terry opened his drawer and pulled out his Ruger. Zach tried to stand. Billy threw him back down.

Terry stood up and cocked his gun. "You think your job is hard? This big loof could do it." He pointed in Billy's direction. "And you talk all big like you should run things around here." Terry shook his head as he walked around his desk. He took a seat on top of the cherry wood and rested the gun on his leg. "Oh, the stories I've heard Zach." Terry looked into florescent light above him and smiled. After a moment, he returned his sinister gaze to his prisoner. "I normally don't do this dirty work, but I'm going to enjoy this." The gun on Terry's leg was pointed at Zach's stomach. The trigger was squeezed, and the room thundered.

Zach screamed in agony. His white shirt turned red as quickly as a watercolor brush connecting with paper. Terry bent down in front of Zach's pained face. "How's this for handling business?"

"*Terry, please!*" the man said in a slurred voice. They were his last words.

Terry stepped back and pointed the gun at Zach's head and squeezed the trigger once more. Brains flew across the room, the majority landing on Billy's face. Terry laughed as Billy tried to clean his large mug.

"Sorry about that." Terry walked over to a couch and grabbed a shirt from the arm rest. He wiped at the few drops of brain matter that landed on him then tossed the shirt to Billy.

"I suppose I gotta clean this up?" Billy asked as he wiped the crimson mask from his face.

Terry gave him a look that said *"of course dummy"*. Then a couple of light knocks sounded at the door.

"What?" Terry yelled.

"It's me," an accented voice said from the other side. Terry nodded for the door. Billy opened it.

Jorge entered the room, showing no surprise or sympathy for the man with the top of his head missing. "Is that Zach Marshal?"

"It was," Terry responded. "Whatcha got for me?"

"He didn't go to the gym today. He's out in Ocean Beach."

"Doing what?"

"Playing basketball with a bunch of blacks. They looked like LPB. I think he just hopped in the game though."

Terry smiled. "I guess Lincoln Park is too hot for those boys these days." He walked over to a small bar and poured a glass of scotch from a snifter. "I have to admit, I thought David would be back by now. Maybe he really is done with us."

"Are we really just gonna let him get away with trying to cheat us?" Jorge asked. "It doesn't look good boss."

Terry downed his drink then went back to his desk and retrieved a cigarette. Jorge reasoned that his boss was buying time for his answer. Finally, after igniting his smoke, he said "I like the kid, alright? When he got arrested back in the day, he could have dimed on me and walked. I'd probably still be in shackles. But he didn't. He did his time like a man. I don't know if anyone in my crew now would do that."

"I would," Jorge said.

"Me too," said Billy.

"Well let's just hope you don't have to prove that to me anytime soon, because I have my doubts. The point is he was good to me. I want him back for selfish reasons. But he's been useful in other ways. He'll come back full time eventually. My coke is too good."

Jorge nodded his head reluctantly. He was bloodthirsty.

"Let's do this," Terry said, pausing to inhale. "You keep an eye on him. If you get word that he's got another fight coming up, we'll pay him a visit. Because, as you and I both know, he owes us one after what happened last time. Let's not kill our cash cow."

Jorge nodded once more. "Sounds good."

"In the mean time, help Billy get Mr. Marshal to his final resting place."

Jorge looked at Billy. They both frowned.

⊷╫⊶

That day turned into a cloudless night illuminated by a full moon, and the owls and hawks were not the only creatures using its light to prowl for precious goods in the Telcolote Canyon. Above the ninth green of the golf course that shared the canyon's name, Mark was fighting his way through brush that had grown significantly over the past fifteen years. When Mark went to prison, the Telcolote Golf Course was a hot commodity. Now it was one of the cheapest and most terribly maintained courses in the county.

Equipped with a headlamp and a shovel, Mark hacked his way through the brush until he came to a clearing. In the center of that clearing was a magnificent old willow tree towering over the area. Its leaves hung like long dreadlocks from the branches, casting waving shadows on the moonlit area. Mark was breathing heavy, sweat dripping from his brow. He began to walk through the clearing when another storm of coughs stopped him cold. He tried to restrain the coughing as best as he could, not wanting to be heard. He was close to positive no one was around, but being caged up with murderers and rapists can turn a man paranoid.

With his coughs having subsided, Mark walked over to the massive tree and gave it a pat on its giant trunk. He looked down at the roots. They were much bigger than he remembered. Also, they had been carved on. *"TS loves JM"* and *"Fuck Spics"* awkwardly shared the same crowded space. There were other signs of activity: beer cans, plastic bags, and cigarette butts to name a few. Mark began to worry that his buried treasure would not be where he left it, that someone had made a hell of a discovery with one of those damned metal detectors. With his paranoia growing, he moved quickly, on the verge of frantically. He followed the large root that pointed in the direction he came from. Starting with his feet touching heel-to-toe, he walked ten steps then slammed his shovel into the dirt and began to dig. The process was slow, understandably so, he was old, weak, and dying of cancer.

After twenty minutes of coughing and digging, Mark was certain someone had found his stash. He was on the verge of quitting and tears when he heard a *clunk* sound under his shovel. He scraped away the dirt and saw the top of the old trunk he buried long ago. Another ten minutes of digging and he was able to heave the old box out of the ground. He cracked it open as he gasped for air. His smile that followed shined bright in the darkness of the willow tree's shadow.

Everything he buried fifteen years ago was still there.

CHAPTER FOURTEEN

Over the next week and a half, David saw Ryan six times. Monday, Tuesday, and Thursday were the days his mother had allowed him to attend. Every time Ryan came, he got better—his punches smoother, his gas tank deeper, his defense sharper. David loved seeing these improvements, but his favorite part of the days Ryan attended was what came after class was over: the three to five minutes he spent talking to Jamie. David could tell that she was always tired from her long day, but she never let that change how she interacted with him or her son. Jaime and Ryan had a special bond. It was like they could speak whole paragraphs just from a look and a wrinkle of the forehead. David admired their relationship. It reminded him of the one he had with his mom before the night they both heard the *crack*.

It was always Jamie who picked Ryan up, never Ryan's father. At first, David was curious about meeting this mystery man. But as time went by, he grew happy that it was only Jamie who seemed to care about her son's new passion for boxing. His absence aided David's fantasy that Jamie was his. He liked to imagine she wasn't married at all. He was pleased whenever he detected the rockiness in Jamie's marriage. Whenever Jamie mentioned her husband, her words were coated with a layer of contempt. And Ryan had nothing to say at all.

On the Thursday that marked Ryan's seventh class, the boy got his first chance to spar. David matched him up with another nine year old boy named Clarence. Clarence wasn't the toughest boy of his age, but he wasn't the weakest either. David thought it would be a good matchup for Ryan. It didn't occur to him that it would be a terrible one for Clarence. The older kids went first, as was custom. Ryan waited anxiously as he watched Xavier systematically destroy his sparring partner (this was nothing new; in three years, when Xavier turned eighteen, fighters around the world were in serious trouble). Eventually it came time for Ryan and Clarence to tango. The two boys entered the ring of students. Their equipment, despite its "kids" labeling, still appeared cartoonish on their child bodies. The clock on the wall buzzed, and a timer of five minutes began to tick down. David sat on the edge of the mat with a sweaty Xavier to his left. They watched with smiles on their faces as the young guns circled each other with their gloves held high. David loved watching his younger students spar; they were the most moldable of the bunch. As the sparring match developed, Ryan impressed his coach once again. He was moving forward on Clarence, throwing "punches in bunches" (as the old-time boxing commentators love to say). Clarence was folding under the pressure. "Fight back, Clarence!" David yelled through the cheers of his students. "You can't hit back when you cover up like that. He's just gonna tee off on you!" Clarence did his best to fend off Ryan's attacks, but every time he went to punch, his head was whipped back by one of Ryan's fists. With ten seconds left and a call from his coach telling him so, Ryan unloaded. Clarence ducked his head and tried to throw back, but he could do nothing to avoid Ryan's shots. The clock hit zero with a buzz, but Ryan kept punching.

David came and peeled the boy away and lightly scolded him in front of the class for not stopping at the bell. But the scolding was a show. What David saw in that moment was the raging internal fire of a true competitor—a true fighter.

David mingled with some parents after class until the gym was close to empty. Several of his students' parents participated in the lax adult classes and thus were fairly acquainted with David. Eventually, with the gym cleared out, David noticed Ryan standing by the door, staring out the window.

"Where's your mom?" David asked as he walked over.

Ryan gave an unknowing shrug of his shoulders. "Do you have a phone I could call her on?"

David's bag was next to them under the bench. He reached into the outside pocket and pulled out his cell phone. He immediately saw that he had a message from Jamie. Surprised at first that she had his number, he remembered he had called her from his cell phone when he first inquired about Ryan's absence.

"Running a little late. Sorry! On my way!"

"She's running late," David said, still looking at the screen.

"Ok," Ryan replied.

David waited with Ryan for his ride home on a bench outside the gym. The dying sun turned the world gold around them. At first, the two didn't exchange many words. Both of them were quiet by nature. Unlike most kids, Ryan could go more than five minutes without telling David an incoherent story that he had little interest in.

"What does your dad do for work?" David eventually asked, breaking the silence. "Your mom said he works late."

"He's in advertising," Ryan replied while looking off into the distance across the parking lot.

David nodded his head up and down, amazed that a nine year old could make him feel uncomfortable. "Cool."

"Yeah. He likes it. Seems boring to me. He's always at work."

"Does he have time to play basketball with you?"

"No . . . and even if he did, he wouldn't. He hates sports, except golf. He loves golf. He's always playing with people from his work. He says he doesn't get the point of guys fighting over a ball."

David smiled and shook his head a little. "A lot of fighters don't like other sports either. They say the same thing. To me it's just another form of competition, one where you don't have to punch each other in the face to prove who's better, you know?"

"Yeah I see what you mean, but I feel like fighting gets to the point."

David burst out in laughter. Ryan looked at him, not realizing he had said something so funny. Eventually David was able to contain himself. "Sports are awesome," he said. "If you can play a sport over fighting, do that. You'll make a lot more money."

Ryan turned and faced David with a look of confusion. "You don't like fighting? You're good at it."

David took a moment to ponder Ryan's question. At one point, he did like fighting. He knew that every time he had his hand raised, he loved it. He might not have been the best talker, but in his profession that didn't matter. He was free from any trace of fear of physical violence from anyone walking the earth, and he took pride in that. "I do like fighting," he finally said. "Deep down, I do. I may not like everything that goes on around fighting. But when I'm in that cage . . . I enjoy that . . . I really do."

"Then how come you want me to do something else? I want to be a fighter like you. You said I could be the best."

David turned and looked at the boy. He saw the same spark in his young face that he knew once existed in him. In that moment, he felt revitalized. "You really want to be a fighter?"

Ryan nodded.

"Ok little man, you're right. I shouldn't discourage you. I'll do everything in my power to get you there. But you gotta realize a very small percentage of people make good money in this game. It's important that you do good in school. Get a degree. No reason you can't kick some butt and get a degree at the same time. Alright?"

"Ok."

Across the parking lot, Jamie's car entered from a wave of passing traffic. As she drove up towards the gym, she saw the guys sitting next to each other, and a smile formed on her face. Her son and his coach had eerily similar mannerisms. Both of them were sitting in the same fashion, with their hands clasped and elbows resting on their thighs. She parked the car, got out, and walked towards them.

"Hi guys!" Jamie said, flipping her glasses up in her now familiar manner.

The guys said hi back. David was smiling; Ryan was not. One of them was smitten; one was not.

"I'm sorry I'm late David. Work has been so crazy."

"Don't worry about it. You gave me an excuse to hide from that crazy guy inside." David turned over his shoulder and nodded towards Mike, who was at the front desk. Mike saw he was being looked at and gave an unknowing wave. Jamie laughed as she waved back.

"Your son killed it today," David said.

Jamie's face lit up. David wondered how a person could be so naturally beautiful. "Did he really? That's awesome. I want to hear all about it, son."

Ryan didn't like being talked about, so he got up from his seat. He turned and faced David and held out his small fist. "See you later, David."

David bumped his fist into Ryan's. "Later bud. See you next week."

Jamie rubbed Ryan's head as he went on his way to the car. It was just her and David now in the empty lot, her standing and

David sitting ten feet away. David looked up at her with inquisitive eyes, hands still clasped together, his usual small smirk raising the corners of his lips.

"How was he so good?" Jamie asked, folding her arms across her chest.

"He had his first day of sparring today. And . . . don't repeat this, he put a decent beating on the kid. Nothing crazy, they were both wearing headgear, but Ryan won. He's aggressive and he's fearless. That's a good combination in this field."

Jamie turned and looked at Ryan in the front seat of her car then turned back. "He gets it from me, you know?"

David sat upright with a chuckle. "I don't doubt it. You seem like a *real* killer."

Jamie raised an eyebrow in defiance. "Is that sarcasm I detect? I can be tough when I have to be."

David smiled and stood up from the bench. "I'm just messing with you. He had to get it from somewhere. He didn't get it from his dad?"

Jamie looked to the ground and shook her head. Then she looked up. "He didn't get much from his father. And I'm not so sure that's a bad thing."

David was left without a response. The two of them stared into each other's eyes for a moment. Usually David hated eye contact. But he felt he could look into Jamie's eyes for the rest of eternity without feeling uncomfortable. This was what he liked most about her. He eventually averted his eyes for Jamie's comfort. As he did, he noticed that Jamie's wedding ring was absent. He looked up again, and her grey eyes were still there waiting for him.

"I better get this boy home," she said softly.

"Ok."

"Thanks again for waiting. Bye David."

David raised an awkward hand. "Bye, Jamie."

She turned toward her car slowly. David admired her figure as she moved away, the muscles along the top of her back, leading to her nice butt and extending to her toned legs and calves, all moving in a fluid motion. He felt like a fool for letting her leave. She either liked him, or he had lost all ability to read body language. She liked him. He couldn't believe it, but she did. And he needed to do something about it.

"Hey Jamie," he called.

She stopped and turned around.

"I was thinking..." he paused. "Maybe some time we can get some dinner and talk about how good he's doing."

Jamie's smile faded from a wide grin to a barely existent smirk. "I . . . uh . . . I don't know, David. I don't know if that would be appropriate, you know?

"Right . . . I'm sorry. I shouldn't have asked," David said, shrinking into his seat.

"I'm flattered. Really, I am. But let's not complicate things, ok?"

"Ok."

Jamie turned and got in her car. David rose and turned towards the gym, feeling an embarrassment he hadn't felt since grade school.

Jamie got into her car and slammed the door shut. Her son next to her saw that she was upset. He saw everything. From her seat, Jamie watched David, ashamed and embarrassed, enter the front door of the gym. From her seat, Jamie was experiencing her own unpleasant feelings. She did like David. There was a softness about him that at first glance she hadn't expected. He was good looking too, especially on occasion when he was shirtless upon her arrival at the gym. But what she found most attractive about him was his relationship with her son and all of the other kids whom he coached. It was like he was one of them, socially awkward but with a kind heart. She wanted very much to go on that date. But she couldn't. She wouldn't stoop to her husband's level.

"What's wrong?" Ryan asked.

Jamie let out a sigh. "Nothing," she lied, putting the car in reverse.

⊰ ⊱

As David rode his bike home that day, he periodically shouted "fuck!" towards the sky while shaking his head in disgust. He wished he could go back in time and swallow his tongue before committing his unbearable error. Jamie probably thought he was crazy, asking out a married woman with a child that he coached. How could he ever see her again after making a fool of himself like that? He wanted to jump out of his skin and beat the shit out of himself. The world was caving in, collapsing behind him as he raced home.

He was drenched in sweat after arriving at his apartment faster than he ever had. He lugged his bike up the stairs and ripped his keys out of his pocket at his door. As he put his keys in the lock, he felt a double buzz from his pocket. He pulled his phone from his pants and saw a text message from Jamie.

"Saturday night?" the message said

David was frozen in place. At first he though she might be kidding (what a deranged joke that would be). He opened his door and went inside. From his couch he looked at his phone, thinking of how to respond and sound cool at the same time.

"*Just say yes you fucking idiot,*" he thought. That's what he did.

"Meet me at Casa Brava in La Mesa at eight . . . I'm looking forward to it."

David unknowingly had a stupid, bewildered smile plastered to his face. He thought of his mother, always telling him to break out of his shell and take a risk. He thought she would have been proud of him now.

CHAPTER FIFTEEN

The Silver Fox was nearly empty that Thursday night. Most of Terry's men were still laying low after what all the news outlets were calling a "Gang Violence Tragedy in Lincoln Park". But Terry didn't see a tragedy. He saw a triumphant victory. Nine of the LPB's highest ranking members had been killed in one well calculated attack. The ambush was such a blow that word was getting out that the Bloods wanted nothing to do with the war they found themselves in. The Perros were now operating downtown unharmed. Terry had San Diego under his polished boot heel, right where he wanted it. He sat at the bar with a glass of whiskey in front of him. Jorge sat on his left with a drink of his own. The only other people present were Steve, the bartender, and a couple of regulars down at the far end of the counter.

Terry and his underboss were laughing and enjoying themselves. They had snorted some coke, increasing their ability for alcohol consumption, and they were taking advantage of this power. They talked passionately about sexual encounters of their past (a surefire way of knowing that the coke was indeed great) when a man wearing a grey hood and aviator sunglasses entered the bar. It was neither cold nor bright outside. The newcomer removed his hood and glasses, revealing the face of a surely dying man. He approached the bar and leaned onto it, aiming to get the bartender's attention. He was only ten feet from Terry and Jorge, who were examining him closely. "Where can I find Terry Watkins?" Mark asked.

Upon hearing the question, Terry killed his glass of whiskey only to pour another. Jorge rose to his feet to greet this mysterious intruder. "Who wants to know?" he asked, opening his coat jacket to reveal the Glock on his hip.

Mark put his hands up quickly. "I'm just looking to place a bet. I don't want any trouble. I heard Terry was the best bookkeeper in town."

"Who told you that?" Jorge asked.

"A Mexican man named Gordo. At least that's what he called himself. I doubt that's his real name."

Jorge looked at Terry. The gang had many Gordos, a Spanish name meaning fat. Terry gave Jorge an approving nod.

"We only deal in big action," Jorge said.

"How's fifty grand sound?"

"Football or basketball?" Terry interposed. A bet of that size garnered his attention. "Sit down Jorge. I'll take it from here." Jorge returned to his stool on the other side of Terry. Terry turned and faced his new customer from his seat.

"I got two things I'm interested in," Mark said, pulling up a stool of his own. "I wanna put two dimes on the Cowboys over the Cards on Thanksgiving."

"That's a bold bet. The boys can't buy a win this year."

"I'm feeling lucky. What odds will you give me?"

Terry pondered the question. Despite the large amount of drugs and alcohol he had consumed that night, the old noggin was functioning just fine. "Vegas has it five-to-one. I'll give you six-to-one."

Mark smiled. "You got a deal."

"What else you got?"

"I bet on fights. I heard you can accommodate."

"Sure," Terry said with a shrug. "UFC or Boxing?"

"Neither. There's some fights being held up at Pechunga on the 23rd of December. Rage Cage Promotions. It's a smaller league—"

"I've heard of it," Terry interjected.

"Vegas has odds on it. There's a guy by the name of David Lewis; he's a four-to-one dog. I wanna go in on him to win. No round selection or method of victory, just to win."

Terry and Jorge shared a glance as they heard David's name. Destiny had come knocking on their door, letting them know it was time to dust off their old toy. But Terry's better judgment strangled his joy. Something smelt fishy here. He hadn't heard about this fight, and he was usually on top of these things. "How'd you hear about this?"

"I'm a fight fan," Mark responded. "I watch em all. Been watching this guy. In his last fight he got robbed. The guy he was fighting just wrestled him to death . . . I saw in the paper last Sunday that he had another fight."

"You're betting three dimes on him? What makes you so confident?"

"He lost the last fight cuz the guy wouldn't trade punches with him. This next guy he's fighting is a badass kick boxer named Arnold Loder. He'll stand and go toe-to-toe with David. I know it for sure. And I think that'll be a mistake on his part. This David kid knows how to throw down."

Terry looked at Mark with a calculating stare. "What's your name?".

"My name's Keith."

"Where you from Keith? How come you're just finding out about me now?"

"I recently moved down from Sacramento. Got in a little trouble with the law up there. Nothing serious, just had to put some people in line. Got my trailer out in National City. I was playing the pony's at Pechunga last week and this Gordo fella said you were the man to see for sports. So here I am. If I'm lucky enough to come through, I'm off to Mexico. If not, well, I'm not much of a quitter. You'll see more of me."

"Unless the cops find you first."

"Correct."

Terry hadn't blinked since he began speaking to his new pal Keith. The duration of his death stare was unnerving, but Keith held up, passing Terry's bullshit detector. That's because Mark was an expert bullshiter. "You got the cash?" Terry asked.

Mark pulled five rolls of bills from his coat pocket and placed them on the counter.

"Jorge, get him a couple slips." Jorge went to the back office. "Would you like a drink, Keith?"

Mark raised his hand and smiled. "Fifteen years sober. But thank you."

Jorge returned with two slips containing the details of Mark's bets.

"It's been a pleasure," Mark said. "I'll see you after Thanksgiving if the boys pull it off."

"You do that."

Mark put his glasses back on and left into the night. Terry counted the bills and looked up at a watching Jorge. They were both thinking the same thing: It was time to pay their old pal David a visit.

CHAPTER SIXTEEN

Saturday night at around a quarter to eight, Jamie Hurley was driving her black, 2013 CLK Mercedes, having her bare legs warmed by the seat's heaters while David was on a raggedy bus eastbound towards La Mesa surrounded by a group of equally immobile individuals. He had shaven his face and gelled his hair. He was trying to sit upright so his shirt wouldn't get wrinkled. It had been a long time since he had a date with a woman. And he had gone his whole life without dating a woman of Jamie's caliber. In his younger, bank-robbing years, he went for the fast types—tattoos, nose rings, hatred for society—those broads. Jamie was a classy, tattoo-free girl, and somehow, someway, he had convinced her to go on a date with him. Accordingly, David was more nervous about this dinner than when he found himself locked in a cage with another fighter.

David arrived early like he had hoped to. Casa Brava was a swank restaurant, but it was also discreet. It was located on the outskirts of town, where there was little chance of this dinner being witnessed. David was positive that's why Jamie had picked it.

He selected a nice table on the far end of the restaurant where a Spanish band was playing Spanish music. The place was dimly lit, the walls a dark yellow with red trimming, and there was an aroma of freshly baked bread throughout. Most of the tables were surprisingly seated, and there was a hum of cheerful chatter. Maybe this date would be witnessed after all. Once seated, David took in his surroundings, sipping water compulsively, thinking of things he would say to this woman whom he was infatuated with.

There was a song change, and then he spotted her. She was illuminated by the low hanging red lights. His heart started beating uncontrollably. She was looking for him, walking slowly through the dark restaurant. Before he came, David was worried that he had overdressed, that he was trying too hard. But after seeing Jamie, he realized this was not the case. She wore a tight, short, black dress accompanied by grey heels with straps circling up her calves. Her hair was done up, and the makeup was on.

This was not a casual dinner.

David rose from his seat, gaining her attention. She smiled and made a gesture that playfully said *how dumb am I?* then walked over towards the table.

"How are you?" she asked with her big, comforting smile.

"I'm good. Really good. How are you doing?"

"I'm doing just fine. Thanks for coming." They hugged, a bit awkwardly, then took their seats. Jamie moved with fluid confidence while David moved like a stiff robot.

"This place is nice," he said.

"Yeah I love it here. You've never been?"

"No. First time. I don't get out much."

"Shocker," Jamie said with a playful smirk. "I come here a lot. I'm somewhat of a *reg'* you could say. But most of the time I'm over there by myself." She pointed towards the bar. David chuckled. Their waiter came to the table, a tall, thin man named Julio. Jamie smiled kindly when she saw him. "Ahh Julio, *Como estas?*"

"*Bien* Beautiful, how are you?

"Very good. Julio, this is my friend David." Julio and David shook hands. "Can we start out with a bottle of Merlot, the best you got?"

"Absolutely dear. I'll be right back with that."

Jamie looked to David and smiled through the awkward silence.

"What's Ryan doing tonight?" David asked.

"He's at a friend's house. There's no school tomorrow, so they're having a gaming sleepover; that's what they call it."

"He loves those video games huh?"

"He's obsessed."

"Well at least he gets his exercise with me now."

"That's true," she said, looking down for a moment then back at David. "He really likes you. He tells me the things that you tell him about working hard and how he can be great. It's very sweet."

"It's the truth," David said.

"It's just good for him to hear those things."

"My mom used to tell me I could be whatever I wanted to be. But she was my mom. I realize now that it's completely true, if you work your tail off. I just needed others to tell me my mom wasn't blowing smoke up my ass. So that's my role here: I'm the person other than mom telling Ryan that he truly can be whatever he wants to be."

"You're a good example for him."

David smirked and shrugged. *If you only knew*, is what he was thinking. But instead he said "Thanks."

Despite the good start to the date, David still had some reservations. He knew he had never told Jamie the details of his past. He figured she would ask him about it. It's what he was most nervous about, and he could sense it was about to become a problem.

"So tell me about yourself, David."

David sat upright and settled in. "What do you want to know?"

"Let's see . . . Do you have any brothers or sisters?"

"Nope. Only child. What about you?"

"I have a sister and brother back in Chicago."

"That's where you're from?"

Jamie nodded as Julio arrived with their bottle of wine. He gave an unnecessary background on the wine's characteristics and where it came from. All Jamie cared about was if it could get her drunk. After presenting the bottle, pouring two glasses and taking their dinner order, Julio left.

"When did you come out here?" David continued as they clanked glasses.

"Right out of high school." She said this very enthusiastically, to show some naivety in her decision.

David politely returned her laughter. "That's when you met Ryan's dad?"

"Right again. You're good," she said, pointing a finger at him.

"It's all coming together now," David joked. "How did that go down?"

"How did what go down?"

"How did you meet him?"

"Well, we met at my work and he kept asking for my number. At first I wanted nothing to do with him. He's one of those guys that thinks he can have whatever he wants." She paused and pondered this for a second. "Maybe he can . . . anyway, his persistence paid off. We started dating, I got pregnant with Ryan, and the rest, as they say, is history."

David nodded and came up with another small talk question. "Where do you guys live?"

"You gonna rob us?"

"No," David responded, a little too quickly.

Jamie laughed. "I'm kidding. We live in La Jolla."

"Nice."

"Yeah . . ."

They both sat and smiled at each other. They were already without much more to say. They were running out of small talk, and they both knew it. It was time for the juicy conversation, the kind of conversation that could get them in trouble if they read the other wrong.

"Well, your husband is a lucky man."

"Oh yeah, how so?" Jamie picked up her glass and leaned back in her chair with an attentive smile.

"Well, he's married to the most beautiful woman on the planet for one thing." David stared into Jamie's eyes, trying not to waver.

Some color rose in Jamie's cheeks. "That's far from the truth. But thank you."

"Not in my eyes."

"Huh?"

"In my eyes, you're the most beautiful woman I've ever seen."

Jamie smiled and looked down. She was still sitting in a leaned back, 'Mrs. Cool' position. "Why are you telling me this, David?"

"I just felt like I had to. I've never felt this before. I'm not a player. Far from it. I don't want you to think I say this to every girl I meet. It took every ounce of courage I had to ask you to dinner."

"I see. But you know I'm married."

"But you don't love him."

Jamie took a moment to respond. But she didn't have to. Her face betrayed any attempt to hide her feelings. "And how do you know that?"

"I can see it in your face when you talk about him."

"Is that so?"

"It is. He's never around. Ryan told me as much. And I mean, why did you come here? Why are we here? It wasn't just to talk about Ryan's boxing. You didn't come here looking that good to talk about your kid's punching ability."

The color began to spread on Jamie's cheeks. Her grey eyes remained fixed on David's blue ones. "No, I suppose I didn't. Since you're being so honest, I guess I'll do the same. I like you, David. You're obviously good looking—"

"I don't know if it's that obvious. No one has ever said that before," David interjected with a smile. He looked good saying it, which defeated his quip.

"—You're attractive in a strange way, a way that's hard to put my finger on. But what I find most attractive about you is how you are with the kids. Ryan especially. I saw you in that fight on TV and I thought you would be . . . I don't know. . . kind of scary. But that's not the case."

"Not even a little bit?" David asked playfully.

"Nope. You're like a puppy dog."

David laughed hard. He recognized that a connection was made, that a mutual attraction was confirmed. "I appreciate that, Jamie. While we're on this honesty train, there's some things you should know about me. Something I have to get off my chest." David cleared his throat while Jamie stared at him with nervous anticipation. "I went to prison for five years when I was nineteen." Jamie's eyes widened as she heard David's words. For all the reasons she had just listed, she found this news surprising. "I was a young stupid kid, but I'm not that person anymore. I've made many mistakes in my life. And I'm far from perfect. But I'm not the idiot I was as a kid. Prison is bad for most people, makes them even worse criminals than they were heading in. I'm one of the rare cases that actually learned from their mistakes in there. I really did."

The deflated look that followed on Jamie's face crushed David. He thought she might get up and leave at any moment. "What did you go to prison for?" she asked.

David cleared his throat again. "Bank robbery."

Jamie laughed a little from shock. "Wow."

"I'm sorry I didn't tell you sooner."

"You're not required to notify everyone that you went to prison. But that is surprising. How long have you been out now?"

"Almost five years. And, for the record, without a single brush with the law, not even a ticket."

Despite David's attempt to soften the blow, Jamie was stunned silent.

David felt the size of a mouse, and when he spoke again he sounded like one. "With me walking Ryan to the gym, I just felt like I needed to tell you."

"I appreciate it," she said distantly.

David looked down at his hands and began to pick at a callus beneath the table. He hated telling people about his past, especially someone he cared about. His most recent confession had gone just about as badly as he'd imagined it would. But something David didn't expect happened. Jamie noticed his despair and felt genuine sorrow for him. She could see a life of turmoil personified in the man across from her. She leaned forward on the table, putting her closer to David, letting her glass of wine dangle from her left hand. "Hey," she said. David looked up. "We are not our pasts."

David nodded. These words and the understanding tone with which they were given made tears start to fill David's eyes.

"I see how you teach those kids. I see how you talk to their parents. And most of all, I see it in your eyes that you're a good man. That's all I need to know. So let's put this in the rearview mirror and just enjoy our dinner."

David's small smile expanded into a big one slowly.

Their food arrived, steaming and smelling delicious. They ate and talked and smiled and laughed until their plates were bare, their bellies were full, and two bottles of wine were empty. David learned about Jamie's childhood in suburban Chicago. They shared a love for the Chicago great, Michael Jordan. The details about Jamie's marriage came out: he was unfaithful, never present, and egotistical. They hadn't shared a bed in over a month and hadn't shared each other's bodies for much longer than that. David told Jamie about the things Mark taught him in prison and how he decided he would become a fighter when he was released. He told her about his fears and his shortcomings, the only things he saw in himself. He told her about his rough upbringing and his juvenile delinquency. He told her about the forces. He told her about his mother dying of breast cancer and how he didn't get to say goodbye. He told her about the great distance he felt from society. He told her everything he could think of, and she took it all in stride.

There was only one thing David neglected to tell. His darkest secret remained untold. He hoped that after all these years of lying to himself, pretending that horrid night never occurred, that he would be able to believe his lie. But that was yet to happen.

Jamie leaned on David as they exited the restaurant. She gave her ticket to the valet driver, who promptly ran off into the night. They turned and looked at each other through their wine induced haze.

"Where's your car?" Jamie asked.

"I took the bus . . . I actually don't have a car."

"Let me give you a ride."

"No, that's alright," David said, casting a carnal gaze upon his date. "I don't want you to see where I live."

"When are you going to stop thinking that I'm judging you?"

"It might take awhile."

They smiled at each other in silence until the valet delivered Jamie's car. Jamie handed the young man who was dressed like Aladdin a five dollar bill. The two blossoming lovers got into her car.

After a short drive of laughter (and no DUI checkpoints), they pulled up in front of David's ugly apartment. He was immediately regretful that he hadn't fought off Jamie's request more vehemently.

"This is me," David said in a sarcastic manner.

Jamie leaned over to take a look. The smell of her perfumed hair before his face made David drunk with lust. "It's nice," she fibbed.

"It's fine for me," David said as Jamie retracted her head from his chest. She moved her gaze from David's shanty to his admiring eyes. "Thanks for coming. I had a good time."

"So did I." The lone streetlight cast shadows on Jamie's face as they sat in silence. All he could see was her red lips and her bright, wet eyes reflecting at him through the darkness. He leaned in, not knowing what would happen next. She leaned in also. He felt Jamie's impossibly soft lips upon his and her hand around the back of his neck. Her tongue collided with his canines as fireworks erupted above Seaworld in the distance. They peeled apart as they turned and marveled at the show through the windshield.

To them, the fireworks were not a coincidence. They were for them.

"Stay the night," David said softly. "It's not as bad on the inside."

"I can't." She laid her forehead against David's, and they kissed once more. "I have to go."

"Can this happen again?" David asked, basking in Jamie's hot breath.

"I certainly hope so."

David lay in his bed that night feeling as if his world had stopped and started to spin in another direction. He had read about determinism in prison—the theory that there is no free will and that everything we do is determined by prior circumstances. The theory had always seemed crazy to David, or at least hard to wrap his head around. But when people like Jamie, Mark, or Mike came into his life, the theory seemed to carry weight. It added to his belief that there was some kind of beautiful order at work.

Things were complicated for David now. He was involved with a married woman who was also the mother of his student. Not the ideal scenario. But what was he supposed to do? He loved this woman. There was no instruction manual for this life he was thrust into. He just knew that Jamie made him happy. Eventually, David's blissful night ended as he drifted off to sleep easily and peacefully.

CHAPTER SEVENTEEN

The following Monday, David was back at practice with an extra spring in his step. This was unfortunate for all of his training partners; he was a wrecking ball. He chocked and punched and kicked the shit out of everyone who was unfortunate enough to train with him. He hadn't heard from Jamie since their date two nights prior, but he still hadn't come down from the cloud he was floating on. During Jiu-Jitsu class—the class David hated most—he was sparring with Alex Martins, an old-school ex-fighter and third-degree Jiu-Jitsu blackbelt. For the last five years, Alex had mauled David every time they competed against each other.

Today, David decided that would change.

The match seemingly lasted for an eternity, going far past the time limit for the class; it continued even as everyone left the mats. Mike, who had been mingling with some of the fighters in the front of the gym, turned and noticed the epic battle that was taking place. He walked over to watch. David and Alex were intertwined in a spinning ball of sweaty bodies. David was going for a choke on Alex when he slipped out and spun around to David's back and attempted a choke of his own. Eventually David was also able to escape from his opponent's grasp. This repeated itself over and over until David finally secured a dominant position and applied what would be the winning choke. He squeezed with every ounce of remaining energy he had left until he felt Alex tap for mercy on his shoulder.

"Aye!" Mike yelled, banging on the cage as David released his grip and rolled to his back. "I never thought I'd see the day!"

The two competitors lay next to one another in a pool of sweat. Alex gave David a pat on his drenched chest. "Good job fucker."

After class, Mike walked over to David on the bench, curious as to what had him operating at this insane level. "What's going on with you today?"

"What do you mean?"

"I mean you're fucking everyone up, more so than usual. I've never seen you this jazzed for practice. Not even since your recent revival."

David smiled as peeled his drenched shirt off of his torso and lugged it into his disgusting bag. "I'm feeling good, that's all. I'm the best welterweight on the planet, remember? I should be fucking these guys up, shouldn't I?"

"No, no, there's something going on with you."

"Beats me," David said as he threw a towel over his shoulder and sauntered towards the shower. As he walked across the empty mats with his back to his curious coach, he couldn't stop himself from smiling.

It was truly a good day in David's life; his world was spinning in another direction. His path had forked away from the grime and the ugliness where it started and was now heading towards a world where the sun always shines and love is an abundant currency. For the first time in his life, David had someone out there thinking about him. And he was certain that was all he would ever need. A part of him thought getting involved with a woman would hamper his ability to compete in his dangerous profession. But he felt stronger than ever. He had won a battle that was far greater than a fistfight with another man. He won a battle within himself. With the help of the compassionate woman he had fallen for, he no longer believed he was incapable of being loved.

═╬═╬═

All highs—especially drug induced ones—are followed by severe lows. When four o' clock rolled around that day, the effects from the drug Jamie's smile and smell had injected into his veins were halted, and his intense come-down began.

He got out of the shower and was putting his pants on when he received a message from the captor of his thoughts and feelings. "Hi David . . . unfortunately Ryan can't make it today. He's not feeling well."

That was it. No "I had a good time the other night," or "I'm thinking about you". Just a message saying Ryan couldn't make it to practice, which, of course, was complete bullshit. David looked at the text solemnly as he came crashing down to earth—to the filthy ghetto he was accustomed to. How could he have been so naive? So stupid?Suddenly, that war he thought he won was raging again in his mind. He wasn't surprised that Ryan wouldn't be attending class that day. And he wouldn't be surprised if he never came back. His paid month of classes was almost complete. The party was over. He would never see the young, talented boy, or his mother, ever again.

David looked into the foggy mirror, glaring at the loser staring back at him with disgust. He punched that loser, and his image shattered with the mirror. The patter of sprinting feet sounded outside the small shower room. Mike entered and discovered the troubling scene. "What the fuck David?"

David was looking into the sink, running his masochistic right hand—bleeding from the knuckles—under warm water. "I'm sorry Mike," he said quietly.

"What the fuck is the matter with you?" Mike yelled.

For a moment David said nothing, just watched the red water fill the sink. "I don't want to talk about it," he finally said.

"Well, tough shit. Let me look at that." Mike leaned over the sink for a closer look at David's hand.

"It's not that bad," David said. As he showed his wound to Mike, he was proven correct. There were two cuts, one between the second and third knuckle and the other atop his first knuckle. The latter was the larger of the two, but neither would require stitches. Training, however, would be out of the question for at least a week.

"Come with me," Mike ordered.

David sat across from Mike in his office several minutes later. A couple of large bandages were securely taped around David's hand. Mike was staring with a scary look, but that was normal. What was abnormal was the hint of concern in that look.

"You need to talk to me David. What's going on? One moment you're happier than I've ever seen you. The next you're punching mirrors, ruining the main tool of your profession."

David was silent, staring at the ground before him.

"Are you back on drugs?"

David shook his head. "No."

Mike stared at the top of David's drooping head, rummaging through possible reasons for David's behavior in his mind. "It's a girl, isn't it?"

David didn't respond. Mike took that as a yes.

"It's Ryan's mom, huh?"

David raised his head, revealing his moist blue eyes. It was all Mike needed to see.

"Jesus Christ, David. What are you doing? What happened?"

Slowly and begrudgingly, David began to tell his somber tale. "We went on a date on Saturday. We hit it off, Mike. It couldn't have gone better. I haven't stopped thinking about her since that night. The past forty hours of my life have been spent replaying different kind things she said, different playful looks she gave me, and especially our kiss at the end of the night. I'm obsessed, right? And then I get this message after my shower." David took his cell phone out of his pocket, retrieved the message from Jamie, and slid the phone across Mike's desk. Mike picked up the phone and read the text. He looked pained.

"Ryan comes every Monday," David said. "She's lying; she doesn't want to see me."

Mike put down the phone and looked at David solemnly. "I've been telling you to get a woman for years. Why do you have to pick a married one who's the mother of one of our students?"

"I love her Mike. I knew it from the moment I saw her."

Mike had seen the spark with his own eyes when Jamie and David first met; he just didn't expect that spark to bring any kindling to a flame. Mike and his wife (*mostly* his wife) had set up failed dates for David on numerous occasions over the years. They had all been disasters—either for David's awkwardness, lack of car and money, or his clear lack of interest in them. Now a date had gone well with a woman he was not permitted to see by society's standards. The whole situation coincided perfectly with the dysfunctional routine of David's life. But Mike wasn't one to care about society's standards, and he cared greatly about the young man he was sitting across from. If there was even the slightest chance David had a shot at obtaining a companion, he was going to support him. "Well Romeo," he said, "do something about it."

"Like what?" David grunted.

Mike pulled a bundle of keys from his pocket and tossed them on his desk. "Go get her. You know where she works, right? It's listed as an emergency contact in the computer."

David didn't have to look it up. Jamie's workplace was another thing he learned on their date. After brief deliberation, David reached out and grabbed the keys.

"Don't get pulled over," Mike said.

David rose to his feet. "You'll teach class today?"

Mike laughed lowly and shook his head in disbelief that he was supporting this stunt. "Yeah. Now get outta here before I change my mind."

David went to the door. Before exiting, he turned back one final time. "Thank you Mike."

"Hurry up and go get her."

CHAPTER EIGHTEEN

In the bustling La Jolla cove The Capital Cafe—an old cottage that had been turned into a successful beach-front restaurant—was unusually busy during the late afternoon transition from the brunch menus to those used for dinner. Jamie, one of the few remaining servers from the morning shift, was moving quickly through the restaurant carrying food laden plates, taking elaborate orders, opening wine bottles, and giving change. She was practically sprinting until she arrived at her tables, where she would slow down and treat each table as if they were the only patrons in the restaurant. Customers from around the world traveled to this restaurant annually. Along with their table location, they requested that Jamie be their server. When backup had arrived and Jamie was finally permitted to leave, she was sweaty, exhausted, and four hundred dollars richer.

She exited down a set of stairs trailing from the back of the restaurant, the endless Pacific Ocean sprawled before her. She turned left onto a secluded hill where all of the employees parked. As she strolled along, she marveled at big blue and listened to the seals barking from their ledges below her. She almost fell over with fright when David stepped into her path, emerging briskly from behind a large truck. There they stood in silent knowing.

"Tell me why Ryan *really* couldn't make it today," David said.

"I made a mistake, David. A *big* mistake. This can't happen." She glanced at David's bandaged hand and felt a strange combination of fear and sympathy.

"Yes it can," David said softly as he moved closer.

"No it can't David. I'm married."

"Look," David began his plea, "I can't give you the fancy house, or jewelry, or cars like your husband can, but I can give you me. *All of me.* And until the other night I thought that wasn't worth anything, but you made me feel like it *was* worth something. I'm in love with you, Jamie. I have been from the moment I laid eyes on you. I feel like I'm magnetized to you. There was a time where I would have let this go. But I can't. I'm willing to fight for this . . . and I'm a decent fighter."

They were practically touching. David had crept upon Jamie. His blue eyes peered down upon her from their deep sockets. She smelled his cologne again and was reminded of the prior night—the night when she too felt a love blossoming. His torso touched her's, and she was incapable of resisting her urge to kiss him. They collided against the truck, faces attached, alone on the secluded hill with only the seagulls and seals to view them. David fumbled around for the handle to the back seat. There was no stopping them as they entered the vehicle at full lust. Jamie peeled David's shirt off, and David pulled down Jamie's pants, revealing her tan legs and pink panties. It wasn't the holiest of ways to have sex for the first time—"making love" is not the right way to describe what happened in the backseat of Mike's truck. They fucked like the two sexually frustrated people they were, and it was good. Jamie dug her nails into David's back as he thrust into her, kissing the sides of her neck. They came to a primal climax together. The world shook around them. In the wake of their passion, they stared into each other's eyes, knowing what they had done.

Afterwards, clothed and flushed, David drove Jamie a half mile further down the hill to her car's location. He put the truck in park then turned to Jamie, who was wearing a bewildered smile.

"This is a tricky situation," Jamie said, still looking through the windshield.

"I know."

She turned to David. "Do you mean it?"

He knew what she was asking. "Yes."

"You love me?"

"I do."

She sighed and shook her head, but she was still smiling. She turned and leaned in for another kiss. They both began to laugh.

PART TWO

CHAPTER ONE

The next day was Thanksgiving. For the first time in several years, David didn't have to think long and hard of something to be thankful for. He sat on the bus with a plastic tray of deviled eggs, a gleam in his eyes, and a smile stuck on his face. He had a full feeling in his chest, like he was being blown up with hot air. And like a hot-air balloon, he thought he might float away. Instead of avoiding eye contact and interaction with the other passengers on the bus, he was looking around and engaging with them. He wasn't angered when children sang loudly and out of tune, when a man smelling fouler than a trash can sat beside him, or when the bus was halted while a cyclist struggled to secure his bike to the front. Nothing could bother him. All was good in his world.

Eventually the bus arrived at David's desired stop in North Park. After walking a couple blocks, he was out front of his coach's home. It was your typical middle class domicile: the grass was green and trimmed, a two car garage sat at the end of a short driveway (where the truck he soiled the day before rested), and the front yard was littered with an assortment of children's toys. David approached the front door on circular stone footsteps. Before he could knock on the front door, a young, blonde, bare-footed girl wearing a white dress opened it for him. She stepped out onto the front porch and screamed "Hi!"

David smiled. "Hi Miley, you look very pretty." Mike emerged with a Heineken in his left hand and scooped up his daughter with his free right. "There he is," he boomed. "Welcome."

"How's it goin?" David replied.

"Good man, Happy Thanksgiving." Mike checked out David's tray of eggs. "What you got there?"

"Some deviled eggs. You like em?"

"Shit yeah. There ain't many food items I don't like. You should know that by now."

From behind Mike, in the depths of the house, the scream of a woman's voice shouted "Watch your language!"

Mike made the face of a worried man then looked to his daughter. "Don't repeat that," he pleaded.

"Shit yeah!" she shouted immediately.

"Stop!" Mike pleaded more severely then turned to a laughing David. "Come on in, man."

David stepped into the house and was instantly struck by the heavy smell of the turkey still baking in the oven. Underneath the seasoned turkey aroma was a fainter hint of cinnamon coming from two burning candles above the fireplace and also an unidentifiable smell from what he would later learn was the resting green bean casserole. A football game was playing out on a large television next to that fireplace. In front of the television was a smorgasbord of various chips, dips, and cheeses laid out on an ottoman in front of the couch. On the couch were a man and woman sitting closely, Mike's in-laws. David walked over and added his deviled eggs to the mix and briefly said hello to them. In the kitchen, Mike's wife, Mariah, was putting the finishing touches on one of her dishes with detailed care, unhindered by the significant baby-bump she was sporting beneath her purple apron. "Hi David!" she called cheerily as she saw her guest approaching the kitchen—her dojo.

"Hey Mariah. Thanks a lot for having me. It smells amazing." They exchanged a hug that was clumsily hampered by the oncoming baby and messy hands.

"Of course! We're glad to have ya," Mariah replied from their embrace.

David smiled at her as they separated. He was glad too. The atmosphere of this home was something he hadn't experienced in a very long time. "When is the baby coming?"

"Should be another month now," Mariah said as she resumed mashing potatoes.

"That's exciting . . . So can I help with anything?"

Mariah glanced away from her bowl. "No everything's just about done. Thanks though sweetie. Help yourself to a beer or soda, or whatever you want dear."

Mike emerged in the kitchen, free from his cute daughter's grasp and with an empty beer in hand. He was on a mission for another beverage. David was pretty sure he had a few already. This was a good thing; David liked his coach more when he was hopped up—everyone did. Mike placed his empty on the counter and opened a door that was covered in paper turkeys, finger paintings, and other various pieces from Miley's prestigious pre-school art collection. Mike buried his head in the fridge like an ostrich buries its head in sand, at least according to the myth. He reappeared with two green bottles of booze, grabbed a spoon from the silver drawer, and popped his beer open with it. David did the same.

"This is a good game," Mike said to David, glancing at the screen while he walked up behind his wife to give her a kiss on the cheek.

Mariah leaned back into her husband's embrace. "Dinner's ready in thirty," she said.

"Ok babe," Mike replied. After an exiting pat of his wife's butt, he led David back to the living room.

The two men settled in on the couch adjacent to the in-laws, who formally introduced themselves as Raymond and Katie. The Cowboys and the Cardinals battled on the field while David and his new friends munched on the assortment of snacks in front of them. Mike and Raymond barked at the TV over what they thought were bad calls and shouted for different plays with their expert knowledge. David really wasn't paying much attention to the game. Instead, he was looking around the room, marveling at the comforts of Mike's home. The family portrait hanging above the fireplace grabbed his attention. In the photo, Mike had a crazed smile, was wearing an atrocious collared shirt unlike any David had ever seen the man wear before, and had the two beautiful women in his life flanking him. David shifted his gaze to the three-dimensional Mike sitting next to him and saw the same man from the picture. He was used to the fearsome Mike, not this teddy bear. Seeing this incarnation put a quiet smile on David's face. Over the last five years, David learned that he and Mike had more in common than not. Mike too had been to prison (for assault), and he also overcame an addiction to heroin in his youth. Knowing all this and seeing where he was now served as a beacon of hope that maybe David could live this life as well.

Maybe he could live this life with Jamie.

The table was set in twenty minutes instead of thirty. David became more amazed and felt more hunger with each steaming dish laid before him. One-by-one, Mariah glided her very pregnant self from the kitchen to dining room with plates of food she had slaved over all day. The menu consisted of mashed potatoes, a honey-glazed ham, roasted Brussels sprouts, a green bean casserole, macaroni-and-cheese, and a big, fat, baked turkey.

The meal commenced. David sat on the end of the table next to Miley and the other child at the gathering, Mike's niece, Abigail, while the rest of the adults circled the far end of the table. David felt right at home at the kids' end. Mike and Raymond chatted about their respective business matters while Mariah and Katie chatted about their daughters' activities. David enjoyed his turkey and made goofy faces at the young girls next to him. They giggled progressively harder with each attempt. Mariah caught this in the corner of her eye and turned to the scene with a warm smile. Mariah was the gentleness that offset her husband's brutishness.

"Are you excited for your fight David?" Mariah asked.

David was caught off guard and in the middle of one of his faces when he was addressed. "Yeah I am," he said, finishing his mound of food he was showing to the girls.

"Mike says he's a tough guy, the guy you're fighting."

"Yeah, he definitely is."

"I don't know how you guys do it," Raymond chimed in. "I could never get in a cage with another man that wants to kick my ass."

The adults at the table chuckled.

"Well, it's all I know really," David replied. "I don't know how you guys do it, running businesses and everything that comes with that. You might as well be speaking a foreign language over there."

"You know I barely know what I'm doing," Mike said. "I miss the good ole days of fighting for cash."

"Much less cash," David added. "The way I see it, you don't got much to miss, Mike. I think you got everything you need right here."

Mariah smiled big in approval, still staring at David with interest. Then a hint of sadness emerged in her expression. "Why don't you have a girlfriend yet, David?"

Mike smirked and looked down like a guilty child. David was able to keep himself more restrained. He was, after all, much more sober than his coach was.

"I'm not sure," David said. "I don't have any takers. Besides, I can barely manage my own emotions, let alone someone else's. You know that. We've tried."

"You're a good man, David. You'll find a good girl someday."

David nodded and said "We'll see,". He went back to eating his delicious meal, knowing he had already met that girl.

The Hurley family was also eating their Thanksgiving meal. Lupe had done the majority of the cooking. Jamie pitched in where she could. The feast was on par with the one David was enjoying across town. The table, however, was much less lively. Lupe stealthily looked around at her silent employers full of stupefaction and sadness. Max plucked away at his plate, pretending everything was right as rain. Jamie looked as if her head was somewhere else. And Ryan—

"I'm full," he said after fifteen minutes of rearranging his food on his plate.

"Maybe if you wouldn't drink so much cider, you could eat more," Jamie said.

"Well, I'm full."

Max looked up at Jamie and shrugged.

"Ok then, get out of here," Jamie said with indifference.

Ryan got up and went to his room, leaving Jamie, Max, and Lupe at the table. The silence was thick. The ticks from the clock and the small clang of forks on plates were the only audible sounds. Lupe looked at the two people she worked for. There was once a time when she saw them happy. That was in the early years, when she was busy changing Ryan's diapers and spoon feeding him carrot mush. In those days, these two wouldn't shut up. Now, Lupe wasn't sure if she had dreamed up this distant fantasy. She wanted to be at that table like a house cat wants a bath. "I'm going to start cleaning the kitchen," she said, rising to her feet. Neither Jamie nor Max attempted to stop her.

Now alone, Max looked at his beautiful wife eating her food in almost a defiant fashion. "Are we even going to try to rectify this thing?"

Jamie let out a sigh deep from her gut. "I don't know, Max." She never looked up.

"You wanted me around, and here I am. Can I get some credit for that at least?"

"One day, a holiday at that, isn't going to cut it."

"I just feel like I can't win."

Jamie didn't respond. When she looked at Max, she felt only anger. Maybe some of the responsibility of this struggling marriage fell on Jamie in that regard. They had engaged in the highly irrational and highly improbable sanctity of marriage, and like the millions of other American couples who entered into this crazy arrangement, theirs was rocky.

Max said something else, but it didn't register in Jamie's mind. That mind was in the back of Mike's truck with David peeling her clothes off and kissing all over her naked body. Her eyes were looking out the window now but not seeing anything. She felt moisture downstairs when Max got through.

"Earth to Jamie."

She turned to him, startled and flushed. "What?"

"Are you alright?"

"Yes," she said in a defensive tone.

"What were you thinking about?"

He knows, Jamie thought. *He's an expert in the art of cheating.* "Nothing."

⊰┼⊱

Imperial Acres Mobile Park, a collection of rusted trailer homes less charming than the name intended to depict, is where Mark chose to go on the lam. It had been three weeks since his escape from the custody of the hospital without a whiff of the police who were searching for him. Mark wanted to think that this was because of his excellent hiding location and his careful, covert abilities. But he knew the fact that he was a man living on a month-to-month life lease was a large reason the search for him was not so intense. Whatever the reason for Mark's long leash, he wasn't complaining. He was free, and even the stale confines of his trailer felt like the Trump Tower to him.

Thus, although his Thanksgiving meal bore no resemblance to Jamie's or David's, he was more thankful than both of them were. He was perched on a smelly couch with a ham sandwich on his lap while watching the Cowboys get whooped by the Cardinals with a smile on his face. A woman came from the kitchen with a glass of green juice. She had similar features to Mark, the same eyes and nose, but she was a good thirty years younger.

"I don't want that shit," he said.

"This will make you feel better, Uncle. And you know it."

He did know it. Whatever his niece put in those damn drinks tasted like shit. But there was nothing that made him feel so much better so instantly. It even made taking a shit bearable, if not enjoyable once again. With a grimace, he chugged the vegetable concoction down.

"Good job," said his niece, taking away the empty glass. "I'm going to run to the store. Do you need anything?"

"No. Just remember what we talked about—"

"I have no idea where my uncle is, alright? Stop asking."

"Love you."

"Love you too, see you in a bit."

Mark planned to hide out in this trailer for the rest of his numbered days. And with the time he had before the cancer got too severe for him to function, he intended to get right with his god. He had a plan for this task. It was infallible really, the most noble thing a human can do—die while serving another.

CHAPTER TWO

David couldn't remember a time when he was happier than he was during the following weeks. Being with Jamie not only made him feel like a better man, but it also inspired him to reach higher. If this level of happiness is possible, what would happen if he beat Loder? He thought he might burst with light like an exploding star. So he trained harder than he ever had before. He stayed off the booze, the cigarettes, and especially the coke. He found that Jamie's naked body intertwined with his was better than any narcotic. He also found that his room, small as it was, still proved more serviceable than the backseat of a truck. Despite their blossoming affair, they were able to keep Ryan in the dark. As far as Ryan was concerned, his mother was simply hanging out with work friends on a more frequent basis, or at least she hoped that was the case. Ryan was coming to the age when a parent is the last person a child wants to see, making Jamie's new boyfriend easier to hide. David felt guilty for not telling his pupil what was happening. He could feel this situation gaining in complexity and feared that a conflict could be on the horizon. But David's guilt and fear paled in comparison to the overwhelming feeling of joy he felt as his relationship with Jamie grew roots.

On a warm evening illuminated by a broken moon, Jamie and David drove to Mission Valley Theatre to see a movie. As a child, going to movies was an escape from physical abuse for David and his mother. The smell of popcorn, the mixture of a cherry and coke flavored Slurpee, and the screen larger than his house— these treasures were all he needed to forget about the tyrant who waited at home. It was easily his favorite place in the world. But since that night he sent the tyrant to his grave, he hadn't been back to a theatre.

They walked hand in hand on their way toward the entrance. The colorful lights and the posters of showing movies seemed to call for them to enter, like a Disneyland for adults. Jamie looked stunning to David, and he was beginning to think that her perfume had to be made from some kind of debilitating elixir. They saw *Nightcrawler* in a packed theatre. They thought it was a pretty good flick. The story was mediocre, but Jake Gyllenhaal's performance was masterful. The movie didn't really matter; what mattered was that they had a companion for the evening. Someone who thought they were special and had nowhere else they would rather be than with them. This was something both David and Jamie had lacked for a long time.

There was a small sports bar in the parking lot that they went to after the movie. David indulged with a beer. A few light beers he could handle; it was the hard stuff he was determined to stay away from. David rested his legs on Jamie's as he faced her at the bar. The lady bartender with masterfully crafted fake breasts brought them their beers and added a "you guys are cute." Later she would get a good tip, and not because of the boobs.

"I haven't been to a movie theatre in . . ." it took David a moment the crunch the numbers. "Probably ten years."

Jamie's jaw nearly hit the floor. "You're lying."

David smirked, knowing how absurd that stat sounded. He drank his beer and rubbed some suds from his lip stubble. "The last movie I saw in a theatre was *Gladiator.*"

"Jesus Christ David. You got out of prison almost five years ago. Why haven't you gone to the movies?"

David shrugged his shoulders. "I haven't had anyone to go with."

"People go alone . . . I do."

David wiggled his eyebrows stupidly. "Not anymore."

Jamie smiled and took a sip of her beer. "That wasn't the best movie to break a ten year hiatus."

"I enjoyed it thoroughly."

Jamie shook her head. "Ten years, wow."

David nodded. The look on his face turned inward as he remembered something from his past. "My mom and me used to go a lot. It was our favorite mother son bonding . . ." He struggled for an expression. "Whatever you wanna call it."

Jamie looked at David with a comforting gaze. "Is that why you haven't gone?"

"Maybe subconsciously. I thought about it when we were driving out here. I wondered if it would bother me or not." He turned and looked at Jamie. "But once we arrived, she didn't cross my mind once."

"I'm sorry you didn't get to say goodbye to her."

"It's my fault."

"It's not your fault that she got cancer, David."

"No, but it's my fault that I went to prison. And it's my fault that I was a selfish asshole for a long time before going to prison. But what's done is done."

There was a brief silence. While David drank his beer in gulps far smaller than he was programmed for, he felt Jamie's eyes on him. She asked him a question. "What if I told you that everything that happens is based on prior circumstances?"

David smiled. She was talking about determinism. Maybe she, like himself, felt that their meeting was preordained by the universe. "I'd say you have a point."

"Then why do you beat yourself up so much about going to prison?"

"I still made the choice to rob that bank, prior circumstances or not."

"But prior circumstances are *huge*—prior circumstances you had no control over. Your home life wasn't good, right?" David shook his head. "You didn't choose that. That's not fair. And, like it or not, at the age you were, your surroundings shape the way you behave. So you went to prison, and for the first time, you have a male figure telling you what you can be good at instead of trying to keep you down. And look at you now. Maybe, as corny and crazy as it sounds, maybe it all happened for a reason. Maybe we do have a destiny."

David didn't know where this philosopher came from, but he liked her very much. Every time he saw Jamie, a layer was removed, and he got closer to the unattainable core of who she truly was. He knew where Jamie was coming from, so he decided to meet her on common ground. "I definitely think that there's something at work here, something beyond our understanding."

Jamie nodded strongly, pointing at David as she took another drink. David smiled and marveled at how when conversations like these take place there is rarely much resistance to these thoughts. It seemed to him that these notions of life's queerness exist in everyone. Everyone is in search for the truth. Everyone senses the magic of this place. It sits on the tip of the tongue and on the fringe of consciousness, letting everyone know that it's there but not quite wholly accessible.

"I've always wanted only a few things," David continued. "And I feel like my life has been a series of obstacles and roadblocks that I have to overcome to get those things I want. So when I do, if I can, the feeling of accomplishment will be sweeter. It's like a game someone is making me play. God, if you want to call it that. But not the one that hates gay people or wants us to keep slaves."

Jamie laughed then put her hand on his forearm. "What are those things that you want?"

"The first is a woman who loves me, despite all of my flaws."

Jamie closed her eyes and smiled.

"The second is to be great at something. Really just to be successful in something that's worthwhile. Not in terms of money—in terms of glory. I could never make up my mind where that glory would come from. I bounced back and forth between basketball and football glory as a kid. Now the mission is fighting, and there ain't much time left. I want it bad Jamie, so bad it hurts. It's right there in front of me, but there's always that fear that it's going to slip away, leaving me to climb a mountain again. It's overwhelming sometimes. I don't want to die having achieved nothing during my life worthwhile."

Jamie smiled and rubbed David's head, sliding her fingers through his short, messy hair. "If you work hard enough, you'll achieve it."

"What do you want out of life?" David asked. "What are your goals?"

Jamie sighed and took a gulp rather than a sip of her beer before giving her answer. "Everything changes when you have a kid. My aspirations have turned towards him. I just want to raise the happiest, smartest, and most successful boy I possibly can."

"You're doing an amazing job. He's an impressive kid."

Jamie's smile faded as she looked down. "It's hard doing it by myself and pretending like I'm not."

"Then stop pretending. Look Jamie, I'm bad at this relationship thing—one of the places I've messed up in the past is not laying out what I want or how I feel. I'm bad at it, but I'm not going to do that with you . . . I want to be with you, Jamie. Very badly. Do you feel the same way?"

"I do."

"Then at the risk of being the guy that turns your world upside down—like you've done to me—I'm going to say something: I think you should get a divorce. I don't want to sneak around like this forever. I want you to be mine."

Jamie took a while to respond. David was having a hard time gauging her reaction. What David just proposed was the forbidden desire Jamie had been considering for the last two years. Although the view on divorce was not as close-minded and rigid as it once was, the taboo of it was still a deterrent for her. She may have been miserable, but she feared being even more so if she divorced her husband. Her friends who had the scoop on her new man were skeptical, and her mother, who had been involved since the beginning of her doubts about her current marriage, was downright against the affair. But somehow these doubts fueled her passion. One of the things Jamie had learned about life is no matter how much you respect someone, how very possible, and very probable it is that that person has no fucking idea what they're talking about. They're just as in the dark as we all are. This was Jamie's life, not theirs. And like David, Jamie hadn't received an instruction manual for this life she was launched into. All she could do was ride this thing called life, and right now it was heading beautifully towards the man sitting by her and resting his warm legs against hers.

Finally, after the painful pause, Jamie spoke. "I think you're right."

CHAPTER THREE

S aturday night, one week before the fight of his life, David had to go to a press conference to promote his fight. He wasn't thrilled. He'd rather be spending time with Jamie, but this was part of the job. All he had to do was go answer some repetitive, uncreative questions, and if that brought more viewers, good for him—good for everyone. At this press conference, he would finally meet face-to-face with Arnold Loder. The event was held just a stone's throw from The Bear's Den at the San Diego Sports Arena. It was a cool, rainy night. David didn't like nights like these; the rain was a bad omen. It was raining the night he killed his father. It was raining the night he heard the cell door slam behind him for the first time. He tried to ignore these thoughts as he rode in the passenger seat of Mike's massive truck.

"You good?" Mike asked.

"Yeah. Let's just get this shit over with." David was feeling several emotions. He was nervous as well as excited to finally look Loder in the eyes and into his soul.

David and Mike arrived at the moderately full lot. They exited Mike's truck to a distorted world created by the shimmering, damp pavement. They met at the back of the truck. Mike gave David a nod and a pat on the back, and they started towards the arena. As they made their walk, a Range Rover blaring music cruised past them and parked in a spot thirty yards ahead. A crew of tattooed men stepped out of the vehicle. Arnold Loder was among them. As David and Mike slowly passed by the group, the future opponents made eye contact, and the verbal warfare began.

"Look who it is," Loder said loudly, smiling his bright-white teeth at David. "It's my next victim, Frank."

The large, round faced man Loder addressed as Frank sniffed the air and said "I smell fresh meat, a wounded deer." Frank laughed heartily at his own joke.

David said nothing, just continued to stare. Mike put his arm around his pupil's shoulder and kept them moving. But as they passed, Mike had something to say. "Keep running that mouth while you can boy."

The gang of thugs burst into laughter. Frank popped off again, "Is that your dad? Daddy sticking up for you?"

Mike quickly removed his arm from around David's shoulder and walked towards Frank. David followed his coach with his hands in his pockets and a small smile now on his face. With Mike now in his grill, Frank realized he had poked the wrong bear. The rage radiated off of Mike as he looked down on the shorter man. "I'm *your* daddy boy. Get it straight."

Frank tried to get some words out but couldn't. He was betrayed by his animal fear of a creature higher in the food chain. He tried his hardest to look tough and once more to speak a coherent sentence. But his open mouth had nothing to say. Loder attempted to break things up and moved towards them. When David saw Loder's move, he removed his hands from his pockets and balled them into fists. "Alright, back off old man," Loder said and then placed his hand on Mike's chest. Before Mike could rip Loder's limbs off, David violently shoved Loder into the side of his Range Rover. Loder's eyes turned crazy and a smile formed on his pointy mouth. A brawl was eminent when a high pitched voice came calling from behind them.

"Hey hey hey! Stop that right now!" It was the promoter of the fight, Brian Holliday, a white haired, leather skinned man. He was accompanied by a posse of his toadies. "What the hell is going on out here?" Holliday shouted from between the groups. "Save it for the fight! You guys are professionals God damn it!"

Tensions were high as the men were separated. With some space between them, Frank started shouting once again. A group of reporters saw the scuffle and ran over. Their camera flashes illuminated the group in the night. Mike had calmed down enough to grab David, who had not calmed down. Mike could feel him shaking with rage. David had come to love Mike, and he wasn't going to allow him to be disrespected by Loder, whom he had very quickly come to hate.

As they walked towards the entrance, David's heart was still beating quickly. His senses were heightened after the exchange. He was in fight or flight mode. Outside of a cage, he hadn't felt this way in a long time. "I'm gonna run right through that mother fucker," he said, clenching his fists and jaw.

"I know," Mike said. "I can't wait."

Fifteen minutes later, David found himself on a stage next to all of the fighters on the card. Loder was strategically placed on the opposite side of the platform. Next to David was a large black man named Jamal "Tank" Johnson. It was David's first time meeting the man, but he knew who he was. Tank Johnson was a local celebrity and was almost certainly on his way to the UFC after this fight—unless he lost. This was a crazy game they were playing after all.

Many of the questions were generic: "How has your training camp been?" or "How do you feel about Arnold Loder as an opponent?" And now, after their parking lot scuffle, many of the questions were about that. While Arnold was brash and talkative, saying things like "This guy ain't shit. I'm gonna run through him like I do everybody", David was calm. He answered the questions respectfully and concisely. He had learned something in his life from being surrounded by *real* tough guys—guys who didn't care about going to prison and guys who had no hopes of getting out of it. Those guys weren't loud; they were eerily quiet. He learned that you could spot a real killer by the look in the man's eyes. "*The eyes,*" Mike had once told him, "*the eyes never lie*".

After a long hour of answering these questions, it was time for the fighters to square off for pictures—a customary procedure in the fight world. The podium in the middle of the stage was removed, and the fighters on the card took turns walking up and facing off. Some were cordial, shaking hands, and some were comically violent.

David and Arnold were second to last. A commotion raised in the crowd of reporters when it became their turn to pose for the cameras. After the near brawl outside, everyone was anxious to see if this stare down would produce another conflict. Across the stage, Loder was pacing, acting as if they were going to fight right there. David stood still, staring at the pacing man and never wavering. Mike stood behind him. "Relax," he said.

"I am relaxed," David replied. Holliday called them to the center. As they walked the stage to meet lights flashed continuously and the murmuring of voices rose to louder chirping. Holliday was prepared for a scuffle, so he outstretched his arms to keep some distance between the fighters. Loder continued his talking as they met. "You ain't ready for this!" he shouted, bearing his sharp fangs. David stepped forward another step, pushing

Holliday's arms closer. He got close enough to smell the onions on Loder's breath from his lunch. He looked deep into the man's eyes, where he saw that despite the show, he was nervous. The eyes never lie.

After the presser, the rain had ceased. Mike and David walked away from the arena with tired eyes while a bright moon peeked through parting clouds, illuminating the wet world around them. When they arrived at the truck, David said he wanted to walk home.

"Don't be silly. It's late," Mike replied.

"I like walking at this hour."

"Yeah, well you're a weird dude."

David returned a smile. "We both know this. I just got some things to think about. I'll be fine."

Mike looked around and saw that Loder's car was already gone. He sighed and spat a loogie on the ground for no apparent reason. "Alright man," he said before climbing into the driver's seat. He fired up the loud engine and looked down at David from his perch. "One week and we get a chance to shut that punk up and shock the world."

David smiled. "I know."

Mike gave a nod and pulled away, giving one final wave out of his window before he disappeared into the night. David waved back then pulled out his cell phone.

"Where are you?" was how Jamie answered her cell.

"I'm in the parking lot. Where are you?"

"Oh, I see you now. I'm parked by Carl's Junior."

David walked over towards Jamie's location. The large plastic star in the sky led the way. He strolled up to the passenger side of Jamie's Mercedes and opened the door.

"What's up beautiful?" David said, leaning into the doorway.

"You looking for a ride stud?"

"What kind of ride?"

"Hop in and see."

David slid into the car. Jamie pulled away into the night.

<hr />

That night, Jamie was supposed to be out in Newport for a friend's birthday party. Instead, she was in bed with a man she enjoyed being with sexually for the first time in years. She could see into David's soul now. It wasn't hard. David had been wanting to put his guard down for a long time. For the first time in his life, he felt comfortable being himself around a woman. He never worried about what Jamie was thinking. He knew her intentions were pure. He smiled, inhaling the scent of her hair and thinking these pleasant thoughts while they lay as naked spoons.

"What are we going to do, David?" Jamie said softly, looking off into the darkness.

"I don't know." He didn't. This love was dangerous, and it involved the life of a young boy. But it was love, and David couldn't control that.

"I'm scared," she whispered.

"What are you scared of?"

"I just don't know what to do. I'm scared for Ryan. I don't want to hurt him."

David took a moment to respond. He didn't want to hurt Ryan or Jamie. Not being sure if he was in the wrong, all he could do is go with his gut. And his gut told him he couldn't go on in life without this woman. "I'll never let anything happen to you two."

"I know. It's just . . ."

"What? Tell me."

Jamie turned and faced David. He pushed her hair out of her eyes gently. "I don't care about money," she said. "You and me could live out of a van traveling the country and I'd be the

happiest girl in the world. But I want—I *need*—to be able to provide for my son."

David was hurt. "You don't think that I can. Is that it?"

"I don't expect you to," Jamie said sincerely. "We will be fine.
I'm tough—"

"I know you are."

"—I'm just nervous, that's all. If I get a divorce, I'm scared Max
is going to fight me to the bitter end in court. I'm nervous about
going through all that shit. It's going to cost a lot of money."

"I'll help you. We'll find a way. And not from robbing banks, either." Jamie laughed. "After I win this fight, I'm gonna make triple
the money. I'll do anything to provide for you guys. I'll work construction; I'll bus tables at your restaurant; I'll deliver newspapers.
I'll do whatever it takes. You and Ryan will never want for anything.
I promise you that."

Jamie looked down for a moment, smiling with tears in her
eyes. When she looked up at David again, she kissed him then
mounted him for round two that evening.

CHAPTER FOUR

When David woke the next morning, he found himself alone. *Strange*, he thought. He was normally a light sleeper whose nights were haunted by various wakings caused by unwanted dreams. But apparently a night of sex put him into a deeper state, allowing Jamie to slip away unnoticed.

On the nightstand was a note: *"Let's do it. I love you."*

David smiled at the note as he rose from bed and headed for the restroom. As he was emptying his bladder, he looked out his window and was instantly struck by an ominous feeling. It was raining again, and a bolt of lightning shot across the sky in the distance followed shortly by the loud crack of thunder. Subsequently, on his coffee table, his phone began to ring. David walked toward the phone slowly, watching it spin on the fake wood. He knew who was calling him. He didn't know how he knew, but he did. He felt it. And when he picked it up, his intuition was confirmed.

The forces were pulling at him.

David let the phone ring and ring until it finally ceased ringing. He started to pace the room. When he slammed the door in

Jorge's face a month earlier, he expected retribution, but he expected it to come much sooner. At that time, he was prepared to kill or be killed. It didn't matter to him. He had nothing to live for. But his life was different now. He had *everything* to live for. After a whole month without this moment coming, he naively thought it wouldn't come at all. In fact, he'd almost forgotten about Terry entirely—until he saw the Lexus at the park. They had been tailing him. *But why?* David wondered. *Why not come for me earlier? Maybe they want me back in the crew. Maybe Terry's money's going south. Maybe he wants me to set some people straight.* Whatever it was, David wanted nothing to do with it. Especially not now, when everything was going so well. As he paced the room considering all of these things, he began to feel unbearably frustrated and angry at the prospect of dealing with this psychopathic caller.

He sat on his couch and looked at the phone, waiting for a voicemail or text. Nothing came. He started to think Terry had accidentally dialed him. Heavy footsteps approaching his door sent him crashing back to the reality he was living in. The footsteps stopped outside his door. Three loud knocks followed.

David quickly walked to his closet and reached into a mess of books and clothes on the top shelf. He emerged with a snub-nose 38. revolver in his hand. As he checked the old relic for bullets, three more knocks came, louder this time. His inspection confirmed that his gun was still loaded. David held it by his side as he approached the door and looked through the peephole. Standing on the other side of the door was a man David recognized. It was Billy. The button up shirt he was wearing had to be custom tailored to fit his ridiculous frame. Drops of water were rolling off of his clean-shaven head, and he was casually smacking gum with his chiseled jaw. "Open up David!" he bellowed.

David shoved the gun into the back of his sweat pants. "What do you want?" he shouted through the door.

"Terry would like a word."

David thought about resisting but concluded it was worthless. Despite his four-lock defense, Billy would bust his door down with ease. Then he'd be forced to blow the big bastard's brains out. He didn't need the mess or the prison time. So he opened the door.

"How can I help you, Bill?" David asked as he opened the door and looked up at the ogre's mug. In the street behind Billy, David could see the Lexus he arrived in. Terry was smoking a cigarette in the back seat. Jorge was the driver.

"Get dressed and come with me," Billy said with no emotion before smacking his gum again.

"I'm not going anywhere."

Billy shook his head. "That's not the right answer here."

The two men stared at each other, both refusing to blink. "What is this about?"

"That's for Terry to discuss."

From the car in the street, an impatient Terry called out. "Come on down David! We'll have you back by lunch time!"

David was debating punching Billy on the chin. Four weeks of vigorous training had put him on edge and in fantastic shape. He felt like giving his fists a test run. He could place two punches on this man's face, and before Billy knew what caused him to be on his back, David's heel would be finishing the job. But then what? Terry and Jorge wouldn't take kindly to that. And then he'd have to deal with them. No, that wouldn't do. He decided his best chance of emerging out of this situation intact was to be diplomatic. So he decided to play ball.

"Give me five minutes you fucking gorilla."

Billy looked at his stolen Rolex. "You're on the clock."

David shut the door, got dressed quickly, then stuffed his revolver in his waistline. Then he called Jamie, hoping she wasn't somehow caught up in this.

After several rings, she answered. David could finally exhale.

"Where'd you go?" he asked.

"I had to pick up Ryan from his friend's house, remember?"

He did. But in his paranoid fog he had forgotten. "That's right."

"I'm doing it today."

"Doing what?"

"Seeing a divorce lawyer."

David smiled. "Ok that's good," he said softly. "Be strong. Call me if you need anything."

"I will. I'll talk to you later."

David and Billy walked down to the car. It was a chilly December day in San Diego. The exhaust from the Cadillac blew out like a cloud from its rear. The rain had turned to a downpour. Terry looked up and smiled at David from his backseat, using a folder to block the rain from hitting him. "What's up David?" he asked loudly over the rain.

"What's this about Terry? I'm a busy man."

"Oh I doubt that. All you do these days is go to that gym. We know that. Sounds boring if you ask me."

David said nothing. Just thought about Jorge spying on him. And wondered if they knew about Jamie.

"Just hop in. Let's take a ride, huh? Get outta this rain."

"I'm not getting in the car until you tell me what you want."

"Well David, it's time we talked about that last fight of yours. And I have a business proposition for you. That's all I'm going to say for now. Hop in."

David clenched his fists. "I don't know who you think you are Terry. I'm not your whipping boy anymore. You got me? I told you guys I'm done. I lost the fight for you, now get the fuck out of my life."

Terry laughed briefly before he turned to David with irritated eyes. "Ok David, listen up, and listen good. As you know, I know where you live. I don't want to, but if I have to, I can make your life real fucking miserable."

"Don't threaten me Terry."

"I'm *promising* you. I run this fucking town. I got eyes on every fucking corner. I've come here with a business offer and have been nothing but kind to you as always. Now I'm asking you one more time, get in the fucking car." Terry scooted over, leaving an opening. Billy opened the door.

"Get in the car," Billy repeated like the giant parrot he was.

David looked around. There was nobody in sight. No one to see David be murdered. Billy attempted to nudge David into the car, but David swiped his hand away. "Don't touch me you fat fuck, or I'll break your nose." The two alphas shared a primal glare. David held that glare as he got into the car on his own. Billy shut the door. Lighting split the sky once again.

They got on the Five-south and drove for twenty minutes. David thought they might be heading to Mexico. Maybe Terry was going to involve David in some sketch drug deal. He wasn't sure. All he knew was that he was pissed off. Throughout this unwanted field trip, Terry sang along to the tunes Credence Clearwater Revival (the music wasn't bad, but the company was). David felt the revolver's heavy steel crushing his balls. He had a strong feeling he might have to use it.

Just ten minutes before they reached the border, Jorge exited the freeway. Shortly after that, they pulled up in front of The Silver Fox. David had heard of the place but had never been. Terry bought the joint while he was in prison. And when David bought coke from Terry, it was always from Jorge at a location closer to his apartment. The sign listing the hours of operation said that it wasn't open until two that afternoon. David doubted the place made much real money; it was just a place to clean his dirty cash, stash his coke, and kill people like him.

The goons led David through the empty bar towards the hallway in the back of the place and eventually to Terry's office. Somebody had done an excellent job cleaning up the mess Zach Marshal's brains had left. Terry went to his leather seat and pulled a fresh cigar from his desk. David took a seat in a chair across from him.

"Give us some time, guys," Terry said. Billy and Jorge obeyed, leaving the two men alone in the room. David sat heavy in his chair looking at Terry, amazed that he found himself back in this world. He hadn't seen Terry in two months, and it looked like his hair had greyed significantly in that time. Terry struck a match and methodically lit the end of his cigar. "What happened with the last fight my man?" he asked between puffs.

"I lost it, just like I said I would," David said stubbornly.

"You certainly did. And I paid you, like I said I would. Even though you and me both know you tried to double-cross me."

David leaned forward and looked Terry in the eyes. "I already told your baboon out there that I didn't try to win that fight. I had to make it look real."

"David, don't insult me, okay? Let's get past this."

David laughed in frustration.

"You could have tapped out in the first round to that chokehold. And also to the one he had you with in the second. Those punches you hit that guy with, I'm lucky, and *you* are especially lucky that that guy had a block-head. Because if you won after promising me you wouldn't..." Terry paused and flashed his whites. "Well my man, this conversation wouldn't be taking place."

Once again, David felt his weapon pressing against him. He really wanted to use it.

"You're not going to cop to it are you?"

"No."

Terry grinned and threw up his hands. "So be it. You don't have to confess. Instead I'm gonna give you a chance to redeem yourself."

David's heart sank. He knew what was coming.

Terry opened a drawer on his desk and pulled out a rolled up poster. He unraveled it across his desk. It was a poster advertising the fight card David would be competing in six days from now. Across the top of the poster was the heading: A CHRISTMAS CARD SPECIAL, and directly below: PECHUNGA CASINO AND RESORT. Below the heading were pictures of all the fighters on the card, David included.

"I'm not throwing this fight Terry. There's no way. If you've brought me all the way down here just for that, you've wasted your time."

Terry reached into his desk once more and tossed a stack of cash on the table. "That's ten grand. You'll get another twenty-five large after you go down on Saturday."

"Are you deaf?"

"Nope, I'm not, but you'll be *dead* if you don't do this."

David stood quickly, pulling his gun from his pants and then pointing it at Terry.

Terry didn't flinch. He couldn't have been less scared. "Go for it sport. You won't make it out of here alive if you pull that trigger."

"Maybe so," David replied, "but neither will you."

Terry spread his hands in a gesture that said "*so be it*". After a moment, he spoke again. "David, this is a no brainer." He rose slowly to his feet, still puffing on his cigar casually as he rounded his desk towards David. "How much are they paying you for this fight? A grand? Probably not even that much huh?"

David was trembling, his gun still aimed between Terry's eyes. His finger tightened around the trigger. In the span of five seconds, his mind processed a large amount of information. He could kill Terry, and try his luck with the other two. The odds were against him, but he had a chance. He could probably get away with it too. He would be doing the cops a favor by killing these cockroaches. Then he thought about what killing his father had done to him psychologically. He walked around with that heavy load everywhere he went. Killing Terry would probably be different, but David wasn't sure that would be the case. He didn't want to see another head explode from his doing. Finally, he thought about the money. Thirty-five thousand dollars was more than he had made in all of his fights combined. Before meeting Jamie, he wouldn't have cared about the cash; he wanted to win this fight that badly. But now he wanted to help Jamie more than he wanted to win the fight. This final thought won the war inside of his head. He slowly lowered his gun.

Terry smiled, biting his cigar with his front teeth. He took the stack of cash from the top of his desk and slid it into the inside of David's coat pocket. "This is the last time. I promise. You'll never see me again."

David looked at Terry once more. "Never won't be long enough."

David took an expensive cab ride home. Fresh off of his sordid payday, he could afford it. The trip seemed to last forever. He spent his time trying to rationalize the decision he had just been forced to make. In the span of two hours, the path of his life had forked in another unpleasant direction. Thinking about buying Jamie a necklace with his new cash comforted him. So did him knowing that Terry wasn't taking no for an answer—that he had no choice. But none of these thoughts could mask the pain he felt for abandoning his dreams for money once again.

When David finally arrived back at his apartment, he paid a visit to the liquor store for the first time in a month. He went for a bottle of Jim Beam and set it in front of Larry without finesse.

Larry set down his Sunday paper on the counter and put his reading glasses on top of it. "How's it going, David? Back on the sauce?" he said jokingly, but David wasn't laughing.

"Back on the sauce," David confirmed. He gave Larry his money and left without getting his change. Larry watched him off. He was slightly concerned for David, but with all the lowlifes he saw on a daily basis it was hard to have a heart for everyone.

David sat on his couch with the bottle and a shot glass. He poured a shot and took it down with a wince. Then he took one more. Liquor wasn't cutting it, so he walked over to his night stand. He opened the drawer and was painfully reminded that he had flushed his coke. An old pack of reds would have to suffice for this date with destruction. He smoked the pack and drank the whiskey until he was numb of emotions. He even smiled as he lay back on his couch and took one last sip before he passed out.

CHAPTER FIVE

Tiffany Snyder's office was neat and organized. The shelves were lined with various law books, and the appropriate credentials hung on the wall. She was in her late twenties, maybe early thirties, and she looked good despite the pack of camel lights she smoked daily. She had a focused look on her face, the look of a woman ready to take down another deadbeat husband.

"We can get him for half easily," Tiffany said. She was writing on a yellow legal pad relentlessly as Jamie gave her the details of the split.

"I told you already. I don't want it or need it. I want this to go as smoothly as possible. All I want is full custody of my son."

"I understand that, and I respect it. But you deserve compensation for sacrifices you have made. From what you've told me here today, he is due to pay a hefty amount of child support."

Jamie let out a long sigh. She hated every bit of this. But she was finally getting the ball rolling on this divorce, something she felt she should have done much sooner.

The two women ironed out the details of the case for about an hour. When they were done, Tiffany presented Jamie some preliminary papers. "Max can sign these if he's willing to speed up the divorce process. I can have these delivered for you if you'd like."

"No," Jamie said, grabbing the small stack. "I'll serve him myself."

Tiffany smiled and nodded. "You're my kind of gal."

⇥⊹⇤

Jamie walked through a row of cubicles filled with men and women who hoped to obtain her husband's position one day. The room was in pandemonium; phones were ringing left and right, above and below. There were people laughing and people yelling. She could smell cigarette smoke—or was it weed? Whatever it was, it was breaking several fire codes. It was this chaos that her husband loved more than his family. She came to the door that read Max Hurley, Senior Agent without anyone questioning her presence. She could have had a bomb or a gun, and no one would have batted an eye.

"He's on a call right now, Mrs. Hurley," Max's secretary, a young, pretty woman said from her desk on the right of the door.

Jamie looked towards the voice's owner—a fresh college graduate with perky tits giving her a look of superiority—and wondered if this bitch was the reason she never saw her husband. "I don't give a shit," Jamie said and entered the room.

Max was pacing his large office and was indeed on a call. He saw Jamie enter and nodded towards a couch for her to take a seat. She did.

While Max discussed matters with one of his clients, Jamie looked around his office—the place he spent most of his time. The room was dark: dark-brown wallpaper, a dark Italian-made

157

desk, and a dark red couch she was now seated in. A Picasso hung on the wall along with some other expensive paintings. A set of golf clubs resided in one corner. A bar loaded with all the essential liquors was tucked in another. Max had built a cozy setup for himself. It showed his dedication. She just wished that he could have shown the same dedication to his family. If he had, maybe this day wouldn't have come.

Max hung up the phone and turned to Jamie. The look on her face told him that she had a bomb to drop, and he was pretty sure he knew what it was. "How can I help you Jamie?" he asked, flipping a sheet of paper on his desk.

"You should sit down."

"No I'll stand." He was calm, resigned to what was about to come.

"Please."

Max shook his head in frustration as he walked over and took a seat on an adjacent chair.

"I'm afraid the day we both knew was coming has finally arrived." Jamie reached into her purse and pulled the legal papers out, placing them on the table.

Max remained leaned back in his chair. He said nothing, just stared at the wife he was losing.

"I don't think I'm asking for a ton of support, but I'm asking for full custody."

"No fucking way."

"Max, you won't win this."

He laughed. "Jamie, you're a waitress."

"Yeah I'm a waitress, a waitress at a high end restaurant. And maybe I'll get another job. But I'm also a very involved parent. Something you're not. This will be proven in court if you want to take it there. I certainly don't."

"Of course you don't," Max said. "You can't afford that."

"I'll find a way. I'm getting full custody of our son. We can make it long and painful or not. It's up to you."

Max leaned his head into his hands and ran his fingers through his hair. Then he turned and looked outside through large windows. Jamie could see that her husband knew she was right. After a long silence, he spoke again. "Where will you go?"

"I've got a few apartments in Claremont I'm looking at."

"What about Christmas? It's in a week."

"I would like to spend one last Christmas together. Then we're moving out."

Max nodded, still looking out the window. "I'm sorry Jamie. I don't know how we got here."

"We're just not compatible. You don't have to be sorry for that."

Max turned and pulled out a pen from his pocket. He glanced over the papers briefly then signed them.

⋙─⋘

Amidst one of the most emotionally draining days of her young life, Jaime had one final task to complete. It was the one she was dreading most of all. She pulled up to After School Matters with moist eyes. After parking her car, she looked in the mirror and practiced looking like her normal self. A moment later, Ryan came walking out the front door, his large backpack bouncing behind him.

The ride home was a quiet one, which wasn't unusual. Ryan looked out the window at the passing landscape with the wonder only a nine year old child is capable of. Jamie decided she would wait until they got home before they had the talk.

When they pulled into the driveway, she wasn't sure she could do it. Maybe she should put it off until after dinner. Everything's better on a full stomach. Ultimately, she decided she couldn't wait.

She had to be strong if she was going to expect the same from her son. When Ryan reached for the door handle, she stopped him.

"Ryan, there's something I need to talk to you about."

The young boy knew the tone of his mother's voice meant there was trouble ahead. He turned to her with his full attention. "What?"

Jamie cleared her throat, sat upright, and inhaled deeply. As she exhaled, she said, "Me and your father are getting a divorce."

After a long silence, Ryan asked, "Why?"

"Because me and your father are not in love anymore . . . What's worse than that though is that we don't get along. It's not fair to you or to me."

"You don't love each other anymore?"

This question was so sincere and naïve that tears rushed to Jamie's eyes and dropped before she could even attempt to stop them. All she could do to prevent herself from losing control and sobbing like a baby was to shake her head with her lips pressed tightly together.

Ryan took a moment to respond once again. He knew his parents didn't get along, but he didn't see this coming. Kids at his age never do. "What's going to happen now? Where will I live?"

"You're staying with me."

"Will I be able to see Dad?"

"Of course. We haven't decided when or for how long, but you will be able to see him whenever you like."

"Where will we live?"

"You and me will find a nice apartment, one down by Claremont High School and the park over there so you can play. You can help me pick it out."

Ryan looked out the window at the house he had known as his home since he started registering memories.

"Ryan, I want you to know that me and your father love you very much. This decision has nothing to do with you."

"Yes it does," Ryan said, catching Jamie off guard. "You're getting divorced because he doesn't spend time with me."

"That is one reason, yes."

Now the tears began to come to Ryan's face, causing a tidal wave from Jamie. "He's just busy. He told me he won't be as busy soon." Ryan wiped the drops from his cheek. A small snot bubble popped in his right nostril.

"Your father is a good man, Ryan. But he is obsessed with one thing over anything else: his job."

Ryan sat in stunned silence.

"I think with us being separated he will realize what he's been missing out on. When you guys hang out, it will only be to do fun things. You don't have to see us arguing all of the time."

Ryan turned and got out of the car. Jamie didn't try to stop him. He was experiencing a life-shifting moment, and the gravity of the event made his stomach feel like it was packed full of rocks.

CHAPTER SIX

*D*avid *is in his childhood bedroom. There's a pounding on his door. David sits up from his bed quickly. Sweat is pouring from every part of his body. He gets out of bed tentatively and begins to walk towards the door that is shaking with each pound from the other side. He wants to open it. He doesn't know why. Maybe to make it stop. Maybe to talk to the person whom he knows is doing the banging. Before he can reach the handle, the door is kicked open. Standing in the doorway is his father, his eyes completely white, blood dripping from the crown of his head over his face like a fountain. In his right hand is the bat that David had used to kill him. At least he thought he did. He knows now that he was wrong. David wants to scream, but he's scared silent. All he can do is back up slowly as his dead father trudges forward towards him. They walk slowly in unison until David's feet back into the base of his bed, sending him falling to his back. As he goes to sit up, he sees his father swinging the bat down on him, lips pursed together tightly, showing his great effort. David has no time to move. CRACK!*

David's eyes opened and he sat up quickly on his couch. For a moment, he had no idea where he was. He rubbed his face and took a deep breath. Just another one of his cursed dreams. The worst part about these perpetual nightmares is how real they always appear to the gullible dreamer. As coherent thoughts aligned themselves, he came to the realization that he had awakened to an even worse nightmare—his actual life. He put his hand over his thumping heart and leaned back on his couch. The clock hanging crookedly over his bed said it was eleven. He was supposed to be at the gym by ten. Mike would be calling him and minute now to cuss him out.

As David slowly climbed up to his feet, his bottle of liquor fell from his lap down to the ground, spilling what little whiskey remained onto his feet. Instantly he felt like his head was lined with shards of glass. His eyes watered, his ears rang, and warm fluids—a mixture of whiskey and stomach acid—rushed to the back of his throat. Somewhere inside his body, a red alarm was flashing above an abort-ship sign. He rushed to the bathroom nine feet away and bent over the toilet where he proceeded to hurl brown liquid into the bowl for several minutes. After no more fluid would eject, he flushed the toilet and collapsed onto the bathroom floor. Then, to his astonishment, he began to cry.

Mike drove his truck with his phone to his ear, a disgusted look on his face. After a long ring indicated that David would once again not answer, he shouted "Pick up the fucking phone!" He pulled his truck into David's apartment complex and parked it illegally across three spots. He stormed up the stairs to David's door and slammed his large, scarred fist against it. "Open up, David!"

The door was opened quickly, and Mike was slightly surprised by what he saw. David was standing with his bag hanging from his shoulder, ready for practice it seemed. "Sorry Mike, I overslept."

Mike stood in the doorway with a skeptical look on his face. After further examination, he began to think something was amiss. David was pale. Red rings surrounded his eyes. But he seemed chipper enough. Maybe it was stress? Mike supposed David was allowed to be stressed a week out from the biggest fight of his life. "Now's not the time to be slacking off man. Just because all the hard work is done doesn't mean this week isn't important. We gotta get this weight off."

I shed some weight puking already, is what David thought of saying but decided to keep that information to himself. "I know. I'm sorry. Let's hit it." Before Mike could press him further, David rolled his bike outside and shut the door.

During the final week before his fights, it was customary that David didn't train hard or spar. Instead, he let his body heal so it could be at its full capability come fight night. This wasn't necessary anymore, but making Mike believe he was still committed was very necessary. If Mike knew David intended on throwing the fight, he was more likely to kill David than Terry was. The main task David faced in this final week was losing a good amount of weight, fourteen pounds to be exact. He weighed a buck eighty-five and would have to weigh in at the welterweight limit of one hundred and seventy-one pounds by Friday. This part of training camp had always been miserable. Combine this with the terrible feeling of treason, and it made for a really shitty week.

David ran for several miles on the treadmill then hit pads with Mike afterwards, all while wearing several layers to sweat as much as possible. There would be no eating burritos for the next five days. Instead it would be small portions of red meat and salads—rabbit food, as David liked to call it.

David tried his hardest to prevent Mike from detecting his melancholy that day, but he couldn't, not completely. The paleness of his fighter's skin was all he needed to see. After their run, while

David was sitting on the bench by the door putting his socks on, Mike approached him. "Everything alright?"

David looked up at him, trying to appear normal. "Yeah, just tired that's all."

"You're feeling ready and fully prepared for the fight?"

David smiled and used an old line: "I stay ready."

Mike smiled back and patted David on the head. "Let's shock the world, kid."

"Let's start with San Diego County. We can shock the world later on."

Mike chuckled slightly. "Just watch out for those leg kicks, and we'll be good."

"If he gets leg-kick-happy, he's gonna get countered with this thing." David held up his balled right fist.

"That's right."

David stood up and hung his bag on his shoulder. "I'm gonna go get some groceries for the cut. I'll see you later."

"Ok," Mike said.

He watched David as he crossed the parking lot on his bike until he rounded the corner and was out of sight. Mike knew something was wrong with his fighter. All he could do was hope he got over it before it was go time.

———

David rode his bike home feeling like a man being torn in two pieces. He wanted so badly to be known—and to be loved, he had come to find—for being a great fighter. This desire went back to the days of his father—and also his peers— telling him he couldn't be great. Fighting was his best chance at rising above mediocrity and proving all his doubters wrong. But David also had to be realistic. The money he was getting from Terry was likely more than he would make in his entire fighting career. And, unlike robbing people, this crime was a relatively safe one. Guys took dives in fighting; fixed fights are part of the sport's history. But David swore he would never be one of those gutless people. He had failed to adhere to his principle by becoming a cheat on more than one occasion. And the resulting guilt was powerful enough to distract him from his insatiable crush on Jamie that had consumed his thoughts for the past several weeks.

All he could think about was the decision he had made, about selling his dreams once again for money, and about the forces derailing the train whose course he was riding on to accomplishment once again.

CHAPTER SEVEN

Ryan lay in his bed staring at the ceiling, full of emotions he didn't have names for. Like David's childhood bedroom, Ryan had posters on his walls. His posters were of strange, new images though. Instead of a Michael Jordan poster, he had a poster of LeBron James. Instead of a *Star Wars* poster, there was an *Avengers* poster. Instead of a guitar, a Playstation three was plugged into a small TV.

Ryan didn't know what to think about his parents' divorce. All he knew is he felt like crying. So that's what he did. He lay on his back while his big, blue eyes let out a steady stream of tears.

In the living room, Jamie, like David, also felt like she was being split in two. She knew she didn't love her husband, but was that a sufficient reason to put her son through such pain? Was her happiness worth it? Would time heal this wound? She hoped so. There was an exciting world outside of her marriage that she wanted to explore. She couldn't convince herself that this desire was wrong. That gave her the confidence to move on with her decision. Before meeting David, she never believed in love at first sight. She certainly didn't experience it with Max. That was more like love after a relentless (but admittedly admirable) refusal of the word "no". But it never truly became love, just closely brushed it. With David, it was the real thing. She had never met anyone like him. He seemed to care about everyone else's feelings far more than his own. This is what she fell in love with. But there was something more than that, something hard to put a finger on. A feeling of destiny, of absolute rightness about this love. She deserved that feeling, like everyone does. And now that she knew it was real, she was going to have it.

⇒⤞ ⇷⇐

Later that evening, Starbucks was not the bustling mad house it was during the morning rush. Instead it was a calm work and study place, a good environment for David and Jamie to meet and discuss the hole they had dug for themselves. David walked over to the table Jamie had claimed with his black coffee in one hand and Jamie's elaborate latte in the other.

"Thanks," Jamie said as David set their drinks down and took his seat across from her.

"Sure thing."

They were both emotionally drained. Jamie's reason was obvious. David's was a secret that he hoped would remain that way. "How'd it go?" David asked as he put his hand over Jamie's and waited for his coffee to cool.

She let out a sigh. "Asking for the divorce was easy, satisfying actually. But telling Ryan was heart breaking. I feel absolutely terrible."

"There are worse things kids have to go through," David said in a comforting tone. It'll be ok."

"I know," Jamie said, padding at her eyes with a napkin then putting on her best smile. "How was your day?"

"It was . . . good." David had always been a bad liar.

"Are you sure? You don't look so good."

"Yeah. I just haven't eaten much today, and I won't eat much this week. I have fifteen pounds to lose before the fight. It's the worst part of this great job I've chosen for myself. Let me drink this and I'll be more cheery." David finished speaking then took his own advice and sipped his coffee.

"I'm sorry babe. I'm excited to watch you fight . . . But I don't want you to get hurt."

David could only smile to mask the pain he was feeling as he heard Jamie's words. "I'm not gonna get hurt. I can pretty much guarantee it."

"Someone's feeling extra confident tonight."

"Something like that," David said, nodding his head.

"I like it. You beat yourself up inside that head of yours too much."

"Inside my *big* head."

"It's not that big!" Jamie said, smiling.

David smirked and raised his eyebrows. "There's a reason I haven't been knocked out."

Jamie laughed. David laughed with her. He couldn't help it. Seeing Jamie smiling gave him temporary relief from the storm in his big head.

"Hey, I got some good news," David said.

"What?"

"The promoter raised my pay for the fight. Because of Loder talking shit in the parking lot at the press conference, people are more excited for it. Ticket sales are apparently through the roof. Even if I lose, I'm making much more money now." The part about ticket sales and increased buzz was indeed true. Fight fans always like a good old-fashioned grudge match, and after the parking lot scuffle, that's what they thought they were going to get.

"That's amazing!" Jamie said.

"When all this is over, we can finally spend more time together. And after a while things will be better."

"Being here with you already makes me feel better about everything."

David smiled at this most pleasant compliment.

"And the fight is on Saturday?"

"Yeah."

"Ok. We'll be watching."

David was afraid they'd be watching, but he accepted it. Still, the idea made him feel sick. At that moment, an idea came to David, one that seemed pleasant to him. Something that could help everyone in this fucked up situation. It would bring joy to Ryan, and it would distract David from the runaway semi truck that his thoughts had become.

"Can I take Ryan to play basketball instead of practice tomorrow?"

A puzzled look rose on Jamie's face. "I was going to take him to look at an apartment that I'm leaning towards renting."

"We'll meet you there afterwards."

"What about the other kids?"

"What about them?" David asked with a smirk. "Ryan's my favorite."

"Where will you guys go?"

"There's a park in Ocean Beach. I play with some guys there."

"You do?"

"Yeah . . . well I have once. Ryan would love it. I think he deserves that right now."

Jamie pondered briefly, then her lips parted in a smile. "You're a good man."

"You're a good woman. The only one for me."

After their powwow, David and Jamie walked hand-in-hand down the street towards David's apartment. They were both bundled up. December in San Diego had brought slightly cooler weather. David looked over at Jamie. Her hair was falling from her blue beanie that had one of those fluffy balls on the top. Her cute, small frame bounded next to him. In that moment of admiration, his head was cleared. He felt substantially better. Despite everything he had been through, he felt like the luckiest guy in the world. It was suddenly easy for him to give up his ambition of beating Loder. He had a much bigger and a much more important prize holding his hand.

After all of this mess was done, she was his.

※─ ─ ─ ※

Lupe was folding clothes in the living room when Jamie arrived home. She told Jamie that Ryan was in his room and that he seemed in decent spirits.

"Thank you Lupe. You can go home. I will take care of the rest of the laundry."

Lupe nodded. "Ok Hermana." She folded one last shirt and then rose to her feet.

Jamie was in the kitchen pouring a glass of wine when she sensed Lupe standing behind her with that extra sense all people seem to possess.

"I hate to ask, but I must be prepared for what is to come. Will I be let go after you and Max are officially divorced?"

Jamie turned around and faced the woman who had helped raise Ryan his whole life. Jamie and Max went through five nannies before Lupe showed up on their doorstep. "I will not be able to afford your services," Jamie said. "But I don't see why Max wouldn't keep you. You've been a blessing to both of us."

Lupe pulled her bag strap up high on her shoulder and prepared to leave. But before she could exit, her face mashed together in an attempt to block her need to cry. "I will miss him so much."

Jamie would have cried if she had any tears left. She walked over and hugged her long time maid, nanny, and friend.

Inside Ryan's room, Batman and Wolverine were having an intense battle on top of their owner's desk when a giant blonde woman stepped into their world.

From behind the action, Jamie watched Ryan making noises as he made the two action figures collide and spin through the air in self-made slow motion. He was mature for his age in many ways, but she was glad to see he wasn't too old to imagine other worlds where a plastic Batman and Wolverine could establish who was supreme. She found it amazing how quickly her son could find joy and put the day's news behind him, or at least shelve it for a time.

She knocked on the open door twice, breaking Ryan out of his trance. He turned to her from his chair. She walked over and sat on the bed next to him. "How are you doing?"

"Fine."

"Did you do your homework?"

Ryan turned, grabbed a sheet of paper with a bunch of repeated words in cursive written on it and showed it to her.

"Good . . . I came in here to tell you something. David is going to take you to play basketball after school tomorrow. How's that sound?"

Ryan stared at Jamie for a moment. Anyone else wouldn't be able to tell what he was thinking. But she could; she was his mother. She knew him better than he knew himself. It was the unconventional look of an excited boy. "When?"

"Right after school. He's going to meet you at After School Matters."

"Ok," Ryan said. Then he returned to the world of make-believe.

CHAPTER EIGHT

The next day, David met Ryan at After School Matters as planned. On their two mile stroll to Ocean Beach, he kept looking over at Ryan. He noticed with amazement that the boy was doing the things he had to force himself to do the last time he made this walk—he was taking in his surroundings; he was in the moment. He was like a super computer downloading an unthinkable amount of information with every passing person, animal, or tree. David thought they might get all the way to the park without speaking a word when Ryan asked a question that stunned him.

"Are you my mom's boyfriend?" Ryan asked, still looking straight ahead.

"What? No-no-no. What makes you think that?"

"It's okay if you are. I want you to be."

"Your mom is married, Ryan."

"But they're getting a divorce."

"Ryan, I don't know if these are things you're supposed to talk about. It's private."

"Just answer the question."

After being addressed this way, David felt he had to come clean, at least a little. "Me and your mom have become good friends. I really like her, almost as much as I like you."

Ryan looked up at David. He had to squint to protect his eyes from the sun, and he had a knowing smile on his face. "Whatever you say."

Fuck this kid is smart, David thought. "Let's just play some basketball, alright?"

"Okay . . . You're going down sucka."

"We'll see about that."

As they approached the park, Darnell and another man from the previous meeting were already playing a game of one-on-one.

"You see that guy?" David pointed at Darnell. "He's amazing." On cue, Darnell sunk a deep three-pointer.

"Yeah, he looks good."

Today the gate was unlocked, and they strolled right in to the court. Darnell and a man named Chris finished their game just as the newcomers walked up. David introduced Darnell and Chris to his young friend.

"How you doing Ryan?" Darnell asked with a cool smirk.

"Good," Ryan said, shaking Darnell's hand. "Don't take it easy on me."

Darnell laughed and shot a glance at David. "Alright little man. I won't."

The game commenced. The teams were Darnell and Chris versus David and Ryan. Of course they took it easy on the kid, but if he knew, he didn't show it. He hustled around, diving for balls, throwing up shots, and using all of his fouls, all the while wearing a big smile on his face.

After a couple of games, David and Darnell took a break on the bleachers while Chris gave Ryan some tips on the court.

"Your fight's this Saturday huh?" Darnell asked.

David sighed. He felt like he was wearing a sign that said TORTURE ME. "Yeah it is."

"You excited? I'm gonna have to tune in for this one."

"Yeah, really excited," David said unconvincingly then desperately tried to change the subject. "How's the free life?"

Darnell let out his own exasperated sigh. After a moment, he responded. "It's tough man. The world moves on without you when you locked up."

David nodded. "It sure does."

"And not for the better either. All I wanna do is keep my nose clean but it seems like everyone is on a mission to send me back to the Big House."

"It's the forces," David said distantly.

"Huh?"

"Nothing. How are they trying to get you in trouble? What's going on?"

"Well of course there's the drugs, which I'm not having a hard time refusing. I don't wanna be a slave to that shit anymore. The hard part is not being out in the streets with my homies. I'm losing a friend every week, mostly to your old boss. And unlike my boys, I'm not doing shit about it."

"Terry's crew is doing this?"

Darnell nodded. "It's a full on war right now." He paused, appearing to stem the flow of tears and doing so successfully. He was a tough man and had no time for tears. "My uncle was killed last week."

David shook his head in frustration. He could trace the majority of his problems in life back to Terry—his drug addiction, his prison stint, and now his marred life after prison—all of these were either caused or perpetuated by Terry. Despite all of these dreadful conditions, he could handle the burden, because the cruelties were happening to *him*. What David couldn't handle was seeing someone he cared about suffer. Jamie was right; David did care for others' well-being above his own. He could see and feel pain in others. He didn't know where he got this sense. A psychologist might tell him it was developed in his childhood from always being hyper aware of his father's moods, the indicators of oncoming beatings. David didn't know why he was this way, but he knew that seeing even an animal suffer irked him. Now, seeing the reach of Terry's evil touch Darnell was almost unbearable, especially since he could have put down the beast two days prior. "Why can't your boys—" David paused to make sure Ryan couldn't hear him. When he spoke again, he was quieter. "—why can't they kill him?"

"They're trying, but he's killed some of our best soldiers. My uncle was one of em. And everywhere he goes he's got bodyguards. He's careful. You know all this. He's got crazy numbers right now and crazy guns from his Mexican connections."

David did know this. He also knew about the demented psychos Terry had working for him better than Darnell did. Killing Terry was not an easy task. He should have done the job when he had the chance. It would have done the city of San Diego a lot of good. "There's gotta be a way."

Darnell sighed again, looking past David into the distance. "If you want something done, you gotta do it yourself, right? I thinks that's what I gotta do. I swore off that life, swore I'd never go back to Donavan. But man, after a few weeks as a free man, I think I prefer it on the inside."

"Don't say that. It'll get better."

"I'll leave it up to God. I'm gonna let him guide me on this one."

David sat and watched Ryan practice his layups for a moment. That boy and his mother were the reasons he couldn't help Darnell with this mission. "I wish I could help you man. I really do." David bent down and picked up his coat. He reached into a pocket and pulled out two hundred dollar bills. "Take this."

"You don't gotta do all that."

David stared at Darnell with his piercing eyes. He wasn't going to be denied.

Finally, Darnell took the cash. "Alright, Alright. Thanks my nigga. I appreciate it."

"I'm a nigga now?"

"You my nigga."

The two friends laughed. David and Ryan said farewell and took off for a meeting with Jamie.

⇒‡ ‡⇐

The two bedroom apartment Jamie toured that day needed some fixing up but had a lot of character. That's what Lorie, the real estate agent, told Jamie repeatedly as they toured the place. Jamie felt convinced enough.

Outside the window, Jamie could see Claremont High School, a school Ryan would be attending in a few years. She also saw a large park where Ryan could play (or shadowbox, it seemed like she could never get him to stop these days). The two women were in the kitchen when the door was opened by two similar boys of varying ages.

"Hi sweetie," Jamie said as Ryan walked over and wrapped his arms around his mother's waist.

David surveyed the empty apartment as he joined them. "This place is nice."

"It sure is!" Lorie chuckled from the corner with her clipboard hugged against her chest. David smiled awkwardly at the strange, insincere lady.

Jamie squatted down. "Did you guys have fun?"

"Yeah, lots."

"Good." She smiled up at David, then back to her son. "I really like this place. What do you think? Walk around and check it out."

Ryan obliged by first exploring the kitchen, gliding his hand across the steel fridge and marveling at the deep-set sink. He looked out the window where his future high school stood across the street. Leaving the kitchen, he made his way down the hallway and turned into what would be his room with David and Jamie trailing him. The room was slightly smaller than his previous one, but it had his own attached bathroom, the kind of little thing that can swing a child's mind.

He turned and looked at the adults. "I like it."

"Do you think you would like to live here?"

He nodded his head.

"You're sure? There are other places we can look at."

Ryan scoffed in slight frustration then let out one of those mature quips that always made David laugh out loud. "It's a fine home, mom."

Jamie smiled and turned to Lorie. "We'll take it."

There was another feature of the apartment—perhaps the most important one. It resided right down the street from an In-N-Out Burger. The three amigos stopped by this champion of fast food eateries after they were done at the apartment. But David couldn't eat much. He got a single patty, free of any sauces and wrapped in lettuce, while Ryan got a double-cheeseburger and David's favorite: animal fries. Normally during his weight cut, David stayed away from places like this where the smell of cooked cows was too intoxicating. But this was the first time the three of them had a meal together, and he wasn't going to pass that up.

"You're going to Temecula tomorrow?" Ryan asked David.

"Yup."

"Why? You're not fighting til Saturday."

"Well, I have to weigh-in on Friday, and I want to be comfortable in that environment. That way, come the night of the fight, I'll feel right at home. Lots of fighters do it."

Ryan nodded his head with a disgusting glob of food sloshing around his mouth while Jamie watched her boys chat with a pleasant smile.

"I saw the guy that you're fighting on TV," Ryan continued. "He looks scary."

David laughed. "He does, huh? Not the best look."

"Are you afraid?"

"No. As long as I got a job and you guys to come back to, I got nothing to be afraid of, right?"

"I guess so," Ryan said. That ended conversation time—his sole focus turned to devouring the delicious meal before him. Meanwhile, beneath the cover of the table, Jamie's hand clasped onto David's.

CHAPTER NINE

F riday morning, David woke up in fancy a hotel room in Temecula, California, courtesy of Brian Holliday. He walked over and emptied his bladder into the clean, pearl-white bathroom. On the way out, he stopped and looked at himself in the mirror. The image he saw was startling: he was emaciated. He was so dehydrated that he could see striations running across all of his muscles, making them look made of corduroy material. His cheekbones, which were always prominent, now looked like they were about to pierce his skin. His eyes were sunk deep into his face and void of any trace of happiness. As he leaned on the bathroom counter, Mike walked through the room behind him on the same mission that David had just completed. As Mike urinated, David couldn't help but to think that his coach's piece was bigger than his just by the sound of the piss stream. David walked over to a cheap scale he bought at a nearby Walmart the previous day. As he stepped on it, the red needle spun to one hundred and seventy-six pounds, leaving him with five pounds to lose to make the limit for his fight. The weight cut that was usually fairly easy for him was proving to be torturous this time around. And David knew why—he was a nervous wreck.

It was eight o'clock. He had three hours until the weigh in. Mike came out of the pisser in his tighty whities, his grey hair spiked in every direction. "Grab your sweat suit; let's hit it."

In the corner of the spacious hotel gym, David lightly hit pads with Mike while wearing a black sweat suit, which was basically a garbage bag jump suit. He grimaced as he threw punches. Even at the low intensity, his body was failing him. Mike recognized David's frailty and called a stop to the activity. He had David take off the suit. As he peeled the nasty bag off of his body, sweat dumped out onto the colorful carpet. Another gym goer looked on with disgust. Afterward, David lay on the ground in his soaked boxers, looking like a dead man. Mike put towels over him to trap the heat and keep him sweating.

While David lay in his towel cocoon with his eyes closed, Mike took a seat next to him. "We gotta keep the pressure on tomorrow. Don't let him get off first."

David had heard Mike give these instructions at least a hundred times during the past week. He had always taken the advice in stride, but hearing it now, knowing what he planned to do, was extremely painful and very annoying. "Got it."

"Give him no hope. From the start, we gotta put it on him."

David nodded. Mike stared at him, knowing that whatever had been bothering David had not been alleviated. He was worried about that.

After twenty minutes incubating under the towels, David walked over to the scale located in the corner of the gym. It was one of those scales with the two black bricks that somehow balanced out the weighee's weight. David set the big bottom brick on the one-fifty-mark and slid the little brick towards the twenty. As the little black brick crept closer to its mark, the metal beam began to bounce. At one seventy-one the metal beam rested, floating in the center of its holster.

David had made weight.

Before he could eat, he would have to officially weigh in before a crowd of reporters and fans. He would also have to square off with Loder again. The press conference scuffle had many people hoping for a repeat at the weigh-in. A large attendance was expected.

David wanted to puke for several reasons. He had depleted his body of every drop of water it contained, leaving him feeling very sick. But what he mostly wanted to puke over was the knowledge of what he planned to do the next night. How could he face this man whom he hated, who was standing in front of his dreams, knowing the promise he had made to Terry? How could he put on this act after all he had been through, not only in the last seven weeks of getting in shape but throughout his entire life? The prospect of this seemed impossible, but he would do it somehow. He would carry on with this conspiracy like the good slave he was.

David never understood the strange spectacle of the weigh-ins. Somehow people found it entertaining to watch fighters take their clothes off and stare at each other with their meanest looks possible. Some people even based their predictions off of the staredowns. It was absurd—yet another facet of this fucked up universe he lived in.

The event's security team wanted to keep David and Arnold as separated as possible during the lead up to the fight. But as the fighters waited backstage for their names to be called, there was no way of isolating them. Every fighter stood single file backstage, trickling out one by one as their names were called.

David was scheduled to weigh in first, so he was positioned in front of Arnold. About ten feet behind David, his rival and a small posse of men stood patiently (Frank was noticeably absent). David thought Arnold was going to badger him the entire time. He was relieved to find this to not be the case. They met eyes only once. In that instance Loder said nothing, just smacked around the wad of gum in his mouth like a horse eating hay. *Must have had a hard cut too*, David reasoned. He, like David, was a big welterweight.

There were only two fighters behind them in line: the two heavyweights who would square off in the main event of the night— Tank Johnson and Khabib Nabokov. These two men looked like cartoon characters to David. Both of them were fresh as daisies. They didn't have to miss any meals leading up to this odd spectacle of man-meat exhibition. There was no weight limit for heavy weights. Tank Johnson was eating a banana. Although he would never say it out loud, David couldn't help but see King Kong when he glanced at the big man having his snack. It was clearly a circus fight, and circuses make money. Plenty of people had paid top dollar to see these two behemoths go at it.

David felt like he was on the doorstep to death as he waited for his name to be called. Mike was watching him closely and rubbing his shoulders. "We're almost there, champ. Then we're going to feast."

"All I want is some fucking water."

"It's yours in five minutes."

What David really wanted to was to go home. Or better yet, he wanted to hop in a time machine and go back to the day he first met Terry and tell him he was a fucking schmuck then follow the insult up with a thick loogie to the face. But he couldn't. He was bound to this miserable place in time in an arena packed with fight-fans, about to pretend to look mean in front of a man he was going to pretend to fight in just over twenty-four hours. And if he didn't make it look good, make it look *real*, he would never have a fight again. *Maybe that wouldn't be so bad*, David thought. He was resigned to the gutter that his life would always be. The man who woke up in his prison cell to read and do a hundred sit ups, push-ups, and squats every day—that man was dead and gone.

The fighter in front of David was hopping up and down, occasionally punching himself in the side of head with good force. He was a small Mexican man, around five feet and five inches tall. David was amazed at the energy he had, but then again, the little guys were known for their stamina. Through the small part in the curtain barrier, David saw lights flashing periodically. Standing by the curtain, guarding it fiercely, was a man wearing a headset. He had his hand in front of the energetic Mexican, keeping him at bay until his name was announced.

The time came. On the other side of the curtain, a man with a microphone called out "HECTOR MARTINEZ!" The man with the headset let the hyper Mexican pass through his curtain.

The man with the headset waved for David to come forward then stopped him in front of the curtain while the two fighters on stage did their duty. David could see through the small slit between the curtains and was astounded by the size of the crowd. There was a small boy holding a sign that read "David versus Goliath" and a rather good illustration of David launching an uppercut into an oversized Loder's grill. David's heart sunk. That boy was going to be robbed from seeing his favorite fighter win the following night, He was going to be robbed from seeing a real fight at all.

The two flyweights squared off in their nearly naked state. Martinez looked meaner and more sure of himself. Immediately, several notebook wielding fat men ran off to place their bets on him. Then it was David's time. The MC introduced the next fight between two local San Diego fighters. David's name was announced, and he and Mike were ushered through the curtain. David was temporarily blinded by the flashes produced by hundreds of cameras. They prevented him from seeing the mob of fans cheering for him. As he climbed a set of stairs onto the stage, his eyes adjusted. Instead of blinding him, the barrage of flashes now created a shimmering field in front of him. He could now see how massive the crowd was. It was a greater sum of people than he would have ever imagined being interested in something he was part of. His heart slightly picked up its rate, but he kept his composed demeanor. It was easy really, for he possessed not an ounce of vigor. He took off his clothes and handed them to Mike before slowly stepping on the scale and waited for his weight to be announced to the fans.

A chubby, mustached scale operator stood on a platform in front of David that was slightly lower than the stage. He flicked the metal blocks on the scale down to the one hundred and seventy-one pound limit and peered through his glasses for a long time. Finally the chubby man called "One seventy-one!"

"ONE HUNDRED AND SEVENTY ONE POUNDS FOR DAVID LEWIIIIIS!" The MC shouted into his mic while pointing at David. Sweat was dripping from the man. David stepped off the scale and took his position where he was to wait for Loder. Mike handed him a bottle of water. He immediately took in three glorious gulps. He instantly felt his organs sing with pleasure as they gained the means to operate once again. Despite his fucked up situation, and his fucked up life, he was relieved this part was over. He did it. He almost died doing it, but he did it. He had made weight.

All that was left to do was lose.

"ALRIGHT LADIES AND GENTLEMEN, LET'S BRING OUT DAVID'S OPPONENT, ARNOLD LOOOOODEERRRR!"

Arnold emerged from behind the curtain, encouraging the fan's cheers by waving his arms and cupping his hand by his ear. David stood in his boxers staring at the man. It was time to put on the first part of his act. He had to look mean. This task would also not be very hard. He really disliked the man who was about to step on the scale in front of him. Arnold stripped, glanced heatedly at David, then stepped onto the scale.

"THAT'S ONE HUNDRED AND SEVENTY ONE POUNDS FOR THE MUAY THAI CHAMPION: ARNOLD LOOODERR!" the sweaty MC called out again.

Loder turned to David and walked towards him quickly. David also took a step forward. They came face to face as the flashes and clicks of cameras buzzed from below the stage. David held his calm, stone-cold face. Loder's was much the same. Both men raised their fists up to the other's chin, shaking them slowly. Loder chomped on his gum harder than ever, showing (or pretending) that he was unafraid. After a long stare down, Brian Holliday separated the two men. As Loder backed away, he dragged his thumb across his throat. David surprised himself when he laughed in return. After what David had seen in his life, there was nothing Loder—or any man for that matter—could do to put fear in his heart. And that had not changed since his deal with the devil.

CHAPTER TEN

Mike and David were at a Bazillion Steakhouse within twenty minutes ready to do some serious damage. It was one of those places where each table is given a two-sided sign. One side of the sign's circular head was green; the other side was red. Green meant bring marinated meat; red meant stop bringing marinated meat. At the table with the two scary, unsociable men, that sign was green all night. David devoured plate after plate but didn't say much, even less than he normally would. Mike remained concerned. He figured that the night before the biggest fight of his life, David would have more to say. He didn't prod him though. He wanted to let David sort out his own mind games before the fight.

"I know this is a lot to ask," Mike said, "but don't eat too much. You'll get sick."

As if realizing his coach was right, David set his fork down and pushed the plate away. "I'm tapped out," he said, sounding like he had just gone for a run.

Mike laughed as he turned around the sign, putting a halt to the incoming meat. "Good," he said. He smiled at David, who had both of his arms stretched outwards on the top of the bench behind him. Mike studied David. He couldn't help it. He wanted to know what was going on in that head of his. Mike had always given David his distance, which is why they had become so close. But for once, he wished his fighter would open up.

After a few seconds, David couldn't take Mike's stare any longer. "What?" he almost laughed.

"I'm just excited man. How are you feeling?"

"Now that I'm not about to die, I feel great," David said without resembling this description of himself. He was full of nutrients now, but he was still sick. Sick as a dog.

"You sure?"

"Yeah I'm sure,» David said angrily, as if Mike was crazy to think there was anything wrong with him.

"Tell me what's going on, David. You're not right. Twenty-four hours from now you have the fight of your life. So talk to me and let's get it right."

David ducked his head. He was failing his important task of acting normal. The burden he shouldered was too heavy. It was impossible to hide. The words *I'm throwing the fight* were on the tip of his tongue, begging to be blurted out, just so the cement block could be lifted off of his chest for the moment. But he couldn't say it. Mike had done too much for him. He had believed in David from the beginning. He let him train for free when he started out, he let him sleep on the mats before he got his apartment, and he gave him the teaching job. David owed everything good in his life to Mike. For all of these reasons, he couldn't tell his coach what he planned to do the following night. He just couldn't. It was out of the question.

"David," Mike said quietly, "there's nothing you can tell me right now that will make me not love you."

Just like his amazement that Jamie could love him, David couldn't believe that Mike could either. David thought Mike *shouldn't* love him. Mike's statement made tears begin to fill David's eyes. He couldn't tell him about the fight. He didn't think it was possible or helpful, but he felt the urge to tell Mike another secret he had locked up inside of him. A secret that only Mark and his deceased mother knew about. Telling this harbored secret wouldn't remove a cement block from his chest—it would remove a mountain. It would also give him an excuse for why he was so down. "Do you want to know how my father died, Mike?" He looked to the ceiling for a moment, keeping the tears from dropping. Slowly he brought his gaze down to Mike's intense eyes.

"If you want to tell me, or if you *need* to tell me, I think you should."

David deliberated and came to the conclusion that he did need to. At least once a day, the thoughts of his mother's face when she was helplessly being raped, or the blood spilling onto the tile floor, or that fucking *CRACK* played in his head on a torturous loop. He winced every time these thoughts swam to the forefront of his mind when he was not in control. When these thoughts arrived, he often compulsively yelled "no!" or "fuck!"—startling those around him and embarrassing himself. He had always felt he couldn't tell anyone his dark secret. He had no one he could tell who wouldn't think he was a monster. Most people thought he was a monster simply because he had been to prison. So as he prepared to speak of this horror for the first time since telling Mark in prison as a young man, he sincerely hoped that Mike had spoken true.

"I was sixteen. I was at home playing my guitar. I heard him come home and start arguing with my mom . . . I ignored it at first; this happened all the time. But then I started to hear my mom scream . . . So I. . . uh . . . I eventually opened my door, to hear better. I heard him throw her to the ground. Also not the first time. But then I heard her voice reach a level of fear I hadn't heard from her. My bat that was signed by Sammy Sosa was leaning against the wall inches from my hand . . . I went downstairs with it . . . and

found my mom being raped while she pleaded for him to stop."
David paused to gather himself. Mike watched in silence with wide
eyes. "I had seen it all. He'd beat the shit out of both of us many,
many times, but this I couldn't take. He was too drunk to either
know or to give a fuck that I was standing in the doorway watching
everything. I lost it . . . I . . ." He couldn't say the words.

"You killed your father?" Mike asked as softly as those words
could be uttered.

Tears flowed down David's cheeks. He nodded and tried to say
"I hit him with the baseball bat,", but it was inaudible.

There was a long, painful silence.

"It must be hard walking around with that feeling," Mike started. "But you did the right thing. This world isn't fair. You didn't
choose to be put in that situation." David was holding his head in
his hands. "Look at me, David."

He slowly brought his head up out of his hands and looked at
Mike with red, wet eyes.

"You did what you had to do. You're not a bad person. You saved
your mom from a heinous act. And I'm sure the courts saw it the
same way."

David nodded, wiping at his face constantly.

"You didn't choose to make your father's choices. He paid a just
consequence for his actions. You must move on from this."

David straightened up. He had his tears under control. "I know.
But like so many things in life, it's hard to do what you know you
ought to do. There's forces that try to take you off of your path of
commitment."

"What do you mean *forces?*"

"You know em. We all do. There are forces—drugs, friends,
work, women, insecurities . . . you've just been able to overcome
them. You've overcome them in a big way. You have a beautiful wife
and family."

Mike nodded, knowing exactly what he meant now. "It's a constant battle, but you're right. I have overcome lots of those things. But you know what? So have you."

"I haven't overcome shit."

"You know what your problem is David?"

"What?"

"You don't give yourself any fucking credit man! Not an ounce of it!" Mike's voice began to rise. "Think about everything you've been through. You've made your mistakes like we all have, but you committed to something in prison and you got some knowledge into that thick skull of yours. Then you got out and you put that plan into action. And look where we are now!" Mike slapped his heavy palm on the table, causing many to look their way. He paid them no mind. "David, you went from being in prison to being on television in five years. *You are achieving your dreams.* And you should be proud of that. But David, that's not what you should be most proud of." Mike's voice returned to a still loud but reasonable level now. "What you should be most proud of is that thing thumping in your chest and that thing between your ears, because you're a good person. *That's* what I love about you. You're a good, caring person."

David processed Mike's words while Mike stared with loving ferocity. He had hoped that telling his secret would alleviate him, and in some respect it did. But Mike's reaction also crushed him. He was sick once again and had to pretend that he wasn't. David got up out of his seat, hating himself. Mike did the same, knowing what it was all about, and the two men hugged.

From the clenched hug, Mike said "Go achieve your dreams tomorrow."

David gripped his coach tight while inside he crumbled with despair. *I'm sorry Mike. I'm so sorry,* his insides screamed.

PART THREE

CHAPTER ONE

*D*avid finds himself back at the Bear's Den, or some version of it where there are no walls, and it resides on the beach, where the sky is red. A heavy bag swings side to side slowly in front of him. He's punching it, but incapable of doing so with any power. He keeps going, trying to hit the bag harder, but the force won't come. He just pushes at the bag with each shot, like he's punching underwater.

He hears laughs coming from the side. When he looks over, he sees his father sitting on a nearby bench watching him. His head is healed, his face free of blood. He smiles and asks his son "Are you serious right now?"

"I can't hit right now. I don't know why. You should see how I usually hit these things. I fucking destroy 'em. People gather round just to watch me hit the bag." David turns and walks over towards his father as large waves crash against the rocks on the beach behind him. David finds his father not intimidating for the first time since he was very young.

"I'm sorry Dad."

Suddenly Walter's face changes. His forehead wrinkles and his eyebrows tilt in anger.

From further down the long bench, another voice chimes in. "Don't worry pops. I'll teach him a lesson." David looks in the voice's direction. It's Loder, putting on a t-shirt after some training of his own. He walks over to them.

"Leave us alone," David says. "We're talking."

Both men stare at David silently. A third voice approaches from behind. "You won't have to work too hard Arnold. You have a guaranteed win."

Loder looked at Terry. "Are you serious? I don't need any help to kick this guy's ass."

"I think he knew that. That's why he took the deal."

"That's not true," David says. "He made me do it. I need the money, that's all . . . You're proud of what I've done, aren't you dad?"

All three of the men start laughing.

David rotates his stare between each of the men who are now crying with laugher. He takes a swing at Loder. His hand connects but once again with no power; he only pushes on Loder's chin, sending him away slowly.

Loder swings back, cracking David in the jaw with the speed of a whip, sending him crashing to the ground. Sparks fly across David's vision. All three men start kicking him. He feels real pain with each shot.

Eventually they stop kicking. When David opens his eyes, he sees his father looking down at him. Walter's face begins to decompose before him. A roach pops his left eyeball out and scurries around the surface of his face, then his head begins to spout blood again. More roaches emerge from the top of Walter's head, sliding rapidly on the blood like a roach theme park. "This is what you get, son. This is what you get for killing me." Walter has his bat now. He examines it with his rotting face. He raises it high into the red sky. He swings it down atop David's head one last time.

David sat up with a short scream that woke Mike in the bed next to him. He looked at the clock. It was only four a.m..

"You alright?" Mike asked in a groggy voice from the darkness across the room.

"Yeah, sorry."

"It's fine. Go back to sleep. You need it."

But there was no going back to sleep.

David put on some clothes and took the elevator down to the casino. Four in the morning and the place was still crowded with degenerates who were either at the end of their day or its beginning. He walked through the smoke infested floor while his emotions destroyed him. He had never experienced an anxiety attack before. Those were for weak people. But he was confident he was having one now. The insane sounds emitting from hundreds of slot machines sounded like children banging away on toy xylophones. He was going mad. He couldn't escape the swirling sounds and colors and faces and beer-guts and stained teeth and mullets and waitresses who hated their jobs and dealers who hated their jobs and pit bosses who hated everyone. His world was spinning, growing and shrinking; he felt like he was overdosing on psychedelics. He was drenched with sweat, on the verge of puking, when he spotted the double doors to the outside world across the casino. He went to them as fast as he could.

He reached outdoor salvation where he hunched and puked into some bushes to the left of the casino entrance. A few people watched in disgust, but otherwise left him alone. For a while he stayed crouched while he took in long pulls of the dry Temecula air. When he eventually rose upright, he felt slightly better. The sun was peeking over the mountains in the east—the eternal morale booster. He started walking away from the casino in that direction. The resort was surrounded by what Temecula was famous for—vineyards, acres upon acres of them. They were coming to life as the morning light kissed the top of the fields. Small birds hopped from vine to vine, enjoying a morning snack. Men in big hats with baskets hanging from their chests set out for harvest on their plots of land.

Now that David was out of the haunted casino, he could think about what he must do. He was frustrated after having another dream about his dad. How was he ever going to stop having them? He had finally told someone about his father's death. Shouldn't that have alleviated his burden? Why won't he go away? Once again he could have used a psychologist. But he didn't have one. It was just him and the birds left alone to handle this crisis. As he walked past the fields, he previewed several scenarios for this dreaded day in his head. Like a game of chess, he tried to predict what moves would unfold as the result of each decision.

Scenario One: he loses the fight on the purpose. He would earn 35,000, and the promise of never seeing Terry again. He could go back to San Diego and start his life with Jamie, who didn't care in the slightest if he won or lost the fight. But that's not all that would happen. He would lose a part of his soul. He would not achieve his dreams. Every mile he ran, every day of sobriety, every positive thought, every promise he made to himself in prison, all that will have been for nothing. Throwing this fight would confirm that David is what everyone thought he was: a talentless, drug-addicted criminal.

Scenario Two: he loses the fight while attempting to win. He will most likely be badly damaged. Terry will know that he tried to win—he couldn't pull that stunt a second time. Terry will track him down and try to kill him. He will have to face the fact that he wasn't cut out for the fight game at its highest levels. He would lose Jamie, Ryan, and Mike, by leaving them to keep everyone safe. He would disappear and drink the rest of his days away. *But* if he tries to win—if he goes down swinging—he will know that he never bowed to anyone, that he lived his life fighting. And that, at least, he could be proud of.

Scenario Three: He wins the fight. He collects a thousand dollars instead of thirty-five. His life enters into immediate danger, as do the lives of everyone he cares for. He will either have to go on the run, or be killed. But, all things considered, that would be ok. He will have done what he wasn't supposed to do. His success that was twenty-nine years in the making will be televised for everyone to see. All of the men in prison that remembered the guy practicing boxing in the yard would see him triumph. All of the women who were disgusted by him might actually recognize him, maybe even say hello. And everyone who ever doubted him will know that they were wrong—that they were foolish—for doing so. His father, whom when David asked as a young boy if he could be a basketball player, told him that he must be seven feet tall and black, whom when he asked if he could be superhero, replied by saying that was fairy tale shit and he needed to stop talking about it, whom when he asked if he could get help with homework, told him he better learn his way around a hammer and nail because manual labor was the only profession he was cut out for, that man would *really* be proven wrong, and hopefully banned from his thoughts forever. Everyone who watched the fight would be witness to a man who overcame everything life threw at him in order to reach his goals. If he won this fight, he will have proven to his father, and everyone else, that he was something special.

With the sky now fully illuminated, David stopped and turned back for the casino, knowing what he must do.

CHAPTER TWO

David was able to sleep a couple hours when he got back to his bed. If he dreamed, he didn't remember the content. He woke up around eleven and had a Denver omelet delivered to his room. He spent the next six hours rotating from armchair to table to ground to bed in a body absent of its mind. The mind he once owned was in another world, a world where fists and elbows were flying at his face. During those six hours, television was watched, phone calls were made, and conversations were had, but David recognized none of it. Mike came and went in his own attempts to pass the time. He played a few hands of poker in the casino, losing a hundred and winning it back. He stared at sharks cruising in a large aquarium in the lobby. And he video-chatted with his wife and daughter for nearly an hour. When he went back to the room for the final time, David was dressed but still had an occupied look on his face. At five p.m., Mike dropped a bag in David's lap, finally breaking him from his spell. He looked up slowly, and Mike noticed something wonderful—the ferocity back in those blue eyes.

David and Mike were escorted through the guts of the arena beneath the bleachers by a tall man wearing a headset, the same man from the weigh-ins. He led them to the locker room where David would warm up and wait until it was time for him to fight. At that time, the headset man would return and lead them to the ring.

So the excruciating waiting game went on a little longer. Mike held pads for David to hit lightly. David was still yet to utter a sentence longer than three words all day. Once again Mike was left to hope that his fighter was okay. It was too late to do anything about it.

There were only two fighters left with him in the locker room—Hector Martinez, who would fight before him, and Tank Johnson, the heavyweight man who would be fighting in the main event after David's fight. A TV in the locker room was playing the fights that were taking place down the hall in the arena. Tank was not yet warming up. Instead, he sat cross-legged on the ground, watching the fights. Martinez was hitting pads with his coach with the same ferocity and zeal he had shown the day before at the weigh-ins. David was only lightly warming up; he had plenty of time. He took a break to wander over to the TV to watch the current fight. Tank looked up at David and held out his massive hand. "Tank," he bellowed.

"I know who you are," David said as he took his hand. "David Lewis."

The black man smiled big, exposing his insanely white teeth. "I gotta admit, I know who you are too man. I'm a fan."

David smiled back politely. "Thanks."

"Aye that guy you're fighting is a live one though. I'm excited for your fight."

"Should be a good scrap . . . but he better pack a lunch."

The big man tilted his head back and snorted at the sky in laughter. It was an infectious laugh. If David hadn't seen this savage put many men to sleep with his mailbox-sized fists, he would have thought he was a kindergarten teacher. He composed himself, but his smile remained. "Let's let 'em fly tonight man. Give the fans what they want."

"I like your style," David replied.

"I mean, that's what they wanna see. And you don't wanna lose a fight knowing you held anything back."

"I agree," David said. He liked Tank. "When are you gonna get bumped up to the big leagues?"

"Hopefully after this fight man. You can do the same. Just go put it on him. There's all kinds of scouts here tonight."

On the television screen, two fighters were waiting for a judges' decision after fighting for three rounds when the headset man entered the locker room. He called for Martinez to come with him. Both David and Tank gave the small man a nod as he left the room still bouncing up and down rapidly.

"Them lightweights never get tired," Tank said.

Three minutes into the second round of Martinez's fight, he was knocked out in one of the most devastating fashions David had ever seen (left high kick, unseen shin-to-jaw action). It was a reminder of the dangers of the fight he was about to engage in. David and Mike began hitting mitts hard. They knew their time was coming. Just fifteen minutes later, the headset man entered the room. "Lewis . . . It's go time."

David gave a nod to the headset man and started on his way. He looked at Tank across the room. Tank, who had finally begun to warm up, raised a fist in the air. "Kill him," he said rather psychotically. The teddy bear now looked like a grizzly with rabies.

David nodded and left the room. They followed the headset man down a long hallway. The muffled sounds of cheers and music grew louder as they walked. Eventually the trio turned left and could see into the arena. David saw the cage two hundred feet away before the lights dimmed and his song "Right Now" by Van Halen began to play. David felt Mike's hands massage his shoulders. He closed his eyes and took a deep breath. Then he began the walk to the cage where everything would be decided.

>==<+ +>==<

Forty-five miles away, David made his walk on Jamie's television. She had told Ryan that he couldn't watch, that it was too violent. But she had clearly been broken because Ryan sat just four feet from the TV. "Back your little butt up, mister. You'll go blind." Ryan didn't know if that was true or not, but he stayed where he was.

"He looks kinda scary," the boy said.

"Yeah . . ." He did look scary. But in Jamie's eyes, he'd never been more handsome.

>==<+ +>==<

David took his shirt off and handed it to Mike. As he walked up the stairs towards the cage, he caught sight of three familiar men in the crowd. He wasn't surprised. The associates in this scandalous ordeal met eyes, and Terry didn't like what he saw.

"He's gonna do it again," Terry said to Jorge.

Jorge dipped his hand into a bag of popcorn. "Don't worry; this guy is going to kick his ass. Look at him."

Loder was already in the ring. Terry heeded Jorge's advice by examining the man upon whom he had a large sum of money bet on winning. After doing so, he felt the same confidence Jorge was showing. Loder looked like a comic book villain. Like David, Loder was much bigger than he was the previous day when he had withered away into a ghost of himself. He was replenished, and by the looks of him, he was ready for battle.

David entered the cage and glanced across the twenty-five feet of canvas at his opponent. He had had fights where knew he was going to win just by looking at his opponent. Tonight was not one of those nights—Arnold Loder was game.

Hank Stillwater, a suited man with grey hair, stepped forward as a microphone dropped from a dark abyss above the arena. He snatched the mic as it lowered to his level and the lights in the arena dimmed once again.

"ALLLLLLLRIGHT LADIES AND GENTLEMEN, THIS NEXT FIGHT IS OUR CO-MAIN EVENT OF THE EVENING. IT FEATURES TWO WELTERWEIGHT FIGHTERS FROM YOUR OWN SAN DIEGO CALIFORNIA!" The crowd reacted with cheers. A spotlight illuminated Loder as Stillwater continued. "STANDING IN THE RED CORNER IS A THREE TIME NORTH AMERICAN MUAY THAI CHAMPION. HE HAS A RECORD OF EIGHT WINS AND ONE DEFEAT. STANDING SIX-FOOT-ONE AND WEIGHING IN AT THE WELTERWEIGHT LIMIT OF ONE-HUNDRED-AND-SEVENTY-ONE-POUNDS . . . LADIES AND GENTLEMEN, GIVE IT UP FOR ARNOLD LOOOOODEEERRRR!" Loder, still bouncing on his toes back and forth, held both hands up as the cheers and boos rained down.

The spotlight swung around the ring clockwise and stopped on David. "AND IN THE BLUE CORNER IS A MAN THAT NEVER STRAYS AWAY FROM A SLUGFEST. HE HAS A RECORD OF SEVEN WINS AND SEVEN LOSSES, WITH ALL SEVEN OF HIS WINS COMING VIA KNOCKOUT. HE STANDS FIVE-FEET-AND-ELEVEN-INCHES AND HE TOO WEIGHED IN AT THE WELTERWEIGHT LIMIT OF ONE-HUNDRED-AND-SEVENTY-ONE-POUNDS . . . PUT YOUR HANDS TOGETHER FOR DAVID LEEEEWIIIIIISSS!"

The crowd roared, but David could hear nothing. Time slowed down as the microphone returned to the blackness above. Hank Stillwater left the cage with two cameramen trailing. Four more cameramen peered in from the top of the cage like vultures on their perches, waiting for he or Loder to die. The sound of clanking metal was heard as the cage door was locked shut. Across the ring, Arnold Loder looked very athletic and very malicious. The referee, a large, tan man with tattoos running down both arms, took a close look at both competitors and knew he was going to have to save someone in this bout.

David paced back and forth one last time. With a glance outside of the cage, he made eye contact with Terry once again. Terry had a very serious look on his face. David nodded to him and looked away.

The fight began with a bell's loud "DING!" and time went back to its normal speed. Both Loder and David plodded forward to the center of the ring with their hands up. They measured each other for a second. Out of nowhere and with lightning speed, Loder threw a piston left hand that David slipped. But immediately after—as smooth as the workings of a fine watch—Loder launched a right leg kick that devastated David. It was by far the hardest he had ever been kicked. David backed away, doing his best to show no pain on his face.

David moved around and Arnold chased after him moving in a creepy back-and-forth way like a cobra. David planted his feet and threw a right-hook left-hook combo like two lightning strikes. Arnold blocked both of them, but he felt David's power on his arms.

David backed away again. In his mind, he began to think about what tactic to employ. He thought that if he could perfectly time the same combo he could catch him. Just as he was thinking this . . . WHAM!—another impossibly fast leg kick brutalized the muscle on the outside of David's left leg and shattered his train of thought. He limped backwards as the crowd reacted. Loder came forward, smelling blood in the water. In the crowd, Terry laughed. David's back hit the fence and Loder started throwing vicious punches in succession, first at David's body, then at his head. David covered up as best as he could, but two punches crushed his body. On the last punch of the barrage, a thunderous left hand cracked David on the Jaw, causing his world to momentarily go white.

David threw back, but he hit nothing but air as Loder nimbly dodged the strikes that were coming slower now. David moved to the middle of the cage again, his right eye already starting to swell from the hard shot Loder landed. Behind Loder, David could see his coach for the first time. Mike's eyes got big as he yelled "Hey!" then mimicked the motion of a double-leg take-down. David had never gone for a takedown in his career and didn't want to start now. But if he didn't, he'd likely be knocked out. He decided to wait for the opportunity. After keeping Loder at bay with some jabs, the opportunity came. Loder telegraphed a right hand, and David shot in for the takedown. It was beau-tiful—like a samurai sword chopping through an enemy torso he scooped Loder up and slammed back to the ground in one smooth movement.

Loder tried to stand vigorously, but David clasped his hands around his body and pinned him down to the ground, feeling like he was hanging onto a shark that was trying to flop off of a boat back into the sea. David was in side control after passing by Loder's legs with the slam. After fifteen seconds of flopping, Loder was gassing out. He put his shoulder blades to the mat for just a short moment. David capitalized. With laser-like efficiency, he swung his right leg over Loder's body. David had him in full mount.

David sat up and began punching his helpless opponent. On the second clean shot, a cut opened up under Loder's left eye. He gave a big buck with his hips, but David planted his hands and was able to keep position. He reset before throwing more bombs down on Loder. A left hit flush and Loder's eyes rolled to the back of his head. For a brief moment, David thought the fight might be over. But his opponent's pupils reemerged, and he continued to flail until the bell sounded, signaling the end of the round.

The ref yelled "Stop!", and both fighters stood up wobbly. They exchanged stares as they slowly turned for their corners, stumbling like drunks.

"He's dead fucking tired!" Mike yelled at David on his stool from a kneeled position, the veins in his neck having never been larger. David took deep breaths, trying to regain some energy.

"I'm gonna catch him this round," David said.

Mike didn't like the idea of standing with Loder at all. "You go catch his ass with a takedown! You got me? This guy couldn't stop a takedown if his life depended on it!"

David said nothing. His eyes were cold and fixed across the ring. Loder was bouncing on his toes again but with much less conviction than he had before the fight. And despite how hard he tried to hide it, his eyes had less life in them.

The eyes, they never lie.

The bell signaled the start of the second round and both men came forward. Right away, David threw a rapid left-right combo, with the right getting through. Loder's head snapped back and blood began to trickle from his cut again, breaking the dam of glue applied between rounds that was intended to keep it contained. Loder threw another leg kick, but this time David barely evaded it. Loder was losing steam. He had spent all of his energy after going for the kill when he had David against the cage. David pushed forward with a plan. He knew what was coming: a right leg kick. His fist would get there first. That was the plan. And then it happened. The slightest twitch—in the hip, or the shoulders, maybe even something in the eyes—David didn't know what triggered it, maybe destiny triggered it. Whatever it was, he let loose a right haymaker as hard as he could. Loder started his patented, vicious kick but never got his foot off the ground. David's fist landed on Loder's jaw like a meteor crashing into earth. Loder fell to his back, asleep, toes curled, arms extended in the air like a zombie.

In the locker room, Tank Johnson put his hands over his mouth and muffled his scream, "OH MY WORD!"

With Loder unconscious before him, time slowed down for David once again. He couldn't hear the massive amount of cheers raining down on him, but as he walked aimlessly around the cage, he could see the people with their mouths open, some with delight, others with shock and concern for Loder's health. He saw Mike jumping over the cage and running for him. He saw several doctors and security personnel spilling in through the now open door. Two doctors ran to Loder, whose severe concussion made him look like he could be dead. Mike collided into David and held him tight, tears in his eyes. He hoisted David above his head and walked him around the ring on his right shoulder. There had been a shift in David's reality. He felt it. For the first time in his life, he didn't succumb to adversity. Extreme adversity. As he was paraded around the ring above his coach's head, he realized his prediction for how he would feel when this moment came was accurate. He was bursting with light—with energy—like an exploding star.

The euphoric bliss ceased abruptly when David again met eyes with Terry. He was standing and staring at David with murderous intent. Time regained its normal speed, if not faster.

David patted Mike on the shoulder forcefully. "Mike let go!"

Mike released his grip, dropping David to the ground. He had a stupid smile on his face until he saw the seriousness on David's. "What's wrong?"

"We gotta get out of here."

"What? Why?"

"We have to go," David repeated as he pulled Mike towards the exit.

Mike resisted successfully, yanking his arm from David's grasp. "They have to announce you as the winner first."

David turned back and shouted "MIKE, WE HAVE TO LEAVE NOW!"

This urgency convinced Mike despite his extreme confusion. He followed David to the open cage door through the crowd of camera men and doctors. A couple of security crewmen tried to stop David from leaving, but he was able to shove them out of the way.

⥤╬⥢

Back in San Diego, Jamie and Ryan were going crazy. Ryan was doing some kind of fast, uncoordinated jig. Jamie was now close to the screen with her son, her hands clasped across her chest and a quiet smile on her face. She watched with joy as Mike carried David around the cage in triumph. She could see the look of accomplishment on her lover's face. But that joy she was feeling quickly shifted to concern when she saw him run from the ring.

CHAPTER THREE

The crowd was buzzing after the stunning come from behind knockout. People were smiling and gossiping as they headed for the restrooms or the bar to replenish their beverages before the final fight of the evening. But Terry wasn't pleased with the ending to the exciting fight that had just occurred. He and Billy watched helplessly as David and Mike sprinted towards the locker room across a blockade of loitering bodies.

"He's a dead man," Terry said to Billy, with Jorge noticeable absent. "I want you to let him know that before he leaves the building." Billy nodded and started to make his way through the crowd as quickly as he could. Terry took his seat and rested his head in his right hand in astonishment.

Four rows behind Terry was a man who had just won a lot of money. He was wearing a large cowboy hat and large glasses, but the largest thing he was wearing was the smile on his face.

⊰┼⊱

As Mike and David walked briskly down the hallway, Mike demanded answers. "What the fuck is going on, David?"

"We don't have time to go into details, but there are men here who very much wanted me to lose that fight. These men will kill me now if they get the chance."

Mike had a million more questions but no time to ask them. If David was telling the truth, and he had never known him to be a liar—until that day, that is—they had to get out of there.

As David and Mike arrived at the locker room, the headset man and Tank were heading out. Tank's eyes got big when he saw David. He raised his large hand in front of David to stop him then leaned in close towards David's face. "You got company hiding in the locker room. Time to bounce."

David and Mike shared a look as well as a mind at that moment. They both looked at the emergency exit down at the other end of the long hallway. "Thank you," David said, backing away. He and Mike turned and sprinted towards the exit. As they ran, David thought about his decision and the consequences he now faced, but even as he ran to evade the men who wanted to kill him, he knew he had made the right choice.

Inside the locker room, Jorge was standing quietly over a pile of David's clothing and his empty bag. When the door was opened he swung his gun towards it—the intruder was Billy.

"Where is he?" Billy asked.

Jorge didn't answer, just shook his head in disgust. A gun to the head was enough to keep Tank's mouth shut when he dropped in on him and his coaches, but the duration of his wait since their departure made Jorge realize what had happened.

Jorge sat at David's locker and picked up his pants from the floor. He rummaged through the pockets and found nothing of use. "They're not coming," he finally said to Billy, who was pacing the room, scratching his large head with the barrel of his gun.

"How stupid can you be? I mean really?" Billy asked.

"He's stupid alright. That's for sure," Jorge said, rising to his feet. "The guy can fight though. Gotta give him that. It's a shame we gotta kill him now." Jorge started for the door. "Let's go. They're gone."

⊱―⊰

The following day was Christmas Eve. David and Mike were not hungover after their victory. The men were up early—just before 5:00 a.m. David sat across from Mike at the table where they dined a month prior for Thanksgiving. There was anger in Mike's eyes, but there was also understanding. Both men had cups of steaming coffee in front of them. Outside the window, David was watching the sky gain light in its corners.

"How did this happen?" Mike asked quietly as not to wake his family.

David maintained his gaze out the window as he dove into the details surrounding his last week. He spoke quietly as well as slowly. "I was being followed by some guys in the gang I used to run with as a kid. I saw them at various places watching me. And eventually, the morning after the presser, they came to my house. This guy named Bill Tremble—big ogre of a man—banged on my door. And Terry—the guy I used to work for—was waiting for me in the street. They took me down to Chula Vista, where Terry has a bar. He asked me to lose the fight for thirty-five large. I tried turning it down—I really did, even with my gun—but he wasn't taking no for an answer. I couldn't kill another man, not then, not after I . . . you know. So I agreed to do it. I planned on it too. Forgive me Mike, but I planned on it. I felt terrible, but the money he offered was more than I'll ever make in twenty fights . . . I was gonna do it. But when it came down to it, I couldn't. I decided I wanted that win more than I wanted my life. And I don't regret my decision. I see clearer now than I ever have before."

Mike shook his head in disbelief. "That's why you were so . . . fucked up."

David nodded. "There's something else I gotta tell you Mike."

Mike didn't respond; he just sat in disbelief that there could be more awful news.

"I'm not completely innocent here. My fight against Miles Toomey, I got paid to lose that fight."

Mike felt the sting of betrayal. "I knew it. I knew something was wrong with you."

"I'm so sorry Mike. That's why I couldn't lose against Arnold. I didn't want to let you down. I couldn't betray you again. I just . . . I can't seem to get away from my past."

"How am I supposed to believe you were forced to lose this fight after you willingly threw away the Toomey fight? How do I know you didn't arrange this whole thing yourself?"

"It's the truth Mike. I was done with those guys. Done with the drugs and the booze too. I was completely all-in for this fight. You know that. You saw it. I hadn't talked to Terry since the Toomey fight. I was literally sick with shame after it. As I trained for Loder, I was able to forgive my actions, because I knew I was finally doing everything right. But they came for me, the forces came back." David looked out the window once more. The sun had breached the horizon. Despite the state of chaos his life had become, he managed to smile. When he was going over his potential scenarios the previous morning, he only gave himself two options if he were to beat Loder: run or be killed. He was wrong; there was one additional, albeit messy, option. "This guy's been the bane of not only my existence but many others'" David continued. "That's gonna change today. It has to if I'm gonna live."

Mike grunted in frustration at this debacle, then leaned back in his chair and looked at David with an expression of resignation. "What are you gonna do?"

"I only see one option."

"Get out of town?"

David shook his head slowly side to side. "I'm not going anywhere. We have more fights to make."

Mike nodded, expecting this answer. He knew what David was going to do. "Do you have a plan?"

"I think I do," David said sincerely.

Mike sighed. "I can't go with you on this David, as badly as I want to. I have a family. I . . . I just can't."

"I don't expect you to. I could never thank you enough for everything you've done for me Mike. You've given me an avenue to achieve my dreams, and I won. I won the fight. I did the impossible. Everything else is a bonus. You've already saved my life once. I don't expect you to do it twice." David stood up and killed his coffee. "All I need is from you is your phone so I can make a call."

CHAPTER FOUR

Later that morning, at The Silver Fox, Terry was up earlier than usual, dealing with an unpleasant chore. After Mark had placed his bet on David, others followed suit, and Terry welcomed it. He had men promoting the bout all over town. As a result, he received over $100,000 in bets on David winning. Today, he was shoveling out over five hundred grand in winnings to his customers, many of whom he had to convince that it was a good bet to take in the first place. Over a hundred thousand dollars, his biggest individual loss, was due to go to the mysterious Keith. He had a surprise for Keith if he came to collect that money.

Terry spent that morning at his desk smoking cigars and handing out envelopes loaded with cash with a smile on his face. Most of these winners had only put down several hundred dollars and were cashing out with several thousand. This was chump change to Terry. They would be back next week, and the week after, and eventually they would lose it all back. The house would eventually win. As the hours passed, the man Terry really wanted to see remained absent. He couldn't stand the thought of him not coming.

He needed to have a chat with Keith. Around 10:30 that morning, his man finally arrived.

An older gentleman wearing a Hawaiian shirt and mean eyes led Mark into the office and shut the door behind him. Mark was wearing the same cowboy hat, the same glasses, and the same big smile as he was the previous night. That smile lost some luster when he saw the look on Terry's face.

"Hell of a fight wasn't it?" Mark asked.

Terry cleared his throat and sat upright in his chair. "Sit down, please."

"I think I'll stand," Mark said as he rested his thumbs in his pockets.

"Sit the fuck down," Terry demanded.

Mark's eyes widened. He didn't like where this was heading. Reluctantly, he circled the chair in front of him and put his butt in it.

After a brief silence, Terry spoke again. "Why did you come to me with this bet? Did you get to Loder and make him lose the fight?"

Mark laughed briefly. "You saw the fight. You know damn well that's not the case. Both of those men were trying to win. Now if you don't mind, I'd like my money."

"You're not getting shit."

Mark was shocked. He had heard a great deal about Terry from David and other inmates in Donavan, but he had underestimated the level of thuggery Terry was capable of. In his day, a bookie always paid his bets, crime boss or not. "What the fuck are you talking about? What is this?"

"I know you cheated me, you slimy fuck! You know David! You know him!"

"Why in the world would that matter? He won the fight—"

Terry picked his arm up from over the table. He was holding a gun. "Shut the fuck up! I'm asking the questions!"

Mark put his hands up "Jesus christ, I can't believe this."

"You're a fucking hustler. You'll be lucky if I let you walk out of here with your life."

"Alright, listen," Mark said. "I'll get out of here, just don't expect a good yelp review."

"You tryna be cute?"

Before Mark could answer, he burst into another storm of coughs. In the midst of the storm, he pulled a handkerchief from his pocket and covered his mouth. This sickening interruption went on for nearly forty seconds. When he was done, Mark leaned back in his chair, looking sicker than he ever had before. On the cloth, he covered his mouth with what Terry saw as blood. "May I please leave?" Mark asked tiredly.

Terry planned on killing him, but it was clear that mother nature would take care of this job for him soon. Eventually he nodded his head. "And never come back."

"And why would I do that?" Mark asked as he rose to his feet. He backed towards the door with his hands up. He had a good feeling that if he turned his back, a hot slug would meet his insides. He fumbled around for the handle and opened it. Before leaving, he had one more thing to say. "You know, this little thing you got going on here, it won't last forever."

Before Terry could respond with words or a bullet, Mark shut the door.

Terry slammed his gun down in anger. He had hoped to sniff out the rat in the room upon seeing Keith. But he couldn't. There was something off about the man, but he could tell he didn't rig the fight. This all fell on David. Terry had more money than he knew what to do with, so he wasn't upset over his green heading out the door. He was upset that David Lewis lied to him and was out walking the streets, still breathing oxygen.

⚔︎

The interior of David's apartment was a wreck. Drawers were thrown on the floor, and clothes and papers were scattered everywhere. Billy was in the kitchen making a sandwich on the messy counter top while Jorge was digging through the junk. To his increasing dismay, he wasn't finding anything useful, just lots of empty liquor bottles and cigarette packs. It was apparent that David lived a very solitary life, and Jorge was beginning to worry that he had left town without a trail to follow. Before packing it in, the Cuban sat on David's bed and began to sort through the papers a second time. There were old bills, bad illustrations, lame motivational quotes, pizza receipts, liquor receipts—nothing he could use. He threw the bundle of papers on the ground and shouted "fuck!" Then something caught his eye: a shoebox wedged behind the bed frame. He wriggled it out of place and flipped it open. The box contained a good amount of cash, a necklace, old basketball cards (valuable Michael Jordan rookie cards), a tall stack of pictures, and, by the grace of a gangster's God, a small piece of paper with something scribbled on it. As Jorge picked up the note, he heard chimes playing in his ears; there was a phone number and an address written on it. He quickly took out his phone and dialed the number listed.

An unenthusiastic man answered the phone: "Mary's flower shop, this is Tony. How can I help you?"

Jorge hung up. A flower shop. But he wondered where the address led to. Did David have a new girlfriend? He moved on to the stack of photos and began to thumb through them. There were several shots of a young David with his mother and some of him and Mike after one of David's early wins. His search was temporally interrupted by a call from Terry.

"Yeah," Jorge answered. He placed his cell between his shoulder and ear and continued to scroll through the photos.

"Any sign of him?"

"Not yet."

"Did you go by the gym?"

"Yeah. It was closed and locked up good." Jorge came to a photo and stopped. It was one of those long strip photos that contains a series of five shots, usually taken in malls (or movie theaters). The shots were of David and a pretty blonde girl. After seeing a joy in David's face that he had never seen before, Jorge knew that he had him. "I know how to smoke him out."

"How?"

"I found his girlfriend."

CHAPTER FIVE

That morning, Jamie was doing chores around her new apartment. There were boxes scattered throughout the barren home, a small radio was playing Destiny's Child, and on the kitchen counter was a bouquet of flowers she discovered on her porch that morning. Jamie hoped that taking care of these tasks would distract her from her nervous mind. She had called David twenty times since she witnessed him flee the arena and became more afraid with each unanswered call. It wasn't just that he ran away after the fight; there was something wrong with David even before he left. She knew it and was mad at herself for not trusting her instincts.

She kept taking glances at her phone while she hung paintings and pondered where she would place her furniture. Ryan was in his room listening to his own music. He was supposed to be unloading the few boxes he had, but he was shadow boxing, imitating his favorite fighter, David Lewis.

When a tap came on the front window, Jamie turned around and let out a startled yelp. A man in a black hoodie was staring at her. He pulled his hood down. She exhaled as she walked over to the door with her hand on her chest, making sure she wasn't having a heart attack.

"What's the matter with you? You scared the shit out of me!" she exclaimed as she opened the door.

"I'm sorry," David said quietly as he entered.

"What's going on? Why haven't you been answering your phone?"

"I had to get rid of it."

His explanation confirmed to her that something very bad was happening. "David, *what is going on?* I saw you running from someone after the fight."

"Some bad people are after me, some very bad people. But I'm going to take care of it . . . today.".

"Why are they after you?"

"They wanted me to lose the fight; that's all I can say right now. There's not enough time to explain everything. I just . . . I can't seem to escape my past. But like I said, I'm changing that today."

Jamie's face turned ghost white. "David, you're really scaring me."

"I know, and I'm sorry. I truly am. I'm going to make this right. But I need you to do something."

"What?"

David pulled a wad of cash from his back pocket and peeled off several bills. "Take this and go get a hotel room for the night."

"Are you kidding?" Jamie asked frantically. "Are these people after us?"

"I don't think so. But I don't wanna take any chances. If they've seen us together, they might be looking for you just so they can get to me. After tonight, it will be safe to come back."

"I'm not going anywhere David. Tomorrow is Christmas! We're going back to the house in a little bit!"

"Jamie, please. These guys don't care about that. Take the money."

Jamie stood aghast in disbelief. The look on her face switched from fear to anger as she took the cash. "Please leave, David," she said, averting her eyes.

David shook his head in pained frustration. "I'm sorry this is happening, Jamie. I love you, and I won't let anything bad happen to you or Ryan."

David went in to kiss Jamie, but she pulled away. She looked at him like a dog that wasn't friendly enough to pet. David nodded solemnly. He told her he loved her and then left. Jamie locked the door, closed the drapes, and began to cry.

David walked through the open center of the apartment complex towards a back fence with a determined look about him—an angry look, the same look his opponents saw across the cage. David jumped the fence and ran down a small grassy hill on the other side. A beat up Honda was waiting for him in the street. He entered on the passenger side.

From his seat, David looked over at Darnell and said "Let's roll."

For close to twenty minutes, Jamie, determined to stay despite David's warning, peeked out the window for any sign of intruders. Every moving body looked suspicious to her. She even had the old man carrying his Christmas dinner groceries pegged as a threat. After realizing the absurdity of her paranoia, she knew she couldn't stay. *God damn you David*, she thought as she walked to Ryan's room.

Outside the apartment complex, a black Lexus came to a stop. Jorge was looking at his coveted piece of paper in the passenger seat.

"Is this it?" Billy asked.

"Yeah, get your gloves on."

Ryan had ceased his shadow boxing. He was listening to the radio and finally unloading his boxes when Jamie entered his room.

"Ryan, grab your bag," she said, trying to keep her composure. "We're going for a ride." Ryan ignored her. He was lost in the mind of a curious nine year old. Jamie didn't have time to bring him out of it gently. She walked over and yanked him by his arm, looked into his startled eyes and shouted "Now!"

"What's wrong?" Ryan asked with a quivering voice.

Jamie composed herself and stood. "Nothing, just get ready."

Ryan did as he was told as he began to fill his backpack quickly. He hadn't seen his mother behave this way before. Jamie threw some boxes into a corner of the entryway as she waited for Ryan to come out of his room. She stopped her mindless wandering in the middle of the kitchen to close her eyes and take a deep breath. When she opened her eyes, the flowers David sent her that morning were glaring at her. She walked over to the fragrant bouquet and threw it into the trash bin.

Ryan came into the kitchen and asked his mom once more what was wrong.

"Nothing. Are you ready to go?"

Ryan nodded his head and adjusted his baseball cap, which made his mom smile. Her son was tough, always had been. Jamie put her arm around him and kissed his head. They went to leave. She wasn't sure where they would go. When she opened the door, she saw a short brown man and a giant white man following him. As soon as she met the brown man's eyes, her heart sunk. He ran up the stairs. Jamie slammed the door and tried to lock it. But before she could, the door was rammed open, knocking both her and Ryan to the ground.

Jorge and Billy walked into the apartment, guns drawn. "Where is he?" Jorge yelled, pointing his pistol.

Jamie and Ryan were scared silent.

"Is he here?" When he again didn't receive a response, Jorge turned to Billy. "Check the rooms."

"You got the wrong place," Jamie said from her seated position.

Jorge shook his head with a smile. "Not going to work, hon." He pulled the picture of her and David from his pocket and tossed it towards her. The long photo strip spun in the air until it landed in front of Jamie face up. She took one look, and knew she was fucked.

Billy emerged from the hall. "He ain't here. The place is empty."

"You guys coming or going?" Jorge asked with his lunatic smile. Once again, his hosts said nothing. "Tape em up Bill. We're going for a ride."

Billy removed a roll of duct tape from his coat. For a brief moment, Jorge looked away to examine one of Jamie's paintings. Ryan took the moment to stand and sprint at the intruder. He leaped into the air and kicked both of his feet into Jorge's back, sending him into the wall. Jorge turned around, blood immediately dripping from his nose. Ryan landed on his back, breathing heavy, with a brave, defiant look on his face. Jorge wiped the blood from his nose and admired his red fingers. He smiled before launching his foot into the boy's ribs. Jamie screamed and tried to get up, but Billy snagged her and taped her hands behind her back as she continued to squeal like a captured rat.

Jorge looked at Ryan and Jamie with his bright smile. "This is gonna be fun."

CHAPTER SEVEN

Darnell drove David deep into an eastern downtown neighborhood. As he was guided through this unfamiliar land, David felt like he had entered an alternate reality. In this new universe, everything had shifted. The world was tinted a new color. His brain was working in a completely new way. There was a queer, satisfying sense of definitiveness with every move he made. He was above the law in the sense that he didn't care about the law. Not anymore.

Things were likely over between him and Jamie. He had ruined her life. But David didn't know what he could have done differently. She had sauntered too close to a jet engine, and it sucked her in whole. A part of David thought he shouldn't have gotten involved with her at all. But he smashed that rogue thought easily. Their relationship was as impossible to avoid as everything else that had ever happened to him. Destiny was real. He knew that now. Beating Loder confirmed this, but he didn't need that confirmation—he'd *felt* it all along. And now, that same feeling gave him the courage he needed to go through with his plan. To protect

Jamie and Ryan, he would fight as hard as he always had, and there were no forces that could stop him.

Darnell's Honda arrived in Lincoln Park in front of the Granite Oaks projects. Despite the bloodshed that constantly swept this area, groups of kids were still playing and jumping rope out front of the decaying buildings. They had nowhere else to go.

As David and Darnell stepped out of the car and walked towards the entrance, David couldn't believe the horrible state of this place Darnell called home. The building looked like it was barely standing. From each window, clothes were dangling. The brick that was once red was now a rainbow of graffiti art, some good, most comically bad. Darnell gave intricate handshakes to a couple of men as he led David to the entrance. David wasn't greeted as warmly. Suspicious, threatening stares were his welcome.

They climbed a dark stairway all the way to the top of the building. Screams from powerful black mothers to their children could be heard at each floor. The smell of marijuana was so robust that David had to laugh at it. It was clear that no police officer dared to step foot in this building.

At the top of the stairs was a door with a sign that said "Roof Entry". Darnell gave a couple bangs. From the other side, a voice called "Who is it?"

"It's me nigga," Darnell said. "Open up."

The door was opened, and standing in the doorway was Jabari. "You remember Jabari?" Darnell asked.

"I do. How's the ankle?"

Jabari laughed. He was in much better spirits than the last time David saw him. "Good as new my white brotha. Come on in."

What David found atop this roof amazed him; a full on party was taking place. And David was pretty sure this party never ended. Circles of men and women were playing dice at various places. Other circles were drinking, laughing, and smoking weed. Music was blaring. A large man with three chins sporting an apron and a chef's hat was holding down a giant barbecue filled with burgers and dogs. Couches were spread throughout the roof. A dartboard was hung on the wall opposite of the door they entered through. A man with a cigarette dangling from his lip and one eye open launched a bullseye shot as David looked over.

On one of the couches, a large man wearing all red was sitting next to a beautiful woman. All the joints and blunts seemed to be passed his direction. This was the man David came to see.

Darnell led David over and did the introductions without much passion. "David, this is Big Berry. Better known as just Big, or Biggie . . . Big, this is David Lewis, the dude I told you about."

Big looked to the girl next to him and whispered into her ear. She turned and looked at David with a strange smirk as she rose to her feet and walked over to another area of the rooftop party.

Big pulled a pack of cigarettes from his back pocket. After retrieving a smoke, he collapsed back onto his massive ass. "So you used to work for Terry huh?"

"When I was younger, yeah. I've been outta the game for some time now."

"He's a dope cage fighter," Darnell added.

"You was locked up in Donavan?" Big continued.

David nodded his head. "Five years."

"What makes you wanna clip Terry now?"

"In short, we've had a disagreement. It's me or him at this point. And I want it to be him."

The big man nodded. "I respect that, but why should I help you?" He looked around at the posse of men who had come close to hear the conversation. "Why should *we* help you?"

"It seems obvious; we have a common enemy. You guys are at war with the *Perros*. A war that frankly they've gotten the better of."

The men around him sneered. If David didn't have Darnell with him, he felt certain he wouldn't be leaving the place alive.

"What makes you think you can kill him?" Big asked.

"Well at least I'm willing to try. Look at you guys, man." David looked around at the party. "No offense, it looks like a lot of fun, but this isn't the way to win the war."

Big took another puff from his cigarette before he spoke again. "What do you suggest smart guy?"

"Take the head off the snake. We go to his bar—where he is right now—and we kill him and anyone else who stands in our way. Not sit around and kill *Perros* every time they come on your turf. That's small-time shit. We gotta go on the offensive."

Some of the onlooking men nodded. David was winning them over. Except for Big, he still didn't look very happy. "This thing has been brewing for some time. I just don't know if it's the right time for this move."

"When is the right time? After everyone you know is dead?"

"You better watch who you talking to now. First of all, I ain't gotta do shit, it's these boys that are gonna be putting their lives on the line, and you don't want to piss them off."

David was asking these men to risk their lives, so he looked around and addressed them. "He's killing you guys left and right. Taking all your business. And you guys wanna just let him get away with it?"

"He's got better guns," one of the men said. "We'd be walking into a buzz-saw."

"But we got numbers. And the element of surprise. Get me in that door, and I'll be pulling the trigger. They're at The Silver Fox—a bar in Chula Vista—getting drunk. We'll catch em with their pants down."

"How do you know he's there?" Big asked.

"He usually is. I'm rolling the dice. Someone will be there. It's their headquarters, like this is yours, and they constantly spill your blood here. Why not return the favor? This is dangerous, no doubt. But this man deserves to die for what he's done to all of us."

Big looked around at his men, examining them. Then he turned to Darnell. "You down for this? I thought you was tryna keep your nose clean."

Darnell shrugged his shoulders. "I wanna avenge my uncle's death. I can't stand around and watch any more friends get got without doin nuthin about it."

David looked at the big man. Everyone was silent now, and the crowd around them had grown in size. "Aight. Get the guns and vests. Whoever wants to go can go." Big removed his glasses, revealing bulging, yellow eyes. "Bring my boys back."

David nodded. "I'll do my best."

CHAPTER EIGHT

J orge and Billy didn't have to take their prisoners far. Terry instructed them to take their captives to his house—which happened to be just a five minute drive—and get information out of
them there.

"You think this'll work?" Billy asked as they made the short trip.

Jorge was polishing his gun in the passenger seat. "Beats me.
But I'm killing someone today. I'll tell you that much."

Terry had a large home in a nice part of Claremont with two empty
lots next to it. The garage door opened as the Lexus pulled up and
was shut as the car entered. Jorge opened the trunk, where mother
and son were piled on top of each other like pieces of luggage.
Jorge, being the smaller man, grabbed the boy. Billy grabbed his
mother. Their screams were blessedly muffled by the tape.

Terry's home was filled with the finest things coke money could
buy, flatscreen TVs, marble statues, heated hardwood floors covered by expensive rugs, and a spacious, open layout. There were
five men in the kitchen having drinks, waiting for Jorge and Billy's

arrival. As those men finally arrived with their hostages, an especially drunk and ugly member of the group said "About fucking time."

Jorge dropped Ryan to the ground and turned and pointed his gun at the loquacious fella. "You haven't done shit today besides jerk off and get drunk. So shut your mouth and come give us a hand."

The crew of men put their drinks down and gave aid—securing Jamie and Ryan to wooden chairs with rope and duct tape.

Jorge put a chair in front of them and straddled it backwards, leaning his forearms on the backrest. He motioned for one of the men to remove the tape from Jamie's mouth. As soon as she could speak, she screamed "Let my son go, *please!*"

"I can't do that," Jorge said. "Not yet. Maybe if you're a good girl we can make that happen."

"What do you want?"

"You know what we want. Where's lover boy at?"

Jamie looked at Ryan strapped down to the chair next to her. Then, quietly, she said, "I don't know, that's the truth."

Jorge looked at the man standing behind her and tilted his head towards Jamie. The goon grabbed her by the hair and yanked her head towards the sky. Jamie screamed in pain and terror. She looked like she was hanging from the ceiling by her hair. Ryan looked on helplessly, tears streaming down his face. He was convinced he was dreaming. He had to be dreaming.

"Where the fuck is he?" Jorge yelled.

"I don't know! He told me to go get a hotel!"

"And what else?"

"And nothing! He just left!"

Jorge cocked his gun and stood up quickly, throwing his chair across the room in the same motion. "You better speak bitch!"

"That's all he said! He . . . He said this would all be over after today! He said he was gonna take care of it!"

Over today? Jorge thought. He smiled and put his gun down. "Let go of her hair you animal," he said calmly to the man gripping Jamie's mane. Then he said to Jamie, "Thanks beautiful."

Jamie put her messy head down and started to scream.

"No, we can't have that," Jorge said. "Tape that bitch back up." He took out his phone.

⟫┤┼⟪

Terry was sitting at the bar with a glass of whiskey in his hand after cashing out thousands of dollars to fifteen different people. As he reflected on the quality of the morning he had just endured, he laughed before he killed his drink in one gulp. He looked from his empty glass to the bartender and said "Just give me the fucking bottle."

Steve the bartender did as told. Then the phone began to ring. He went and answered it, then immediately extended it to Terry. "It's for you boss."

Terry took the phone. "What?"

"He's coming your way," his Cuban underboss said emphatically.

"What? How do you know that?"

"Because he told his slam-piece he was gonna take care of his problems *today*."

Terry processed the news. "How do you know he wasn't lying to her? Maybe he just split town."

Jorge looked at Jamie. Even after all the stress she had been through that morning, he could see her extreme beauty. "No way boss. He wouldn't leave this girl."

Terry smiled. "Ok. Good work. Keep them alive for now. Send those other schmucks this way. You and Billy watch the house. He could come to you if he thinks I'm home."

"Got it."

Terry handed the phone to the bartender then climbed atop the counter. "Everyone listen the fuck up!"

Poker games ceased, conversations dwindled, and Steve muted the television after a couple fumbles of the remote.

"That double timing, two-faced, snake in the grass David Lewis is on his way!" There was a low murmur of conversation as the news was delivered. "Apparently he thinks he's gonna show us who's boss. Show *me* who's boss!"

"Bring it on baby!" one person yelled in the crowd, generating laughs and whistles.

"Now I don't know what he's got planned," Terry continued, "but we're gonna be ready to give him a welcome. It's time we sent that motherfucker to his grave. So get your guns, and fucking load 'em!"

CHAPTER NINE

David and Darnell were once again cruising in Darnell's car. But this time, the car was filled with three men in the back, and two additional cars packed with people were following them. All fifteen men were wearing bulletproof vests. It was one technology the Bloods had in abundance.

"Ok hit me with the plan one more time," Darnell said.

"It's what the Germans called blitzkrieg," David replied. "Were going to storm their asses."

"Like Junior Seau blitzing off the edge?" a man in the back asked.

"Yeah, kinda like that . . . Now be ready for anything. If they're outside when we get there, start firing, or you'll be fired at. We don't look like friendly customers of the bar, and I'm not sure if they ever get any of those. If no one is outside, we'll get ready at the front door then storm in. If I can get to Terry without killing anyone else, great. We wanna cut the head off the snake, remember? But if his men try to be heroes, by all means, dust em."

The men nodded in agreement. Each of them had fierce looks on their dark faces. David faced the front and took a deep breath. In all of his robberies, he had never killed a man. Now that he was on his way to do just that, he didn't feel a shred of guilt. All he felt was a surge of adrenaline, like he was walking out for another fight.

With the rest of the men gone to give aid to Terry, Jorge and Billy were alone with Jamie and Ryan. Billy was once again eating, this time some old mashed potatoes in the kitchen. Jorge was sitting in his chair again, looking back and forth at his prisoners in a psychopathic fashion.

"I hope lover boy hurries up," Jorge said to his silenced guests. "I think we might get to reunite you guys. That would be very sweet."

Jamie was paying Jorge no attention. She was looking at her son. A steady stream of tears was pouring from his eyes still. *He's got to run out at some point* she found herself thinking.

Jorge looked at Ryan. "Where's your dad at young man?"

Max Hurley was lining up a twelve-foot putt at that very moment. To him, it looked like the line would break right to left. That was the most concerning thing he had going in his life. He finally got up from his haunches and lined up the shot.

"Hurley for birdie," an onlooking friend said in a fake British whisper.

Max laughed as he lined up for the shot. He connected with the ball and watched it roll a good distance across the tightly trimmed plain of grass before circling into the cup.

David and his backup arrived at The Silver Fox and parked across the street from the entrance. David was eyeing the lone window the bar possessed. It was hard to see through it during the bright day, but he saw no moving objects. All fifteen men exited the trio of cars. David had his .38 revolver and a glock provided by Big Barry. Everyone else was also wielding dual pistols, with the exception of Jabari; he possessed the group's only automatic weapon—an Ak-47. The group huddled in the middle of the street.

"It doesn't look like there's many men here," David said, "which could be good, unless . . ."

"Unless what?" one of the men asked impatiently.

"It would just be unfortunate if Terry wasn't here. He's gotta be here."

"What's the plan nigga?" one of the other men asked with equal impatience.

"We go in guns drawn. If anyone flinches, or even gives you a look, blow em away."

The men nodded and headed for the door.

David's inspection failed to notice Steve peeking out the corner of the window with his shotgun in hand. "They're here!" he called in a loud whisper. All twelve men inside the bar had their guns drawn. Five had automatic weapons (M-16's, far superior to the AK Jabari was wielding). Terry was standing at the back of the bar with a burning cigarette in his mouth and an M-16 of his own in his hands.

"Go get em," he said. "I don't want my bar getting fucked up. If they're smart, they'll drop their weapons."

The clicks and clacks of readying weapons sounded as the group moved towards the front door. The lead man held up three fingers and began to count down.

David and his crew of Bloods were halfway across the street when a stream of men filed out of the bar and took cover behind two parked cars.

Each party aimed their guns at the other, stuck in a Mexican standoff.

One of the men who had emerged from the bar called out "Drop your guns or die niggers!"

The Bloods and David backed up slowly towards the cars they came from. For a moment, the rumble of the highway was the only sound that filled the tension packed air. David felt the sun's hot rays on his shaking forearms and the wind blowing his hair. One gunshot from Darnell's pistol—piercing the skull of the man who called his family niggers—set off a war zone.

The street erupted in gunfire as the bloods took cover behind their cars. Windows shattered and tires popped as the cars turned into swiss cheese from the gun fire.

David slid across the hood of the car and ducked down behind the tire. Darnell was already there (amidst the chaos he had time to think that black people really are faster). He noticed that he was bleeding from his shoulder. A closer inspection revealed that he was only grazed.

"Use that gun mother fucker!" Darnell yelled at him.

David obeyed his friend. He stood up and emptied both guns with no regard for being shot again. He managed to hit two of the men with M-16's. The sounds of the enemy's barrage were reduced significantly as the men fell to the pavement. David ducked down again to reload. He turned and looked down the line of men he had brought to an ambush. He would have felt great despair had he had time for it. He didn't. Before rising again to fire, he looked in the opposite direction. An idea occurred to him. He turned to Darnell and shouted, "There's a back door! I can get behind them!"

Darnell looked at him and nodded. He had a scary look in his normally cheerful eyes. "Aight!"

"Cover me!"

Darnell got up and began to fire. David turned to his left and hustled behind a long line of parked cars that went all the way down the street. From this distance he was able to cross the street unnoticed. As he did, he passed a car that an old friend was sitting in.

Behind the corner deli was an alley that led to the rear of the bar. David ran down the alley and came to the back door of The Silver Fox while the gunfight continued on the other side of the building. He looked to the sky and said a short prayer to his part time god as he tried the door handle. His prayer was granted. The door was unlocked.

The bar appeared empty. But he knew it wasn't. Out the front door he could see the carnage he had just left, now from the enemy's perspective. The *Perros Locos* were crouched down behind their cars, firing at the Bloods. He moved slowly through the bar, looking around for anyone in hiding. As he peeked out the front door, a bullet whizzed by his head from the crew of bloods. There were seven *Perros* still living. With all the commotion David thought it was possible to take the remaining men out from behind if he shot quickly and accurately with both guns—they wouldn't know what hit them. He took a deep breath then headed for the door again. He began to count down from three in his head. But he only made it to two before the butt of Terry's rifle knocked him unconscious. Terry stood over David with a smile while Steve hopped over the bar and walked over. The two men took him by the feet and dragged him away as the gunfight raged on outside.

As Darnell reloaded for the fifth time, he looked around and realized it had been ten long minutes since David left. He immediately assumed the worst. Only six of his friends remained alive.

The others were dead and soaking the street with their blood. Jabari was down the line of cars. "Let's get the fuck out of here!" he shouted. Darnell shook his head. Their cars were useless now. All that was left for them to do was to die fighting.

CHAPTER TEN

David came-to deep in the warehouse portion of Terry's office, hanging by his wrists from chains that ran to the ceiling. He staggered to his feet, giving some slack to his restraints. He noticed that the floor of this impromptu torture chamber was painted with dry blood. One blinking circular light hung above his head. His shirt was soaked with fresh blood from his shoulder wound and a large gash on the back of his head, the origin of which remained a mystery.

Down the street in a parked car, Mark watched this entire battle with amazed horror, trying unsuccessfully to come up with a way to help. But after seeing David go into the bar and not return, he knew it was time to take action. He fired up the engine, crossed his chest, and slammed on the gas petal.

Darnell heard the tires screech but didn't see the car coming. Neither did Terry's men. Mark's sedan roared down the sidewalk and bowled a strike, plowing through all of the *Perros* at fifty miles per hour. Three of the men flew twenty feet in the air—they were the lucky ones. The other four resided under the car.

"Holy shit!" Darnell shouted as he walked around the vehicle that he had been taking cover behind.

Mark stepped out of the car with a shotgun in his hands. He walked over to one of the lucky ones. He was screaming in the street, his shins were sticking out of his flesh, and his neck was bent in a sickening right angle. Mark strolled up to him and blasted him, putting the wounded man out of his misery. The remaining Bloods walked over to Mark, breathing heavy, eyes wide open.

⊱⊰

"Ah, he's awake. Excellent," said a shadowy figure in the corner of the room where David had been brought to die. A flash of light illuminated the speaker. The flashing light was coming from a taser in his right hand. It buzzed violently as he rose to his feet and walked towards David. Terry didn't look well. His hair was un-characteristically messy, shooting in various directions. His eyes were red, and David could smell alcohol coming off of his breath. "David, David, David, why did it have to be this way?"

David made no response. He only looked on with frustration and hate. Terry wanted some resistance, so he plunged the taser into David's abdomen, causing him to stand upright and scream in agony until Terry mercifully pulled the electric contraption away.

David huffed loudly. The electric shock amplified his other wounds. "Just kill me," he pleaded.

"Oh, no, no. That wouldn't be very fun. I'm too excited for this." Terry punched David in his stomach, causing him to hunch over as far as he could before the chains restricted him. "You're not the only one with a good punch, huh?"

David looked up at Terry slowly. His anger was starting to over-power his pain. "Unchain me and let's find out," he wheezed.

Terry cackled. "I don't think so," he said before walking over to the corner of the room from where he originally emerged and grabbed his chair. He dragged it across the cement floor, produc-ing an incredibly unpleasant sound. He took a seat in front of David, folding one leg across the other. "This is so much easier than I thought it would be. I thought I was going to have to search the whole the county to find you, which I was prepared to do. Even kidnapped your girlie and her little boy as ransom. But you came to me, proving your stupidity even further."

David lifted his head after hearing this news. "You're lying."

"No, I'm not. I'm going to have some fun with them once I'm done with you here. I hear she's a sight to behold."

David saw the world go dim around him. He instantly felt nau-seous. He looked up with his blue eyes swimming in fresh tears. "Let them go. You got me. Leave them out of this. I'm begging you."

"And I'm loving it, but I'm afraid I can't do that."

David made one last ditched effort to rip the metal chains out of the walls. He thought the anger he felt might give him super-human strength, like the stories he'd heard of mothers picking up cars to save their children. It didn't happen. Terry removed his jacket and draped it across the back of his chair. He turned back to David and pulled what appeared to be the hand of a large switchblade from his pocket. With a press of a button on the wood-en handle, a sharp blade ejected. David stared at Terry as he ap-proached, sure that he had come to the end of his life. He vowed to die honorably. He was soon going be let in on the best kept secret of the universe. But first, he was certain, that he was going to go through some serious pain.

"Where would you like me start?" After Terry asked this ques-tion, both men heard a distant bang outside of the office. Terry turned and looked at the door beyond his desk. After a moment, he turned back to his toy and shrugged. "I think we may have killed the last of your new black friends. Valiant effort by those guys."

Terry was face to face with David, gassing him with his foul breath. David was awaiting great pain when he suddenly felt a burning in his stomach. He looked at the location of the burn and discovered that Terry had his knife in him. "Oh yeah," Terry said in a whisper. "In the next life, when you encounter evil like this, just bow down." He pulled the knife. The pain was tangible, too extreme to yell. Blood spewed from David's gut. He could feel himself slipping away almost instantly. It was his body's reaction to such a devastating wound.

The door behind them swung open swiftly, slamming against the wall with a loud bang. Mark stepped through the door with a shotgun in his hand. "Howdy!" he yelled. The room exploded with light and sound as he fired a shot into Terry's crotch.

"AAAAAHHHHHHHH!" Terry shouted as he fell to his back in excruciating agony. Mark started coughing forcefully as Darnell entered the room behind him with a few other Bloods.

"Mark?" David said distantly, not sure if he was hallucinating.

Mark looked up from his storm of coughs and winked at David as he walked over. "Good to see you, bub. I've been keeping tabs on ya." He turned to Terry, who was lying on the ground, writhing in pain. "Keys," was all Mark said. When he didn't get an answer, he placed the barrel of his shotgun on Terry's face. The metal was still hot from the shot that had relived him of his package. "Keys or die champ."

"They're. . . They're. . . They're in my pocket.

"Which one? I'd like as little of your dick-blood on my hands as possible."

Terry slowly reached his trembling hand into his right pocket and produced a set of keys then tossed them into the middle of the floor. "Please . . . don't kill me. I'll . . . I'll give your ma . . . money."

Mark ignored the man he had just castrated as he picked up the keys. He walked over and unlocked David's shackles. As David looked into Mark's eyes, he still wasn't convinced this was happening. Mark embraced him tight, confirming that he was really there.

"Let me see that," Mark said, separating from David and looking at his fresh wound. "We gotta get you to a hospital."

"No," David said, then grabbed the gun from Mark's hands and pointed it down at Terry. "Where the fuck are they!"

"They . . ."

David cocked the gun. "SPEAK!"

"My . . . house . . . please . . . don't—"

BLAM! David pulled the trigger, vaporizing Terry's head.

CHAPTER ELEVEN

Mark, David and Darnell did a hundred miles per hour on their way up the five freeway in Mark's niece's bloodstained car. David had been to Terry's home—it's where he got his coke on several occasions. The trick was staying awake to give directions.

"Keep pressure on that fucking thing!" Mark yelled to Darnell, glancing over constantly at his bleeding friend.

"How did you . . .Why . . ." David mumbled, attempting to get answers from Mark.

"Story for another time bud."

"He's going out," Darnell said.

"I ain't going nowhere," David fired back quickly. The determined look on his face said the same.

Jorge was pacing the room, biting his nails, sweat dripping from his brow. He kept taking nervous glances over at Jamie and Ryan, who had been strapped to their chairs for almost two hours now.

During that time, he put a large amount of cocaine up his nose. He put his phone to his ear and dialed for the fifth time in the last ten minutes. Again he received no answer. "What the fuck is going on?" he said quietly to himself. He went to the balcony where Billy was smoking a cigarette and enjoying the view like a man on vacation. "Something's wrong Billy. I can't get a hold of anyone."

Billy turned his head to Jorge slowly. "He's taking care of our guy right now. He told you that. What are you freaking out about?"

"That was almost an hour ago," Jorge said in an almost child-like fashion.

"He's taking his time," Billy said. "I bet he's cutting extremities off until he bleeds out. You know, enjoying himself."

"No one at the bar is answering either."

"The cops are probably all over that place Jorge. Little Jimmy got his fucking brains blown out. Just calm the fuck down and come take a load off."

Jorge shook his head in disgust as he walked away. With his hand to his chin, he paced the room some more. Jamie and Ryan watched helplessly as their psychotic captor spun his wheels. Finally, he stopped and turned to them. "I think it's time for you guys to go."

"This is it," David said as they arrived at Terry's place.

Mark parked the car four houses down from the house. He looked in the back at his passengers. David's face was pale as snow, but he looked stable.

"The bleeding's stopped for now," Darnell said.

"I don't think the knife hit any vitals," Mark said. "You'd be gone already."

"That's terrific," David groaned. "Let's get moving."

When Mark popped his trunk open, both men's eyes also popped open. The cavity contained an arsenal of weapons: shotguns, assault rifles, high powered pistols, and a sniper rifle. Mark grabbed the rifle. "Alright let's scope this bitch out."

"Where did you get all this shit?" David asked.

Mark looked at him with his eroding face and smiled, "Shoulda gone to the willow tree."

David's eyes widened. "Jesus."

"Let's hurry up," Darnell said.

"If we can sneak around to the back yard, it's got huge windows that look into the entire house," David said.

"Sounds like a good spot."

Darnell shook his head. "It's no good."

"Why not?" David asked.

"We gotta blitzwhatever them. Look at the guns we got. There's no cars out front. Can't be many in there. If you don't want your girl and that kid to end up like my uncle and the eight friends I lost back there, we gotta move fast."

David looked to Mark for his input.

"It's your call bub."

"Let's go through the front."

Mark switched the sniper rifle for the shotgun that had been the demise of Terry Watkins. David and Darnell grabbed two assault rifles.

They jogged down the street towards the house.

Jorge bent down close to Jamie and examined her with his bloodshot eyes. "God you're sexy," he said. "Do you find me sexy?" He wanted an answer, so he removed the tape from Jamie's mouth.

"Fuck you!" she shouted.

"I'd like that. Wouldn't you?" He turned and looked at Ryan. "Wouldn't *you* like that, little boy?"

Ryan squirmed in his seat, trying uselessly to break out of his restraints.

Billy emerged from behind. "What are you doing, Jorge? Let's just leave em and go get a drink in the village. All Terry's got is Maker's Mark. I hate that shit. They won't be able to break out."

"This isn't good Bill," Jorge repeated. "Something is wrong. The cops could be on their way right now."

"You're being paranoid."

"This bitch has seen our faces; she's heard our names. It's time for her and her little mutt to go." Jorge rubbed his hand across Jamie's cheek. "But first we're gonna have a little fun, aren't we gorgeous?"

"You serious right now Jorge?"

Jorge rose to his feet and turned around. "Come on. You're telling me you don't want a piece of this? You were butt fucking guys in prison and you're gonna turn that down?"

"You don't know that!" Billy yelled. Then he looked past Jorge at Jamie. Her grey eyes called him. "I suppose you're right. Turn the boy around though."

"No fucking way," Jorge said.

Billy rolled his eyes. "Whatever."

The two men started to untie Jamie as she squirmed fiercely like a lizard trying to evade capture. Ryan watched with horror, screaming beneath the tape, his face turning a dark purple. Jorge took Jamie by the feet while Billy took the arms. They carried her to the couch and threw her on top of it.

Ryan's eyes darted around the room, looking for anything to help his mom. He prayed to every god he had ever heard of. If a god existed, surely this was the time for he or she to show themselves with a miracle. Just at that moment, he caught sight of David crouching as he moved through the front door, a massive gun in his hand. Behind him followed a black man and an old guy. Ryan met eyes with David and then tilted his head vigorously in the direction of his mother.

As David moved further into the house, he saw what was about to take place on the couch. He aimed his gun at Jorge's back, but he couldn't fire. The risk of hitting Jamie was too high. Darnell and Mark saw the same thing. So David improvised. He flipped his gun around and walked briskly towards Jorge. Once he was within ten feet, his pace turned into a sprint. Jorge turned towards the patter of footsteps just as David's gun came down on his head, producing another murderous *CRACK*. Jorge fell limply to the floor, bleeding into his unblinking eyes.

Billy released Jamie and reached for his gun. Mark and Darnell were in the same predicament David had been in; they couldn't fire without risking David's life as well. All they could do was run to give aid.

David, now gunless, sprinted for the big man. As he collided into Billy, they went barreling through a floor-to-ceiling window. The two men fell ten feet down onto a grass patch in the back yard, glass shards raining over them. The top of David's head smashed Billy's nose to pieces, causing him to instantly scream in pain. The big man's gun was left dangling on the edge from which they had just fallen. Darnell ran over to Ryan and started to cut him loose. Mark ran over and checked on Jamie briefly then peered down on the two fallen men.

Billy shoved David off of his chest. They both staggered to their feet slowly. Billy touched his broken nose and winced with pain then examined his sliced arms. David was relatively free from cuts. They looked at each other. An I-know-death-has-arrived smile rose on Billy's blood-drenched face.

"Don't move big fella!" Mark shouted from the broken window above.

Billy looked up at Mark with his smile still in place. Then he turned back to David.

"I said don't move!" Mark yelled again.

Billy ran for David and swung at him with his large right hand. Mark fired his gun and missed his target. David used the last bit of energy he had in his body as he ducked Billy's punch while simultaneously launching his own right hand. The sound of bones shattering was distinct as David's fist found its mark on another jaw—the biggest one yet. Billy fell face first into glass shards. David looked down on him then collapsed onto his knees.

Darnell and Mark climbed down from the window and kneeled in front of David.

"David you good?" Darnell asked, quickly realizing it was a dumb question.

The sound of police sirens could be heard approaching in the distance. Mark looked in their direction, and a smile touched his lips.

David fell to his back. He saw Darnell and Mark looking at him, but that's not where his attention was. Behind them he could see Jamie and Ryan looking down at him. They looked terrified, but also concerned. David pointed a shaky hand up at Jamie slowly. "Tell her I'm sorry," he said. Then he looked at Mark. "I did it Mark . . . I beat em. I beat the forces."

Then David's world went black.

CHAPTER TWELVE

Eight hours later, Jamie was sitting on the front porch of her former residence, rocking on a swinging bench, examining the stars and listening to the crickets, when a motion light was switched on by Max emerging from the front door.

"He's finally asleep," Max said as he took a seat next to Jamie on the bench.

"Thanks," she said quietly, still looking towards the night sky.

"How are you doing?"

"I'm alright."

Max could sense that she was far from alright as he rested his hand on her shoulder. "Don't blame yourself, Jamie."

Jamie responded with a low grunt. Max looked at the shadow-draped side of his soon to be ex-wife's face for a while as they rocked on the creaky bench. He realized that this insane day had done nothing to repair their relationship. Eventually he quietly rose to his feet and went back inside. Jamie was relieved. She needed this time alone. Don't blame herself? How was that possible? She should have run for the hills the moment David told her about his past.

People like David can't change. The streets are in their DNA. She felt all of this to be true now. But somehow she also felt that these notions were absurd. Because David *was* a good man. There was no denying that. He apparently was a dangerous man, but a good man, whose life had been plagued by tragedy. And Jamie, like David, didn't think their relationship was avoidable. It was going to happen. She couldn't stop it any more than she could stop the sun from rising. Love and hate are so closely related. As she rocked on the bench while marveling at the stars above, she tried to decipher which of these emotions was burning a hole in her chest.

Christmas day. David woke up in a hospital bed in the Intensive Care Unit of the same hospital where Mark had made his escape.

He looked around the white room in a drug induced haze. With his blurry vision, he scanned past the television and medical posters until he came to a black man in a grey suit sitting with his legs crossed.

"Merry Christmas," the man said, putting his cellphone away and rising to his feet. "You're a lucky man, David."

"Who are you?" David asked.

The man removed a badge and held it before David's eyes. "Detective Tim Curry."

David closed his eyes. Why couldn't he have just died?

"I'd like to ask you some questions."

"I need a lawyer," David said with a cough.

"No you don't, David. Trust me. Just answer a few questions." Detective Curry pulled a photograph from his coat and held it in front of David's face. "Do you recognize this man?"

The photo was of Terry, before his head was blown off. David reluctantly answered. "Yes."

"Did you know that he's dead now?"

"I want a lawyer."

"Well he is," the detective continued. "And we found your blood on the scene, along with some other folks' who've been reported as missing and are now confirmed as dead." Detective Curry tossed Terry's photo onto a table next to David and pulled out another. "Now I know you recognize this man, your old cell mate." He held the photo of Mark in front of him.

"That's correct."

"You did a good thing David—"

David looked at the detective, surprised by this last statement.

"—You did a good thing saving that girl and her boy. But I need to know who killed Terry."

"I *want* a lawyer."

"Did Mark kill Terry? He says he did."

David looked at the man with skepticism. "Then why are you asking me?"

"Because I need to hear it from you. Did he kill him?"

"Where is he?"

"Mark? . . . He's dead. Died in his sleep last night. He gave us a statement, but seeing how he's dead now the jury will be skeptical of his confession. I need your confirmation since I know you were there. And I know you were chained to the wall when Terry stabbed you in your side there and when Mark killed a man we've wanted dead for a long, long, time. So say the words, and I'll leave you be. That doesn't mean you won't have to come down for questioning when you get out of here. But truthfully, nobody wants to find the murderer of Terry Watkins, especially when we got a confession. As for the others killed in that shootout, that's just being chalked up at another terrible instance of gang violence. Nobody cares who murdered them either . . . I know about everything David, and I'll see to it that you are not punished for doing the right thing . . . So, one more time, did Mark kill Terry?"

David looked out the window towards the blue sky. He wished with every cell of every fiber of his being that that he could believe

Mark was up there sitting on a cloud with his mother, waiting for him to arrive. People who truly believe this to be the case are relieved of a great burden when they lose a loved one. David wasn't relieved. He was crushed. Mark never got to say goodbye, or tell him why he was looking after him. But he didn't have to now. Mark was his guardian, and even now, after death, he was still protecting him. Finally, without facing the detective, David said, "Yes, he killed him." Then he closed his wet eyes.

Detective Curry jotted a note into a small book and turned for the door. "Thank you David. It's time I got home to my kids. Take care of this girl now."

This girl?

David turned back towards the detective. As he left the room, he bared his handsome smile while he held the door open for Jamie to enter.

David met Jamie's eyes as she walked over slowly.

"Jamie, I'm so sorry . . . You shouldn't be here."

She didn't respond, even after she arrived at his bed.

"I never thought this would happen," David said. "Please believe that."

Jamie rubbed her hands through David's hair and finally spoke. "I know," she said. Then she removed an envelope from her pocket. "This is for you."

David took the envelope from her skeptically. "What's this?"

"I don't know," Jamie said, still speaking very quietly. "It's from that man. Your old cell mate. He gave it to me before the cops came."

David peeled his eyes away from Jamie and ripped open the envelope. Inside was a note written in Mark's neat handwriting.

Dear David,

There comes a time in a man's life when he has to make a stand and tell the forces to go fuck themselves. I saw in your eyes the day you visited me that that's exactly what you intended to do. And even though my body was withering away, I felt a surge of energy from your visit, My hair stood erect, goosebumps lined my skin (I think moments when you feel that way—when the space between your brain and skull is buzzing pleasantly—those moments are indicators of divine experience). They messed up by taking me to that hospital. It was <u>my</u> time to take a stand after serving fifteen years for growing a plant in the ground. I'm sure you're wondering why I didn't come see you sooner. Well, I didn't want to distract you. You were a man on a mission, and at the speed you were traveling, any shift in course could have taken the wheels out from under you. I wanted to watch from afar, until after the fight. I'm writing this from a car outside of Terry's bar. I knew he was keeping tabs on you, so I'm keeping tabs on him (he really is a slimy fuck). I know he has men looking for you, but I have a feeling you will come to him. I won't make it much longer. Days, weeks at most. But, despite the fifteen years that I had taken from me, I lived a good life. I made it to the race. And it was a hell of a ride. Soon I will know the answer to life's greatest mystery, the secret that makes it all worthwhile. And I'm not the least bit afraid. Either I will go back to the unknowing state I lived in before I was born, or—and this is what I believe to be true in my heart—I will carry on somehow to another life with all the knowledge and experiences from this one retained . . . with everything you taught me. I couldn't be more proud of the man you've become, and the fierce fighter you've turned yourself into. Take care David. And live the life you deserve.

-Your Celly

P.S. —There's still money under the tree dummy.

David looked up at Jamie and folded the note. He wiped his eyes as they stared in silence. He still didn't know how this visit was going to go.

"He told me how your father died."

David closed his eyes in anguish. "Jesus."

"I wish you would have told me. And I wish you would have told me about these people."

"I was ashamed. I've always been ashamed of who I am."

"Well, your shame almost got me and Ryan killed."

David couldn't respond.

"Until you saved us."

David turned to Jamie, surprised. "It doesn't matter," he said adamantly. "That doesn't change what I did. You should hate me and leave me forever. I'm clearly not safe to be around."

"I tried to hate you. I spent my whole night trying to bring on the hate. Because that's what everyone expects of me. But I don't hate you David. *I love you.* And despite how crazy the past twenty-four hours have been, I still love you. We didn't choose this life; it chose us. I can feel it. And I know you can too. We're both blessed with second chances here. You get a second chance at life. And I get a second chance at love."

David was shocked at what Jamie was saying. Shocked that she was there. Shocked that he was alive. He had nothing to say, but the dumbfounded look on his face made Jamie laugh. She leaned in and kissed David, injecting life back into him. When she pulled away, he marveled at every feature of her gorgeous face and at the summit of his life where he now resided.

Heaven wasn't in the sky. No, he was in heaven now.

⇥┼⇤

Ten years later.

The MGM Grand Garden Arena is packed for a championship fight. Many stars are in attendance: Denzel, Charles Barkley, Justin Bieber and David Spade are just a few of the celebrity viewers. Amongst these millionaires is a happy couple, David and Jamie Lewis, here to see their son fight for a world boxing title.

Ryan stands in the ring, waiting for his name to be announced. He is as stoic as ever and has become very handsome with age. Standing with him, massaging his shoulders, and uttering inspirational messages in his ear is his longtime coach, Mike Thompson. Ryan took his stepfather's advice by steering away from mixed martial arts and going into the much more lucrative sport of boxing. Judging by where he is now, he made the right choice. Win or lose, he is walking away with a million dollars for this fight.

Jamie clasps David's hand with hers. "I'm nervous," she says.

"He'll be fine," David replies confidently. David has some grey in his hair now, some wrinkles on his cheeks. But the happiness that radiates off of him helps to retain his youthful looks.

Michael Buffer steps forward with a microphone in his hand to give his patented introduction with his silky voice. "Ladies and Gentlemen... LET'S GET READY TO RUMBLLLLLEEEEEEEE!" The crowd applauds the spectacle of Buffer's voice. As the fighters' entourages clear from the ring, Jamie and David can see their son well. He turns to them and puts his fist in the air. As the bell sounds, Ryan turns to his opponent. He walks towards the doomed man fearlessly on his quest for a championship belt, on his way to become the best.

AUTHOR BIOGRAPHY

Casey James, an only child to a single mother, spent his childhood moving from Idaho to Montana to Alaska and ultimately to California. The contrasts of lifestyles he witnessed as a youth forged a fascination for people within him, along with a curiosity for what their story was like. A lifelong lover of writing, James, an English major at San Diego City College, previously wrote screenplays. He believes this practice influenced his fast-paced style, but enjoyed the descriptive freedom that came with writing *A Defeated Man's Destiny*—his first novel.

Made in the USA
San Bernardino, CA
08 September 2016